DEAD MAN'S THOUGHTS

Carolyn Wheat

BERKLEY PRIME CRIME, NEW YORK

Lines from "The Lawyers Know Too Much," appearing on page vii, from *Smoke and Steel* by Carl Sandburg. Copyright 1920 by Harcourt Brace Jovanovich, Inc.; renewed 1948 by Carl Sandburg. Reprinted by permission of the publisher.

Lines from "The Death of the Hired Man," appearing on page 123, from *The Poetry of Robert Frost*. edited by Edward Connery Lathem. Copyright 1930, 1939, © 1969, by Holt, Rinehart and Winston. Copyright © 1958 by Robert Frost. Copyright © 1967 by Lesley Frost Ballantine. Reprinted by permission of Holt, Rinehart and Winston, Publishers.

Lyrics from "There but for Fortune," by Phil Ochs, appearing on page 230, copyright © 1963, 1964 by Appleseed Music, Inc. All rights reserved. Used by permission.

DEAD MAN'S THOUGHTS

A Berkley Prime Crime Book / published by arrangement with the author

PRINTING HISTORY
St. Martin's Press edition published 1983
Berkley Prime Crime edition / September 1995

ISBN: 0-425-14933-1

Berkley Prime Crime Books are published by The Berkley Publishing Group, 200 Madison Avenue, New York, NY 10016.
The name BERKLEY PRIME CRIME and the
BERKLEY PRIME CRIME design are trademarks belonging to Berkley Publishing Corporation.

PRINTED IN THE UNITED STATES OF AMERICA

10 9 8 7 6 5 4 3 2 1

*Praise for Carolyn Wheat's novels
featuring Cass Jameson . . .*

"THE MAIN CHARACTERS LIVE AND BREATHE . . .
Cass Jameson [is] a strong and welcome addition to the
mystery field."   —*Raleigh News & Observer*

"AN AUTHOR WHO EQUALS AND EVEN OUTSTRIPS
MANY ESTABLISHED MYSTERY WRITERS in depth of
plotting, intricate character development, and especially
in intriguing, well-realized atmosphere . . . a new kind
of courtroom drama."   —*Booklist*

"AN ACCURATE AND FAST-MOVING LOOK into the
legal mind and the criminal courts of New York."
—*New York Times*

"VERY GOOD SUSPENSE INDEED."
—Dorothy Salisbury Davis

"WHEAT DRAWS THESE CHARACTERS WITH NO-
NONSENSE REALITY and a lot of heart. She's terrific,
too, on the hard-bitten judges, lawyers, and court personnel who slave under an imperfect legal system that
would turn Bambi into a cynic."   —*New York Post*

"AN ADMIRABLE HEROINE whose toughness and vulnerability are perfectly balanced."   —*Mystery Scene*

"ENGROSSING . . . well-crafted, rich in detail, and
most rewarding."   —Harold Q. Masur,
author of *The Morning After*

"HER KNOWLEDGE OF THE COURT, THE LAW, and
the dirty tricks and conspiracies of the ambitious lends
enormous flavor to the narrative . . . a believable cast
of characters and a plot that unfolds with clarity and
logic."   —*Newsday*

"A REAL, WONDERFUL HEROINE."
—*Hartford Courant*

For Carl, who knew the sound of one hand clapping

The lawyers know a dead man's thoughts too well.

Carl Sandburg,
"The Lawyers Know Too Much"

ONE

There were eighty bodies in the system; eighty defendants, here or at Central Booking, on the treadmill that led from arrest to arraignment. Half were charged with family assaults. Definitely a full moon.

I scrawled my name on another notice of appearance, stood up, and put my card case in my pocket. I was dressed for action—old pants, comfortable shoes, and stud earrings. You never knew whether some nut in the back would go berserk and rip a hoop earring right off your pierced ear.

Other than the full moon, it was a typical night court. Started slow, no bodies produced, then picked up right before the dinner break. Now Nathan Wasserstein and I were taking turns in front of the judge. His cases had been called, so he sat at the Legal Aid table, his Ben Franklin reading glasses tilted on his nose, doing the *Times* crossword puzzle.

Nathan loved night court. He enjoyed the game, the give and take of plea bargaining. Me, I didn't love it. I just did it.

"May we approach, Your Honor?" I asked. The deferential part of lawyering no longer bothered me; it was as ritualized as mumbling your way through the Our Father in Sunday school.

"Certainly, *Ms.* Jameson. Come on up." Di Anci was one of the few judges who called me Ms. But he gave it a slight ironic twist; he didn't say it as if he meant it.

I scooped up my file and stepped between my client and

1

the court officer. I got to the bench before the assistant district attorney, who was hampered by her tight skirt and high-heeled shoes. She could afford to dress. She didn't have to go into the pens and interview a defendant who'd just puked on the floor.

"Judge, this is a case involving—" I began.

"Good evening, Miss Hagerty." Di Anci interrupted, not even looking at me. "Did you enjoy your vacation?" The district attorney, a tiny woman whose sharp features were softened by a cloud of artificially blonde hair, looked up at him and said, "Oh, yes, Judge, just fabulous. My—ah—friend and I went to the restaurant you recommended and had a great meal. Thank you so much for mentioning it."

"A pleasure, Miss Hagerty." Di Anci beamed. "And did you tell Rocco I sent you?" She nodded, smiling a secret smile.

"What are you looking for in this case, Miss Hagerty?" All at once Di Anci was Mr. Business. I was used to his sudden shifts in mood, so I was surprised when the D.A. colored and fumbled open her file.

"Ah, Judge, she was caught with a leather coat worth one hundred fifty dollars. She has an extensive record—"

"Are you kidding?" I broke in. "Extensive record? Three priors—one dismissal, one conditional discharge, and she just finished one year's probation. If you think that's an extensive record, honey, you're in for a disillusioning night."

The D.A. was stubborn. "Judge, I think it's time she had a taste of jail."

"Oh, you do, do you?" I retorted. "And what about her kids? I don't say what she did was right, but put her in jail and the Bureau of Child Welfare will have her kids in a foster home before she's done five days. Is that the penalty for shoplifting these days—losing your kids?"

"She should have thought of that before she took the coat."

"Have you ever been poor, Miss D.A.?"

"Ladies, ladies." Di Anci was avuncular, amused by a cat-fight between two women lawyers. "I'm sure we can settle this amicably. Ms. Jameson, you don't want your client in jail. What do you suggest?"

"Three years' probation, Judge. She successfully completed one year; I think all she needs is supervision."

"Sounds fair to me," Di Anci agreed, and I breathed a sigh of relief.

But the D.A. was a sore loser. "Judge, I can't go along with that. My policy is to get jail time on shoplifters."

Oh, God, I groaned inwardly, how many assistant D.A.s do I have to break in? Any damn fool could have told this kid Di Anci's mind was made up.

But she got on her high horse, telling Di Anci the sentence "wasn't fair." Telling him he couldn't let this woman escape the consequences of her crime just because she had children.

Well, of course my client, Roberta, wasn't escaping anything. If she blew probation, she'd do a year in the slammer, but more to the point, the little D.A. had lost Di Anci completely. Nobody told him what he could or couldn't do. His plump, pinkish face clouded with anger.

"Let me remind you, Counselor," he told her, "that I am the judge in this part, not you. Ms. Jameson's client is pleading to the entire information, so sentence is entirely within my province. Step down, please."

We stepped down. I had a hasty conference with Roberta and then said the magic words, "My client authorizes me to enter a plea of guilty to violating Section 155.25 of the Penal Law in satisfaction of the only count of this information." Then I scrawled P/G 155.25 *promise prob.* on the file and tuned out while the D.A. questioned Roberta. I didn't have to listen. I'd heard it a hundred times before. This week.

So I did what photographers call dry shooting. I roved the courtroom with my camera eye, searching for images. The motto above the bench—IN GO WE RUST—a perfect symbol of deteriorating justice? No, too trite. Maybe a shot of the court reporter, slumped over his machine, himself becoming a machine as he reduced justice to tiny symbols on long, thin strips of paper? Not bad. Shot from below—

just the hands, carefully blurred to show movement, with the rest of the courtroom out of focus in the background. Photo-realism. *Life* magazine stuff.

"*Ms.* Jameson, are you still with us?" Di Anci's light, sarcastic voice brought me back to reality.

"Yes, Judge," I lied. Dick, the court officer, kindly clued me in to what we were doing. "Date for sentence, Counselor?" I flipped through my diary. It was March twenty-first now . . . they need six weeks for a probation report. . . . "May fourth, Your Honor?" I asked. May fourth. Kent State Day.

"May fourth it is, Ms. Jameson." Di Anci looked straight at Roberta and spoke in a deliberately menacing tone. "And let me tell you, Missy, you've been lucky this time. If you fail to appear on the adjourned date, or fail to keep your appointment with the probation department, or if you are rearrested on another charge, all bets are off and I can and will sentence you to one year in jail. Is that understood?"

Roberta nodded. I translated. "All you have to do is go to probation, come back on this date, and stay cool. No more five-finger discounts. Okay?"

She smiled, a wan, weary smile, but probably the first since she'd been busted. "Thanks for everything," she said.

"Good luck, Roberta," I answered. I hoped to hell she'd be back for sentencing—and not before.

The next case was three guys busted in a stolen car. No big deal usually, but this time the car had been taken at gunpoint, so it was Rob One. Two had no records; I was hoping to get them released on their own recognizance. The third guy had a long sheet, so what I had to do was concentrate on the other two and hope he'd go along for the ride.

The D.A. started the ball rolling by announcing, "This is a red dye case, Your Honor. No possible disposition."

That panicked the troops. "What does she mean?" "Can't I get probation?" "I gotta get outa here, miss. I'm gettin' married this Saturday."

"Shut up, guys," I hissed. " 'Red dye' doesn't mean shit.

Just that the case is going straight to the Grand Jury. So just stay cool and let me do my job."

The D.A., meanwhile, was halfway through her bail pitch. Or, rather, her no-bail pitch, since she wanted bail set high enough that none of them could make it.

"Judge, these three men are charged with a serious crime," she said. "If convicted, they face up to twenty-five years in jail. I note that one, Colin Dennehy, has a long record, including two prior felonies." She proceeded to ask for bail in the amount of $25,000 while Dennehy clutched at my sleeve.

"I can't stay here, miss," he pleaded urgently. "I'm gonna have a baby." It took me a minute to realize that he was the one who'd said he was getting married Saturday. Better late than never. I considered laying it on Di Anci, in the hope that it would engage his sense of humor. It was about the only chance Dennehy had of becoming a husband before he became a father.

The D.A. finished her pitch, and Di Anci looked at me expectantly. It didn't matter that I hadn't heard the litany on the other two. I could guess. No jobs. Unverified community ties. But no records. The one and only thing to be said for them. So I said it. Several times.

Di Anci decided he'd heard enough. "You mean they've never been caught before," he said. The sting was taken out of the words by a slight smile on the pudgy face. Di Anci one, Jameson nothing.

I tried again. "Judge, Mr. Vinci is scheduled to begin a job training program next week."

"Why is it, Ms. Jameson, that so many unfortunates are arrested immediately *before* they are to start work?" Di Anci asked, his voice sweet with exaggerated innocence. Di Anci two, Jameson zip.

Desperate measures were needed. The boys were named Vinci and Paculo; the judge Di Anci. It couldn't hurt. I turned to the front row, where an anxious-looking woman sat, leaning forward, straining to hear every word. Her hair was elaborately styled, a throwback to the fifties.

I gave it a try. "Your Honor," I said, after a quick con-

sultation with my clients, "Mr. Vinci's mother is in the
courtroom. Would it be possible for her to address the
court on her son's behalf?"

Di Anci nodded. The woman stood up, smoothed her
skirt, and looked expectantly at the judge.

"What is your name, madam?" he asked, in a calming
voice.

"Gloria Vinci, Your Honor," she said nervously. "I'm
Joey's mother, and I'm also Paulie's aunt."

Watching Di Anci talk to the woman, I relaxed. He
asked about her family, where they lived, what part of Italy
they came from.

"You'll see to it that they both come to court?" Di Anci
finally asked. Gloria Vinci nodded vigorously.

"All right. Paculo and Vinci are released on their own
recognizance. Dennehy, bail twenty-five hundred dollars
bond, one thousand cash. March twenty-fourth, AP4. Next
case."

"Wait a minute, Judge. I need at least two 18-b attorneys." I told Di Anci I'd keep Paculo; we'd need non-Legal
Aid lawyers appointed for the other two to avoid a conflict
of interest.

Meanwhile the cousins were being reunited with the
family. The motherly woman held up her arms to the boys
as if to embrace them in a warm Italian hug. Then she
slapped her son across the face so loud it resounded
through the courtroom. She was shouting something in
Italian that sounded dirty as hell. She turned on the
nephew, but the rest of the family was gesturing, shouting,
trying to remove her from the courtroom before the court
officers did.

Di Anci was loving it. He laughed till the tears ran down
his face. "Maybe I should've set bail after all. I think those
boys'd get more protection in the slammer."

Morrie, the court reporter, spoke up. "And that's just
the mother, Judge," he said eagerly. "Their old man'll put
a steel-toed boot to their ass." He cackled in a high-
pitched voice, then looked at the judge, expecting a laugh.

He didn't get it. In another sudden change of mood, Di

Anci's face had gone rigid. He was lost in a private, bitter memory.

I wondered why. I knew Di Anci's father was a judge on the Appellate Division, which was why people called him Di Anci the Younger or Di Anci Junior. Or, since the elder Di Anci was reputed to have the brains in the family, Di Anci the Stupid. Maybe that was it, I thought. The man must get tired of overhearing people say he wasn't the lawyer his father was.

The last cases before dinner break were the girls. They were brought out in a string by the pross cop, a huge black dude with an earring and a black T-shirt with silver glitter letters that read IN THE SYSTEM. The girls matched his flamboyant, ironically pimpy chic with their hot pants, platinum wigs, white boots, and other working clothes. They stood in a row in varying poses of defiance.

I hate prosses. Not the girls, but the system. As Judge Diadona says, any judge collecting fines on a pross is just a pimp for the City of New York. How the hell do other judges think those fines get paid?

All the girls pleaded guilty except one. Honey Macomb, stunning in red wig and silver lamé gown. Six feet three, with size twelve silver pumps and long fingernails painted purple. True name Harold Melvin.

He had warrants. Most transvestites do; they don't have obliging pimps to pay their fines and keep them in business. Di Anci, barely glancing up from his paperwork, executed sentence. Forty-five days all told. Honey would do the time rather than pay the money for a lot of reasons, not the least of which was that he/she could earn a few bucks in Riker's. Typical case, even down to the black eye and the cut on Honey's head. I put his injuries on the record just for the hell of it. I knew it made no difference to anyone except me.

The court officers and the cops went into their usual bag of he/she jokes and sniggers as the pross cop led Honey back into the pens. It would have been no big deal except for the little D.A. cheerfully remarking, "Looks like your

client fell down the precinct steps, doesn't it, Counselor?"
She had a conspirator's smile on her face.

"Yeah, it's funny how Officer Perkins's defendants fall
down the stairs so often. What makes me really sick,
though, is D.A.s who get off on it." Full of self-righteous-
ness, I stalked away and headed for the Legal Aid table,
where Nathan waited to go to dinner with me.

"A little hard on her, weren't you?" he asked mildly.

"Did you see her face?" I was still furious. "That little
bitch thought it was cute that the cops beat that guy up."

"She hasn't been in the D.A.'s office very long, Cass.
Maybe it's just a defense mechanism. 'See, I'm in the system. I know what goes on.' That's all she's saying, really."

"Oh, Christ! Sometimes you kill me, Nathan, you really
do. Psychoanalyzing the D.A.s. I don't *care* why she said it.
All I know is I'm hungry. I need a break. I don't want to be
kind and understanding anymore."

But that, of course, was the difference between Nathan
and me. For him, kind and understanding was a way of life.
For me, it was a job. One I needed a break from every so
often.

TWO

The only thing to be said for the Kings County Criminal Court is that it's about three blocks from Atlantic Avenue. Every time the Middle East hits the news, some enterprising TV correspondent takes a minicam there to sample local Arab opinion. Personally, I'd rather sample the food.

Nathan and I walked from the courthouse to the restaurant in silence. A companionable silence, the kind you only have with someone you know very well. A silence so rich, so full of meaning, that if I had those few minutes to live over again, this time knowing we were on our way to the last meal we'd ever share, knowing that in two days Nathan would be murdered, I wouldn't wish for talk. I'd stick with the silence.

We'd been colleagues at Legal Aid for four years, lovers for about two. He was older than most of us, forty-eight, with graying Brillo hair and a face that somehow, despite the crags and wrinkles, belied his years. About two inches taller than my five-five. Not exactly the tall, blond, all-American boyfriend I'd dreamed about back in Chagrin Falls, Ohio. But then I was a long way from Chagrin Falls in more ways than one. For now, Nathan was what I wanted, a cozy old-shoe affair. Maybe not passionate but safe and comfortable.

He'd been a successful criminal lawyer in Manhattan for about fifteen years. Name in the papers, heavy cases. Drug dealers. Black Panthers. Then he'd had a nervous breakdown. Quit practicing law. When he was ready to take it up again, he came to Legal Aid.

His cases were legendary. Like the time he crumpled his client's written confession into a ball and kicked it around the courtroom to show the jury how worthless it was. Or the time he compared the People's witness, an informer, to Barabbas—which meant his client was Jesus. He was one hell of a lawyer. Maybe in some ways I was dissatisfied with myself because I compared myself to him. I didn't have what he had. What it took.

We turned from Court Street onto Atlantic Avenue and went into a place called The Casbah. Indian-print wall hangings, tin lamps with cutout holes for the light to flash through, spicy smells, and high-pitched, oddly soothing music. It wasn't crowded; Monday night at nine o'clock isn't exactly prime time in Brooklyn. I ordered a glass of white wine; Nathan raised his bushy eyebrows at me but said nothing.

"I can't take this anymore, Nathan." I tried to say it matter-of-factly, but a certain shrillness crept in. "All this game-playing with people's lives. I'm burning out."

"Why do I have the feeling I've heard this before?" He said it with a smile, but there was a hint of weariness too. He was right; I'd been complaining to him far too often lately.

"I got sick of law once myself," he said. "You probably heard I quit for a while."

I nodded. He was speaking casually, yet for all our closeness he had never mentioned his breakdown before.

"One reason why was an arson case I had. An abandoned building. A derelict died from smoke inhalation. My client, the owner, collected a bundle in insurance. I'd represented some pretty nasty people in my time, but this case got to me." His brown eyes were locked with mine. His voice was low but full of a passion I'd never heard before.

"When I was a kid, about ten or so, we were burned out of a building. In Brownsville. Nobody was hurt, but we lost everything. I can remember my mother crying into her apron. Over the lost photograph albums of her family. She said it was as if they'd been put in the gas ovens all over again." He cleared his throat. "For the first time in my life,

I was face to face with the kind of work I was really doing. And I hated myself for doing it."

"What did you do?"

"Won the case," he said simply. "Then I threw up in the toilet and left the job for a while. I was pretty messed up. Started doing some crazy things—" he trailed off. I had the feeling he wanted to say more, to tell me something even more personal. But I could only wait until he was ready.

The hummos arrived. Nathan tore a piece of chewy pita and dipped it, stirring the orange-colored oil into the paste and lifting the bread to his mouth. Hungry as I was, I didn't follow his example. Instead I sat back expectantly, waiting for him to finish his thought.

"I came back," he told me, "when I realized that it really doesn't matter so much what you do in life as how you do it."

"What do you mean?"

"There's a Zen story," he began.

"Oh, no. Not another Zen story, Nathan, please," I begged. Zen stories are the Oriental version of Christian parables, only more obscure. "You're plucking my last *nerve,*" I joked, quoting Lily, Nathan's secretary, whose last nerve was plucked at least once a week.

"There's a Zen story," he repeated insistently, but with a smile. "However, I'll skip the details and go straight to the punch line. The point is that you must bring two things to whatever task you set out to do in life—concentration and compassion. Concentration on the thing you're doing and compassion for the people whose lives you affect by doing it. That's what it's all about, for me anyway. Doing my job the best way I know how but never losing sight of the fact that I'm dealing with people, not just cases."

"What if you don't want to *do* that job?"

"But that's the whole point, Cass," he answered. "You can't go through life picking and choosing: I'll walk through this part of life, but I'll give myself heart and soul to that part. You either give all you've got to whatever you're doing at the moment, or you'll find you have nothing left to give when the 'right' thing comes along."

"That's crazy!" I retorted. "You mean in order to be a good photographer I have to be involved in law?"

"Involved is involved," he shrugged. "Do you realize you'd be one hell of a lawyer if you ever decided to stop holding back and go for it?"

The waitress brought our main dishes. I started eating my lamb stew, partly because I was hungry and partly to forestall further conversation. It didn't work. Nathan asked me a question.

"Why did you go to law school?" He asked it conversationally, like a guy coming on in a singles bar. Then, before I could answer, he said, "Because you wanted to save the whales, end the war, and stop pollution, all in your first year of practice?"

"Something like that." I smiled in spite of myself; it had been exactly like that. "After the shootings at Kent, which the legal system did nothing but cover up, I decided to learn the language, get my union card, and do what I could."

"Funny," he said. "You went to law school to be a more effective rebel. I went to law school to get respectable. My old man was a Communist. Really," he added, as I gave him a skeptical look. "Guys in long black cars followed us around. He took me to party meetings all the time. Even as a kid I could see that half the people there were poor deluded schmucks and the other half were FBI agents. It made me sore, what a schlemiel he was, believing in the glorious revolution. I went to law school to get away from that, to get into something normal."

"You're saying that's a better reason?" I challenged.

"I'm saying it set up fewer expectations," he replied. "When I came back to law after my hiatus, I could set limited goals for myself. I couldn't save the world, but I could get, maybe, one kid into a program and on the right track. I try to do what I can and forget about what I can't."

"What's this got to do with my becoming a photographer?" I asked.

"Same thing," he said. "I get the feeling photography for you is an escape. Taking pictures at block fairs on weekends. But nobody makes a living doing that. Can you accept the idea of becoming a working photographer—the kind who does weddings and takes high school graduation pictures?" He smiled. "Or is it Ansel Adams or bust?"

I smiled back, a little ruefully. "Berenice Abbott or bust." Then I sighed. "I get the point, Nathan. I don't like it, but I get it."

"Sorry for the lecture, Cass," he said, though he didn't look sorry. "I just hate to see you putting yourself through this. If you could work things out, I think you'd be a lot happier." He took my hand. "And I'd like to see you happy."

Then he looked at his watch. "Back to the salt mines."

"Are you kidding?" I asked. "Salt mining is a clean, wholesome occupation next to being a Legal Aid lawyer."

We walked along State Street in silence. In spite of the damp cold, there were kids hanging out in front of the St. Vincent's Home for Boys. The stars that seemed to twinkle in the pavement were really hundreds of shards of broken glass. In the distance, the red hands of the clock on the Williamsburg Savings Bank pointed to ten o'clock. Three more hours of night court. My stomach knotted up, and I shivered, not entirely from the cold.

THREE

_____■_____

"**H**ey, lady, you my Legal Aid?" the kid with the huge Afro demanded.

"Ain't you got my name on one of them files?" his buddy asked, pointing to the stack I was carrying.

"I gotta see you about my case, and I mean *now.*" This from a black man with dried blood caked on his face and shirt.

I held up my hands. "I'll be with you as soon as I can, okay?" I was back in court, in the holding pens, interviewing prisoners. It was like working in the dog pound, trying to decide which hungry puppy to feed first. I felt as though dinner had never happened. For them, of course, it hadn't. While I'd been eating lamb stew and drinking white wine, they'd had stale bologna sandwiches and watery soup.

Dick, the bridgeman—the court officer responsible for calling the cases—gave me the court papers on an ROW from New York County. When a guy gets returned on a warrant—which means he failed to show up in court when he was supposed to—we don't get the usual defense papers. In fact, the court doesn't have papers either. So nobody knows anything about the guy's case. In this instance, neither did he. He sat on one of the stools in an interview booth, rocking back and forth, singing a tuneless tune. I tried to ask him some questions, but he waved me away, still singing, his wrinkled white hands flapping like dying butterflies. Even in the fetid pens, his smell stood out. He hadn't bathed in months.

He was clearly a loony tune. They'd 730 him—send him

to Kings County Hospital to be examined by psychiatrists. But that's all. Just examined. Not treated, except for pumping him full of thorazine. Then he'd be sent back to court to face the charges against him. Whatever they were.

I put the wacko's file at the bottom of my pile and looked for my next client. Nathan sat in one of the booths talking to a middle-aged white guy who looked like a defrocked cop. The guy was hunched over, his face distorted with intensity. That wasn't unusual; most skells have an exaggerated sense of their own importance. What *was* unusual was that Nathan, nodding solemnly, seemed to share that sense. I wondered what was so special about the case.

I called out a name: "Thomas Boynton." A short black man with the name "Tom" embroidered in red over his shirt pocket stepped forward. Mechanic, I guessed. His hands were balled into fists and held rigidly at his side. I motioned him into the booth next to the one where the 730 candidate sat, still rocking. You could smell him faintly even in this booth.

"I ain't *had* no gun." He punctuated his words by pounding one fist into his other open hand.

"Calm down, Mr. Boynton, I believe you." I did, too. I'd seen it before. Common-law divorce. A woman wants her man out of the house. He won't go. The cops are no help, Family Court is no help. So she has him arrested for something the cops will take seriously—like a gun. The judge usually gives the guy an ACD, which means the charges will be dismissed in six months, on condition that he moves out. If he doesn't, the charges are restored. If he does, everybody's happy. Except that the whole thing's been a lie and he's spent a night in jail for a gun he never had. Justice, Brooklyn-style.

I gave Boynton the spiel about staying away from his wife and told him I'd probably be able to get him an ACD. He relaxed visibly, unclenching his fists and flexing his fingers. "I surely do hope so. I'll lose my job for sure if I'm not there tomorrow morning. I can't let that happen."

"Don't worry. I'll do my best."

I had one more file. "Digna Gonzalez." A thin young

girl with dark circles under her eyes raised her hand as
though I were her homeroom teacher. She was charged
with possession of a weapon. It was a big night for guns.

"Who'd you shoot?" I said it lightly, to break the ice.
She wasn't charged with assault, and the idea seemed in-
congruous, like asking a rabbit if it ate wolves.

Her eyes filled with tears. She whispered, "I try to shoot
myself." I felt rotten, irrationally angry that the complaint
had given me no clue. Once it would have. Once trying to
kill yourself was illegal.

"Why?"

"My husband, Ramon, he leave me and go back to
Puerto Rico. That is bad enough, because I have no money
and the Welfare, they will not help me. But then Ramon
brother, he come in the middle of the night and take *los
ninos,* my childrens, to go to Puerto Rico with their father.
I cannot live without my childrens, my babies."

"Don't worry," I told her. "I'll get you out of here." I
was sure Di Anci would let her go. She had no record, and
her story would melt a stone.

Big deal. I could get her out of jail, where she never
should have been in the first place. I couldn't get her back
to Puerto Rico or on welfare, or get the kids back. Or stop
her being poor and young and helpless.

That was it. Nathan and I had interviewed everyone in
the pens. I stepped out to put my finished cases on the
table and glanced at the clock at the back of the courtroom. 11:25. Another hour and a half and we'd be sprung.

Nathan was before the bench, pleading out a driving-
while-impaired, a Puerto Rican with a blue-around-the-
edges look of a chronic alcoholic. The defrocked cop was
next. He looked panicky, clutching at Nathan's sleeve just
as Nathan moved to approach. I was surprised at his ner-
vousness; I hadn't figured him for a virgin.

While I waited for my turn at the bench, I dry-shot a
portrait of a young junkie nodding out, a trail of mucus
dripping from his nose past his slack mouth onto his
T-shirt. I squinted to read the words printed on the front.
Then I had it. "I looted this T-shirt."

I came back to attention when I saw Di Anci suddenly fly off the bench. He didn't even call a recess, just took off.

I looked inquiringly at Nathan, but he only shrugged back, then came over to the table, tossed his files in the box, and sat down. Picking up one of the files, he took his little spiral notebook from his jacket pocket and began to make notes.

"Another special project?" I asked him, teasing a little. He looked up and smiled. "I think maybe I can get this kid into Hope House."

"Which kid?" I asked. "Not the tall, skinny one who ripped off his sister's TV for dope money?"

He nodded. "All he needs is to kick dope. He's not a hard-core criminal."

"What are you?" I laughed. "A lawyer or a social worker? You can't get all of them into programs."

"Maybe not," he shrugged. "But, Cass, you know as well as I do that just keeping them out of jail isn't enough."

"Hell, Nathan, I'll settle for that. But I see what you mean. I just think you go too far. Having clients come to your apartment isn't the smartest thing to do."

"I don't do it often. But the office isn't open on weekends, and sometimes that's the best time to get a kid and a program together."

"Have you had much luck?"

"Had a case recently. Di Anci," Nathan gestured toward the now-empty bench, "was going to put my kid in for six months. Horrible probation report. The worst. But I convinced him to let me work on a program."

"Found one yet that'll take him?"

"No, but at least the kid's out of jail while I look."

"Until he gets busted again."

"Cynic."

"Bleeding-heart." We both smiled. It would have been a moment to end with a kiss if we'd been alone.

Di Anci burst back into the courtroom, took the bench, and said, "All right, let's go. Haven't we wasted enough time?" Dick, the bridgeman, gave him a sour look; it hadn't been *his* idea to take a break. Then he called my

730. It took less than thirty seconds to convince Di Anci that the guy was a wacko. The cop took the guy back inside to wait for the padded wagon. He was still singing his little song.

Boynton came out next. The little man looked even smaller flanked by a court officer. He was trembling, his hands in fists inside his pockets. The court officer behind him said nastily, "Take those hands out of your pockets." Boynton jerked them out as though his pockets were on fire and let them hang at his sides as if they belonged to someone else. I whispered to him to be cool and stepped up to the bench. I started my pitch for an ACD, told Di Anci he'd move out and leave his wife alone, the whole bit. Then the little D.A. piped up, "Your Honor, this man had a gun. I don't intend to reduce this case unless he gets jail time."

Di Anci gave me a bland look. "Ms. Jameson, what do you have to say to that?"

I was pissed. The D.A. was being serious in her dumb way. She just didn't know the score. But Di Anci was playing games, and it was late and I was tired. "Oh, for Christ's sake, Judge, there was no gun. The cops never recovered one. All his wife wants is for him to move out, and he agrees to do that. Give him his ACD." I knew it was a mistake the minute I'd said the words. I'd made the same dumb move the D.A. had made earlier—telling Di Anci what to do.

"Ms. Jameson, it is not necessary for you to talk to this court as though I didn't know what was what." Di Anci's face was rigid with anger. "I understand a lot of things you don't, like the fact that this man put his wife in fear of her life. Now step down and address yourself to bail."

I knew Di Anci's mood had shifted against me, but I wasn't sure how far he'd take it out on Boynton. The D.A. pulled out all the stops. The wife was "adamant" about prosecuting. Boynton had a "long record." He faced "substantial jail time." The usual litany.

Finally I got a word in. I pointed out that Boynton's record was all several years old, that he had a job now, that the gun hadn't been seen by the cops. It cut no ice with Di Anci. "Bail one thousand dollars." Boynton sucked his breath in sharply and turned to me, panic on his face.

I tried another tack. "Judge, this man works. He could lose his job. Can we have a cash alternative?"

"Cash alternative is one thousand dollars, Counselor." He said it as though he were talking to a child, as though it wasn't obvious.

Boynton burst out, "Your Honor, I can't *make* no thousand dollars. If I don't be at work tomorrow morning, I won't have no job. Please don't lock me up." The man was near tears. If that didn't move Di Anci, nothing would.

It didn't. "You had a gun, Mr. Boynton. You used it to threaten your wife."

Boynton was crying now. "I never *had* no gun, Your Honor. Not since I left the army." He was sobbing as they led him away to the back, to make his own phone call to raise the thousand bucks.

I was furious. Because Di Anci was mad at me, everybody would lose, even the woman who'd brought the charges. She wanted Boynton out of the house, not unemployed. I wished I could convince the D.A. that her little victory would mean no support payments for the very woman she thought she was protecting by locking Boynton up.

Given Di Anci's mood, I dreaded Digna Gonzalez's case. She came out. I went up to the bench with the D.A. I tried to keep my voice steady as I told Digna's pathetic story, trying to keep out of my mind the image of Digna behind bars.

Di Anci raised one arm as though it held a violin and with the other dragged a mythical bow across it. Hearts and flowers. "Don't break my heart, Counselor. This woman had a gun, and guns are dangerous. Aren't they, Miss Hagerty?"

The D.A. looked uncomfortable. "Actually, Judge, my office has no opposition to ROR in this case." I gave her credit. It took balls to refuse Di Anci's obvious hint to ask for bail.

Di Anci gave her a look of disgust. "Step down, ladies."

We did. I was ready for a strong bail argument, but Di Anci started talking first. "Let the record reflect that we have had a bail conference at the bench." This wasn't true, but I let it pass, figuring I'd get my chance later. "I am constrained to disagree with the assistant district attorney's position that release on recognizance is appropriate here. Having a gun is not to be treated lightly. This woman has only been in Brooklyn nine months. That gives her an excellent motive to flee the jurisdiction." He finished, "Bail two thousand five hundred dollars." It might as well have been a million.

I was opening my mouth to begin my argument, when Di Anci stood up, tossed the court papers at the clerk, and proceeded to walk off the bench. I was stunned. I had an absolute right to make a record, and I was going to do it if he held me in contempt. My voice shook as I asked, "Judge, may I be heard?"

He stopped, bowed ironically at me, and stood with his arms folded, waiting.

My voice broke occasionally with the effort of keeping Digna's face out of my thoughts and at the same time suppressing as much as I could my hatred of Di Anci. I finally stopped, not because I was finished, but because the certainty that Digna would go to jail caught up with me. I clenched my fists under the counsel table and blinked back tears.

"Bail stands. Court is adjourned till tomorrow morning." He swept off the bench without a backward glance. I pulled a Kleenex out of my pants pocket and wiped my nose.

Digna was already in the back. I hoped it wasn't too late. I went over to the clerk. "Harry, do me a favor?"

"Sure, Counselor. That was a tough one."

"Put her on suicide watch. I don't want her to succeed next time."

He nodded. "I'll get Di Anci to sign it before he goes. It's the least he can do, huh?"

"He couldn't do any less, that's for damn sure."

I went into the pen. Digna was calmer than I. I told her I'd try for a bail reduction, but I didn't hold out much hope. I patted her arm and turned to go, only to notice that the gate was locked. The correction officers were joking loudly, so I called out "on the gate," and one of them came over and opened it with his huge key. The gate swung open, then clanked shut behind me, leaving Digna's small, serious face, like that of a cloistered nun, staring at me through the grate.

FOUR

I was still mad as hell when we walked out of the courthouse. I wanted to smash Di Anci's fat, complacent face. Yet there was a weariness, too, a sense of having been here too many times before.

"I feel as though people have been spitting on me," I said. Nathan didn't answer. He just squeezed my hand. Finally, I laughed. "You know," I said, "this job reminds me of when I was a waitress. You leave with sore legs and a lousy attitude. The only difference is now I don't have to refill ketchup bottles."

We walked again in silence, mine seething with pent-up anger. So it took me a while to notice that Nathan's was a broody, thoughtful silence. Then, as we turned onto Clinton Street, a pleasant, tree-lined street of well-kept brownstones, Nathan said, "I don't suppose you remember the Burton Stone case." I tried to recall the name. Then it came back.

"Burton Stone the Fixer. My last year in law school. I was doing welfare hearings at the World Trade Center, and a bunch of us trooped over to the courthouse one afternoon."

"Remember who represented Stone?"

"Yeah, sure. Matt Riordan. He did a great job—Stone lived to fix another day."

"The prosecution's chief witness was a guy named Charlie Blackwell." Nathan was talking slowly, either relishing the memory of the Stone trial or trying to remember it more clearly by savoring its details. I couldn't figure out why we were talking about it, unless it was meant to divert me from the bitter anger I still felt at Di Anci.

"Charlie was a skell of the highest order. Always ready to make a deal to save his ass. It's a wonder he lived long enough to testify against Stone."

"From what I've heard, it's certainly a wonder he lived *after* testifying against him."

"That's another good point." I couldn't figure out what Nathan meant by that, so I kept listening. We were across Montague Street now, facing the high-rise building Nathan lived in. Its modern starkness was in sharp contrast to the shutters, carved doors, and garden fronts of the Brooklyn Heights brownstones that surrounded it. It looked like a medium-security prison.

"Charlie was great on direct examination, with the prosecutor asking the questions. Beautiful." Nathan pronounced it "beauty-full." "Laid it out like a carpet. Stone had given him a payoff to deliver to a Judge Wallingford, who conveniently dropped dead of a heart attack before the trial. When the direct was over, that jury didn't have to leave the box—Stone was as good as dead. Then Matty gets up to cross. He asks the usual stuff about Charlie's criminal record, his bad habit of ratting on his friends to catch a break, and then he starts asking crazy stuff. Like 'Didn't you tell Joe Schmo that you took a ride in a flying saucer?' 'Yeah, I told Joe that,' Charlie answers. 'Why did you tell Joe Schmo that, Mr. Blackwell?' 'Because it's *true*. These guys came down from Venus. . . .' Well, you can guess the rest. On direct, Charlie was Mr. Solid Citizen. More or less, anyway. On cross, he turned into a fucking space cadet. The jury couldn't believe a word he said after the kooky stuff."

"So? The guy was a flake. Did he have a mental history?"

"A couple 730s. Charlie's a nervous guy. Of course, if you spent a lot of time informing against fairly heavy people, you'd be nervous too. The shrinks at Bellevue didn't see it that way, though. Whenever they see Charlie, they write down 'paranoid schiz' and find him fit to proceed.

Anyway, long story short, a lot of people were wondering just how Riordan knew to ask Charlie about the flying saucers. It's not exactly standard cross-examination technique."

"I see what you mean. You don't ask questions like that unless you know what the answer's going to be. And Riordan wouldn't know the answer unless he got to Charlie?"

Nathan opened the gate to his apartment compound; it clanked shut behind us automatically. "On the gate," I murmured.

"That's the theory," Nathan went on, "but Charlie had been in protective custody for four months. Nobody could get to him—supposedly. But the Special Prosecutor, then and now, would give a lot to know just how Riordan got that information."

Nathan was opening doors and collecting his mail as he talked. We walked past a bored desk attendant, pushed the elevator button, and waited.

"What brings all this to mind tonight?"

"Charlie Blackwell was in the pens tonight. On a drug rap. He wouldn't say a word about that case. All's he said was, 'I got something the Special Prosecutor would be interested in.'"

I digested the implications of this as we rode up in the elevator. We came to Nathan's door; he unlocked it, switched on the hall light, and plopped his mail on a small table in the hall.

"This could get heavy," I finally said. "Do you think he wants to give the Special Prosecutor the dope on Riordan?"

"I don't know what he has to say. Charlie can keep his mouth shut when he wants to. He's still paranoid as hell; insisted on administrative segregation, so I got him on suicide watch. Only in his case, it's more like murder watch."

"That sounds a little melodramatic," I protested. "I mean, what can the guy really do? Nail some middle-level hood? He wouldn't have anything on Stone himself, would he?"

"Like I said," Nathan answered, "he wouldn't talk. In

fact, when I tried to approach the bench to get Di Anci to give him the suicide watch, he didn't want me to go up. But of course, I had to say something to the judge to get him put in segregation."

"If he won't talk—" I began.

"I'll go to the Brooklyn House tomorrow or Wednesday and get the story," Nathan answered. "Then if he's really got something, I'll call Del Parma. He's an old buddy of mine from my D.A. days. Hell, I knew him when he was still Delos Parmaklidis."

"I keep forgetting you used to be with the enemy." I smiled when I said it.

"Long time ago. Besides, the way Mike Ponce ran that office, it was the best D.A.'s office in the country. None of the shit Del's doing now. Special Prosecutor, my ass. Special Persecutor. Your buddy Di Anci used to work for him."

"That doesn't surprise me. He had to learn how to be a pig somewhere."

Nathan went into the kitchen, opened his bronze refrigerator, and pulled out a bottle of Beck's. He opened it, drank deeply, and passed it to me. I tipped it back and let the crisp, bitter brew flow down my dry throat. It tasted wonderful. We finished the bottle in thirty seconds flat. Nathan took out two more bottles and we carried them into the living room, dumping our coats on a chair as we went.

Nathan opened a sandalwood box on the battered coffee table and took out a joint. The half-beer I'd drunk had barely touched the surface of my tension, so I swallowed the smoke greedily, trying to suck in peace and tranquillity as quickly as possible. I passed the jay back to Nathan and drank more beer. I could feel myself unwinding, and I rolled my head around to unkink my neck. I was slowly turning back into a person after a night as an arraignment machine.

Nathan reached over and put his hand on my neck, kneading the tight muscles. I sighed gratefully and rolled my head around again. That plus a couple more hits on the jay and finishing the beer brought me down a few more notches.

I panned around the rooms, trying to see it as though for the first time. A photographic exercise, deliberately making the familiar new. If I were to photograph the room so as to reveal the character of its occupant, I wondered, what would I shoot?

Nathan's desk—not a desk really, but an old-fashioned library table with a shelf over the writing surface, handy for stacking papers or books currently in use. Only Nathan, in addition to stray bills, magazines, legal briefs, and other papers, had cluttered it with family photos. Of himself as a teenaged debater, the short haircut of the period flattening his curls and making him look all nose. Of his two sons—one at age three, blowing out the candles on a birthday cake; the other, aged about eight, with a bat and glove, a Yankee cap over his long hair. Of himself at four on a pony, his mother in a housedress by his side. Of his father amid a group of solemn-faced men at a union picnic. And one of the two of us, holding hands on the Promenade, taken by a passing Japanese tourist. Nathan was wearing an open sport shirt, his deep tan emphasizing the vigor of his wiry body. I had on an Indian-print sundress, my brown hair cut short for summer, a sunburn warming my usually pale cheeks. We were both squinting into the sun; the Japanese was a lousy photographer.

The bookshelves—books on Zen philosophy next to a pictorial history of the Lower East Side I'd given him for his birthday. Tolstoy, Isaac Bashevis Singer, J. D. Salinger, *The Great Gatsby*. Books on running, on art—lots of those, big coffee table books, but looking well-used. Some of the books everyone gives a lawyer—*My Life in Court, The Brethren, The Art of Cross-Examination*. Lots of science fiction, but the few mysteries were all books I'd either given or lent him.

In between the books were records that had been played and not put back. Pete Seeger. The Weavers. Baez. *Fiorello*. Propped up against the books and records were mementos—a woodburned plaque that said World's Greatest

Dad, a pottery chalice, the king from a now defunct ivory chess set. A framed Get Out of Jail Free card from a Monopoly game.

For the paintings, I reflected, I'd have to change my mental film from black and white to color. A Hopper-style rendition of a country highway, checkerboard farms in primary yellows and greens, sliced by a two-lane blacktop. A scene at a masked ball, lurid and mysterious, disturbing in its implication that anyone could remove a mask and be revealed as someone entirely new, totally different from the person who had originally entered the room. And my favorite—a huge painting in washed blues and greens, repeating over and over again, in varying sizes, the cryptic message: NON-WORD. I had no idea what it meant, but something in me responded to its cool, cerebral quality. Concentration and compassion.

Nathan went out to the kitchen for more beer. I sighed, leaned back on the couch, and looked out the huge picture window at the Brooklyn Bridge. It was lovely, a giant, sparkling necklace strung between Brooklyn and Manhattan. I had picked up a guy in arraignments who'd stolen a bicycle on that beautiful bridge. At gunpoint, from a twelve-year-old kid.

Nathan came back, put down the beers, and sat close to me, his strong arm around my shoulders. I began to drift and drowse in a haze, my senses taking over from my mind. We sat a while in silence, just touching, each in our separate yet companionably shared world.

I was the one who broke the spell. "Boy, do we need baths," I said. "We both reek of the pens." It was true, if unromantic. You can't spend several hours sitting with people who've been locked up for two days and not smell pretty raunchy. Nathan went first, since he takes showers. When he came out, drying his hair with a huge yellow bath sheet, I went into the bathroom and filled the blue tub with water as hot as I could stand it. A little baking soda for softness, and I was all set.

It was ecstasy. Bilbo Baggins was right; Water Hot *is* a noble thing. I eased myself into it inch by inch, shuddering as the heat tamed my aching muscles. The steam curled up around my head, and I closed my eyes and felt deeply relaxed and at peace.

When I came out, I went straight to the bed where Nathan lay. I was naked and steamy, and he ran his hands over my soda-softened skin.

I groaned as his hands roved, touching me with delicate, cool strokes. I began to glow, my mind floating deliciously on sensual awareness like a dragonfly skimming over a still pond. He increased speed and pressure. My body began to sing inside, louder and louder, climbing an invisible peak of pleasure until climax. I turned and smothered Nathan's body with my own. We coupled, then lay exhausted in each other's arms.

As we drifted into sleep, I heard Nathan murmur that he wanted to talk to me. "In the morning," I murmured back. Then we slept.

I woke first. The plastic alarm clock said 7:45. I lay in bed wondering what to do. I was late. I had things to do at work, and I still had to go home and change.

My gaze wandered around the bedroom. Less decorated than the living room, it still had touches of Nathan's personality. The pictures on the walls were mine, photographs of a fall hike we'd taken on the Palisades. Variations on a theme—silver river, colored leaves, jutting stones. There was also a framed artist's sketch of Nathan as a fiery trial lawyer—the kind they show on TV in lieu of camera shots of the actual trial—given to him by the artist.

I got up, stiff with cold, and padded into the bathroom. Sleeping naked makes me feel vulnerable; in the cold light of early morning, my body seemed white and gross.

When I came back from the bathroom, Nathan, lying in bed as soft and sweet as a child, almost tempted me. I nearly pulled off the blanket and snuck in to cuddle up to his warm back.

But that would mean being late for work. If I'd known—but I didn't.

I leaned over and kissed him awake. He stirred, barely

conscious, and I whispered, "Bye, love. See you at work." I ruffled his surprisingly soft gray hair and dashed out the door to catch the IRT.

I never saw him alive again.

FIVE

"**T**raffic cop with the Iceman," Sylvia Mintz remarked. "Better you than me."

Traffic cop is what you do on the third day after you work arraignments. All your jail cases are on anyway, so you might as well answer the calendar. It's called traffic cop because you're supposed to make order out of chaos. I was traffic cop this Thursday morning because my—and Nathan's—cases from Monday night dominated the AP4 calendar.

We were waiting for the elevator in Criminal Court. Sylvia was on her way to the tenth floor, where she was on trial. A drug case. Cocaine. The undercover cop was due to testify, and she was pessimistic.

"I can't believe I'm trying this case," she grumbled. "They've got everything but a *movie* of my guy selling to the undercover." She was dressed for trial. Navy suit and gray blouse, a far cry from her usual bright colors and far-out designs.

"Cheer up, Syl," I said. "In a couple of days, it'll be all over, and you can go back to spending your afternoons shopping at A & S."

"Kiss the Iceman for me," she retorted sweetly, crowding into an elevator.

Kiss the Iceman. Fat chance. The Hon. Perry Whalen wasn't called the Iceman because he had the milk of human kindness in his veins.

I pushed into the next elevator and closed my eyes. Some day I'm going to go berserk in a Criminal Court elevator from the lack of air and the smell of crushed humanity. I'll lose control and bite the neck of the person in front of me, and they'll take me away to a nice place with a big green lawn and adult-sized swing sets.

But not this time. The doors opened; I stepped out onto the sixth floor, and headed for AP4.

I was already late. The Iceman was a stickler. He didn't even waste time chewing me out, just glared at me over the tops of his rimless glasses and went on with the calendar.

The case before the bench was People of the State of New York v. Gaylord Squires, a/k/a Maverick Kent, a/k/a Junior Butts. The defendant looked like every other black street kid you ever saw. Skinny. Jeans. White T-shirt. Felony Flyers. But there was something in him that wasn't dead yet. You could see it in his outrageous aliases. Gaylord *Squires,* for God's sake. As if he owned a country seat and rode to hounds in an impeccable hunting jacket.

But the future was clear. Someday the system would burn him out too. Someday he'd come through and give his name as Junior Butts, and it would be all over from then on. He'd be as dead, as defeated, as most of my clients.

Digna Gonzalez's case was up next. The Iceman didn't even bother bringing her down from the pens. He denied my bail application *pro forma,* which means as a matter of course. For him it was a matter of course to keep people in jail, no matter what the circumstances. I was angry but not surprised. How many headlines do you read that say "Frightened Girl Denied Bail Hangs Self in Jail," compared with those that read, "Judge Frees Killer"?

Boynton was out. His boss had put the bail up for him. I was trying to explain to him why he had to come back to court even though his wife didn't show up, when Judge Di Anci wandered into the courtroom. He was looking for a D.A. attached to the Sex Crimes Unit.

"Must be important," Mario Richetti remarked. "Di Anci the Lazy actually left the bench to do his own D.A. hunting."

"Maybe he wanted the exercise," I said.

"Maybe it's that female D.A. with the big tits," Mario answered.

Paculo, Vinci, and Dennehy were up next. The two defendants who had been released stepped out of the audience, freshly dressed and looking sheepish. Dennehy, still dirty and truculent, still wearing the clothes he'd been arrested in, was brought out of the pen.

The case was put aside to be called again. Dennehy's lawyer was in another courtroom and would be there later. I told Vinci and Paculo to sit down and wait. As they turned to go back to the audience, I noticed a dark-haired woman at the railing. Paculo's mother. She asked me if I could talk to her about her son's case.

I nodded to Mario to handle the calendar and turned to walk out with Mrs. Paculo. Then the pen doors opened, and Nathan's defrocked cop was led out.

I hadn't heard his name. It wouldn't have mattered if I had. For some reason, I didn't have any of Nathan's files. As traffic cop I was supposed to cover everyone's cases, which meant I needed all the files. Without them, I was at a disadvantage. Everyone in the courtroom knew more about the cases than I did. It was unusual, since conscientious Nathan never made mistakes like that.

The D.A. was talking. "Your Honor, this is a narcotics case. There has been a voted and filed indictment." He gave me the number. I wrote it down. I cooled down at Nathan; that had been nice and simple.

It didn't stay that way. The client kept plucking my sleeve the way he had when Nathan arraigned him. His face was pasty, and his mouth worked nervously. I whispered impatiently that I'd see him in the pen; the Paculo family was still waiting for me in the front row. The defendant shook his head. Stammering, he babbled something about administrative segregation and having to be protected from his enemies. I asked the judge if we could approach.

"Is it necessary, Counselor?" Judge Whalen tapped his fingers on the bench. His querulous voice went on, "You have your indictment number. This case has been transferred to the Supreme Court. This court no longer has jurisdiction." I assured him it was necessary, but it wasn't until I got up to the bench and confirmed my suspicions that I knew how necessary. For it was only then, looking at the court papers, that I realized the defrocked cop was Charlie Blackwell. I remembered what Nathan had said about the suicide watch being a murder watch, and I shivered slightly, knowing how close I'd come to putting Charlie back in custody without the special instructions that would segregate him from the mainstream of the prison population, where his enemies lay in wait. I watched carefully as Judge Whalen wrote the instructions in his crabbed hand and then stepped down to reassure Charlie, satisfied that I'd done what Nathan would have wanted.

It struck me suddenly as very odd that Nathan had neglected to get this particular file to me. I had almost missed getting Charlie protected, and I *knew* how important it was. What if I'd been out of the room when the case was called? Charlie might have lost his suicide watch through sheer inadvertence. It wasn't like Nathan to let that happen.

I turned toward the Paculo family, having done what I could for Charlie, but I wasn't let off so easily. Blackwell wanted to see me inside. Throwing Mrs. Paculo an apologetic glance over my shoulder, I followed Blackwell and Vinnie, the court officer, into the pens.

Blackwell's first question was predictable. "Where's Mr. Wasserstein?" He spoke in a low, guttural whisper, so low I had to lean my head against the bars to hear him, giving me the full impact of his foul breath. His teeth were yellow; he was probably afraid they were poisoning his toothbrush.

Falling into Blackwell's conspiratorial head, I lowered my voice. What the hell, even a paranoid can have real enemies. "He has an appointment today with the Special Prosecutor about your case. He'll be there at twelve thirty." At least that was what Nathan had told me on the phone the night before. Blackwell nodded. "Good. I seen him yesterday, at Atlantic Avenue. I told him everything.

Everything." His gray eyes stared at me like a cat's, steady and unblinking. "Charlie Blackwell told it all. Charlie Blackwell tells the truth, the whole truth, and nothing but the truth." He was still whispering, as though his muttered remarks were too hot to be heard by the other prisoners.

"Charlie Blackwell ain't afraid," he went on. "Charlie Blackwell don't fear no man. Charlie Blackwell ain't got nothin' to fear but fear itself."

I had no time for a fireside chat. The Paculos were waiting. "Mr. Blackwell," I asked politely but wearily, "is there anything else you want me to do for you?"

He began to stammer again. I'd been wrong to press him; anything he had to say he'd say in his own time. He finally said, "Tell Wasserstein for me. Tell him to get me out of Atlantic Avenue. It ain't safe for Charlie Blackwell over there. It ain't safe on the Rock neither. Charlie Blackwell should be in protective custody. Like before."

I was about to suggest that these were hardly the sentiments of a man who had nothing to fear but fear itself when a look of sheer panic came over the man's pasty face. It was as if he'd heard his own words for the first time.

"Not like before," he babbled, "not like last time. Tell him. Tell him it's gotta be better than last time. Someplace where nobody can get to me. Not nobody nohow. Tell him!"

I assured him I'd tell Nathan as soon as possible, and turned to go. He still wasn't finished. Sighing in exasperation, I turned back. "One more thing, honey. Make sure you check my yellow card." I nodded and fled.

When I stepped back into the courtroom, the judge had taken a break. It looked like a *Twilight Zone* episode. There were open files on the tables, people's coats in the pews, an open pen on the counsel table, but the human beings had all disappeared. I walked over to the clerk's desk and looked through the pile of yellow commit cards. Blackwell's had *suicide watch/admin. seg. ctd.* in the right place. Everything was okay.

I walked out to the hall to see Mrs. Paculo and nearly

knocked Judge Di Anci down with the door. "Seen my D.A.?" he asked.

"No," I replied curtly. As long as Digna was in jail, I had no desire to be polite to Di Anci. I didn't even bother to tell him the courtroom was on a break; let him find out for himself. As he reached for the door, he said, "By the way, *Ms.* Jameson, they want you in Jury One. Return on a warrant."

Just what I needed. A case upstairs. But I owed it to the Paculos to see them first. They were waiting in a corner, impatient for news.

They didn't like it much when it came. Paulie Paculo was facing Rob One. Two-to-six minimum. No possibility of probation.

Mrs. Paculo was a stark contrast to her sister. Where Gloria Vinci had struck her son for disgracing the family, Theresa Paculo wanted the world to know her boy was innocent. It was all the fault of that white-trash Irishman Dennehy, and the sooner he was behind bars for good, the better. She wanted her son's case dismissed today, and if it wasn't maybe they would hire a real lawyer for the next court date.

I was still seething as I climbed the stairs to the eighth floor to get to Jury One. What a woman, I thought; her precious son's a passenger in a car stolen at gunpoint, and if I can't make it all go away in one day, I'm not a real lawyer.

Jury One was on a break too. Like a dummy, I'd left my Dick Francis novel downstairs, so there was nothing to do but sit and wait. When the bridgeman came in, I told him I'd had a message about a warrant. At first he looked puzzled, then said, "Oh, yeah, we got a guy returned on a warrant in the back. We don't know whose case it is, just that it belongs to Legal Aid."

Oh, great. Dragged out of AP4 to come up here, and it's not even my case. The trouble with judges is that they think Legal Aid lawyers are fungible. "Fungible" is my favorite law school word. It means interchangeable goods, like nuts and bolts, where one shipment is just as good as

another. Unlike say, Picassos. We're nuts and bolts, not
Picassos.

When I got back to AP4, court was already in session.
I stood up on more cases. The red light on the phone
blinked. I picked it up, talking softly so as not to disturb
the court. "AP4," I said.

"Who is this?" It was my office-mate, Bill Pomerantz.

"Hi, Bill. It's me, Cass. What's up?"

"You've been elected chairman—or should I say
chairperson—of the Cozzoli committee. Got a pen and paper handy?"

"That sounds like one of those orange Monopoly cards.
You know, congratulations, you have been named chairman of the public works program. Pay each player fifty
dollars."

He laughed, then read off a list of sandwich orders. It
was an established tradition; whoever was in Criminal
Court picked up hero sandwiches from Cozzoli's on the
way back to the office.

"See you soon." I hung up just before the court officer
ordered me to. Judge Whalen was glaring at me over his
rimless spectacles. "If you've quite finished, Miss Jameson," he said in his dry, thin voice, "maybe this court can
conduct business. With your permission, of course?" I
mentally stuck my tongue out at him.

The court officers were rushing to call as many cases as
possible before lunch, but still people were coming up to
me to beg me to get their cases called. "Please, miss, I have
to get to work." "I have to pick up my child at school." "I
got a clinic appointment." And my personal favorite, "I
can't be sittin' here all day. I got things to do on the
street."

On the way out of the building, I ran into an elated
Sylvia Mintz. "My guy copped a plea," she said happily.
"Thank God! I'm free at last. Wanna go to A & S later?"

"Can't," I told her. "I've got things to do on the street."

SIX

"**H**ey, C.J., my favorite lawyer." Flaherty stood as I entered the lunchroom. He greeted me with a kiss so theatrical that it proclaimed to the world the platonic nature of our friendship. He was a huge, red-bearded Irishman with a wife and three kids, and he was my best friend at Legal Aid.

"You mean Hi Cozzoli, my favorite lunch," I answered, taking out his turkey and bacon with extra bacon, extra mayo, and extra pickles. That's Flaherty. Extra everything.

I put the food down, sat in a chair and listened to the usual lunchtime conversation. I'd interrupted a story Flaherty was telling.

"I just thought she ought to see a rat," he was explaining. "She was standing there in her fucking designer jeans and I thought to myself, 'There's a little white girl who never saw a rat.' You know what I mean?" Jackie Bohan nodded solemnly, missing the gleam in Flaherty's eye. Jackie's heavily political. She's only working at Legal Aid temporarily. Till the revolution.

"So I point the rat out to her," Flaherty went on. "It's down the end of the subway tunnel. Big mother too, all black and hairy. She doesn't see it. She does *not* see the fucker. Right in front of her, and she can't see it. Freaked me out, man." He shook his head.

Jackie nodded. "The obliviousness of the bourgeoisie," she agreed. "The refusal to see what they don't want to see."

"I may wink a jury on the Perez case," Sylvia said. "What do you think, Pat?"

Flaherty turned his attention to Sylvia. Deke Fischer glowered. He's our other supervisor, and it bugs the hell out of him when people turn to Flaherty for advice. Or to Nathan, who's practiced law for nearly twenty years.

"Who's the judge?" Flaherty asked.

"O'Malley. We already agreed the guy shouldn't have to do more than two-to-four. But the D.A.s won't come down. They insist on a plea to assault one."

"Sounds good," Flaherty said. "What's your client think about it?"

"Whatever I tell him to," Sylvia answered. "That's the problem. I think it's the right thing to do, but he doesn't understand enough to know what his options are. He may have delusions that he can win this case."

"What'd your guy do, Sylvia?" I asked.

"Stabbed his best friend," Sylvia replied matter-of-factly. "Trouble is, he's convinced it was self-defense. Because the dead guy insulted him. And if he didn't avenge the insult, he wouldn't be a man. Everybody on the street would know he could be pushed around."

"You know," Bill Pomerantz mused, "that's the exact same thing a cop said to me the other day. I asked him why he beat my guy with a nightstick, and he said he had to get respect on the street or he was as good as dead. I was surprised as hell that he talked to me at all, but when he said that! Jesus!"

"Yeah," Flaherty agreed. "It's hard to tell the good guys from the bad guys out there."

"Meanwhile," Sylvia said pointedly.

"Waive the jury," Flaherty advised. "O'Malley's a mensch. He won't burn you. If he has to give your guy more time, he'll let you know."

"Yeah, it's a good deal," Deke added. Sylvia ignored him. Bill gave him a look of mingled scorn and dislike.

Office life is funny. It's like one of those English villages in mystery stories. Everyone knows everyone else's business without really being close. I couldn't stand Deke, but I knew all about his rocky marriage. I wasn't a friend of Mario's, but I'd heard stories about his flaky girlfriend. The one exception was Bill. I shared an office with the man, but I knew less about him than anyone. No personal phone calls. No gossip, except for the persistent rumor, never confirmed, that he was gay.

Flaherty was a different story. Not just an office friend, but a real friend. He finished a story about a robbery at McDonald's. His guy had said to the girl behind the counter, "I deserve a break today, honey. Give me all your cash."

As we all laughed, Mario intoned in a deep announcer's voice, "There are eight million stories in the Naked City."

I disagreed. "There are eight million *clients,*" I corrected him. "There are *three* stories."

"Yeah," Flaherty agreed. "Story Number One: 'I found it in the street.' "

"Story Number Two," Mario chimed in, " 'He lyin'.' "

Before anyone came up with Story Number Three, one of the secretaries called out, "Is Nathan in there with you all?"

"No, Lily," I called back. "He's at the Special Prosecutor's office."

"No, he ain't," she shouted. "This *is* the Special Prosecutor's office on the phone, and they wantin' to know where he at."

I got up and went to the phone. I told the woman at the other end that Nathan had expected to be there at twelve thirty and as far as I knew he was on his way. It was quarter to two. I hung up the phone with a strong sense of foreboding.

On impulse, I picked up the phone and dialed Nathan's number. I didn't expect an answer, so the busy signal surprised the hell out of me. Nathan was home! What was going on?

I put the receiver back on the hook and looked at the clock again. Twelve to two. My prisoners wouldn't be produced in AP4 till two thirty. I could get to Nathan's in five minutes.

It had seemed like a good idea in the office, but as I approached Nathan's building, I began to feel silly. Nathan was a grown man. If he was sick, he could take care of himself. On the other hand, if he was sick, he'd call the office or call Parma's office, neither of which he'd done.

I didn't have a key, so I waited until someone else opened the door and followed him into Nathan's apartment complex. I walked quickly past the desk where visitors were supposed to sign in, trying to look as though I belonged there.

The ambivalence I'd been feeling grew stronger. I felt like a fool as I walked down the dim, impersonal corridor toward Nathan's door. What the hell was I doing here? There had to be a rational explanation for Nathan's absence from work. Hung up on the trains. Forgot the appointment. Was sitting in Parma's office right now, better late than never. The busy signal was only because I'd dialed the wrong number. Yet, as I stood before Nathan's door, I knew deep inside that none of those things were true. Something was wrong.

I knocked and waited. No answer. I knocked again. I was about to leave, when I decided to try the door. To my surprise, it opened. That fact alone primed my paranoia. I pushed the door open and gingerly stepped in.

The place looked as though a huge, powerful child had thrown the tantrum of his life. Books had been ripped open, the pages torn and scattered, and the bindings flung across the room to land in dejected heaps. The photograph of Nathan on the horse had been thrown at the wall near my feet, the glass cracked and the antique frame twisted with the force of the throw. Records had been smashed, the shiny black shards littering the floor. Playing cards had been ripped and tossed like confetti; the pottery chalice had been crashed beneath an angry shoe. Food had been opened and dumped. There were rice grains everywhere. Brown dried puddles where Coke had been poured over everything like gasoline at an arson site.

And the paintings—Nathan's beloved paintings. Slashed with a vengeance I couldn't begin to comprehend. Who could hate Nathan this much? The cool, detached NON-WORD painting was detached no longer. It was stuck over a lamp, the sharp lamp top sticking out through it like a spear.

My first thought was of burglary, yet I could see otherwise. A burglar would have stolen the paintings, not destroyed them. And the stereo, too, why not take that instead of throwing the turntable against the wall, leaving a twisted wreck? But then nothing made sense in that unholy mess. The viciousness of the attack paralyzed me; I just stood there noting the damage like an appraiser, trying not to focus on the important question.

Where was Nathan?

I wanted with all my heart to believe he was at the police station filling out forms. But the sheer violence, the stupendous anger of the vandalism told me differently. Whoever had done this had not left Nathan to go to the police.

Slowly, reluctantly, I stepped into the hallway, passed the kitchen, and turned toward the bedroom. My hands were cold and shaking, and my stomach was jumping. I stopped and took a deep breath before looking into the bedroom.

The deep breath probably kept me from fainting. There on the bed, where we had made love three nights earlier, lay Nathan's naked body.

I knew he was dead right away. There was a heaviness to him, the flaccid look of a thing out of which all life had drained. The muscles had no life to give them tautness. He was spread-eagled, face down, tied hand and foot to the bed frame.

The bedroom had seen the same blind malice. My photographs had been taken from the frames and torn into pieces, then scattered on the floor. The phone had been thrown against the wall. That explained the busy signal. The news drawing of Nathan had been cracked and propped, with a macabre and brutal humor, at the head of the bed, as though to identify Nathan as the corpse.

SEVEN

I don't know how long I stood there, leaning against the door jamb, my breath coming in little jerks. Part of me wanted to to Nathan, dead as I knew he was, and touch him, my touch miraculously bringing the pinkness of life back to the gray skin. Another part of me wanted to turn around, walk out of the apartment, and start over. Maybe this time when I turned the knob I'd find everything in place, cheerfully messy. Or maybe Nathan would be sitting on his ugly vinyl couch giving a statement to a stolid but helpful member of the Burglary Squad. It's not fair that you can open a door, and in those ten seconds your whole life turns upside down. It's not fair.

Finally, I turned away and, clutching the wall for support, made my way back to the living room. My knees were so shaky I was afraid I'd fall on the slippery papers. So I made for the green plush chair, only to find when I got there that cans of soup had been opened and dumped into the seat. It looked like vomit.

My stomach lurched, and I raced to the bathroom, sliding on the way and nearly falling. I barely made it. I was on my knees, in a cold sweat, hugging the blue toilet and throwing up my Cozzoli sandwich. It felt like the worst morning after of my life. I hung over the bowl, panting, coughing, retching, trying to pour into the toilet bowl all the ugliness I had seen.

Finally I hauled myself up, threw cold water on my face and rinsed out my mouth, then looked around for a towel. I found one buried under *The New York Times* crossword puzzle shower curtain, which had been pulled down and left crumpled in the tub. Still shaking, I lifted the towel to my face, then threw it away with a scream. There was blood on it.

I had to get out of there. That was the only thing I could think about. I took a deep breath and strode through the debris with my eyes fixed straight ahead, like a self-conscious bridesmaid walking up the aisle. I stumbled a few times, but I kept going. Getting out, shutting the door behind me, those were my only thoughts.

When I'd done that, when I stood in the hallway breathing in its institutional calmness, it was with some annoyance that I realized getting out was not the whole story. The police had to be called. I would have to see the man at the sign-in desk. I panicked at the thought. How could I find words for what I had just seen?

My knees still wobbly, still holding onto the walls, I made my way to the elevator and pushed the down button. When the door opened, I saw a young woman with a toddler and a laundry basket. She smiled at me, then saw something in my face and shrank into the corner of the elevator, pulling her little boy with her. She must have been relieved to see me get off at the lobby.

I went straight to the sign-in desk. The attendant put down his paperback book and looked at me with annoyance.

"Whatcha want, lady?"

I opened my mouth, but the words wouldn't come.

"Hey, lady, what's the problem? I ain't got all day."

"Nathan," I began, and then the enormity of it hit me. Nathan dead. My dear, good Nathan, lying up there naked and dead. I began to cry, noisily and violently. I reached for my purse and a Kleenex, only to remember that I'd left it upstairs in the bathroom of the apartment. In my near-hysterical state, this seemed as tragic as Nathan's murder. I cried even harder, wiping my nose with my shaking hand.

Something in my voice got through to the attendant. He guided me to a little office, sat me down, and provided me with a box of Kleenex.

When I could talk, I told him as calmly as I could what had happened, and then waited while he called the police.

When he finished the call, the desk attendant gave me an apologetic look and said, "I gotta go back outside, lady. It's the rules. You gonna be okay in here?" I nodded and he left.

I was grateful for the solitude. Relieved. I took a couple of deep yoga breaths to steady myself, then got up and began to pace. The room was about the size of a prison cell; it took me four paces to go from one wall to the other. I must have logged a good five miles before the cops arrived.

Finally the door opened, and a black plainclothes detective came in. It was easy to see he was a cop. The bulge under one arm where the gun went. The old man comfort shoes. The eyes that had seen it all. He extended his hand. It was small and neat and brown, like an animal's paw. "I'm Detective Button," he said. "I'd like to ask you a few questions."

He sat in the other chair. It felt a lot like being in the Criminal Court interview booths. Only this time I wouldn't be the one asking the questions.

Button took out a pack of cigarettes and offered me one. When I declined, he put them back in his pocket without taking one himself. "Gave it up," he explained. "I just carry them for witnesses."

And prisoners, I added mentally. It's standard cop tactic —offer a guy a smoke and win his confidence. It's especially effective if you're the good guy in a Mutt and Jeff routine. I tensed up in spite of myself. Now I really felt like a defendant.

He started with the easy stuff. Routine. Name, address, phone number. He wrote them in his memo book. My lawyer's mind flashed ahead to a future trial—how many cops had I cross-examined on their memo books? Somehow that made it even more real. "How did you know the deceased?"

"His name," I answered, between clenched teeth, "was Nathan Wasserstein."

"Yes," Button replied blandly, "that's what the desk attendant said."

I explained that we'd worked together, that he hadn't come in to work, and that when I found out he'd missed an appointment, I came over to see what was wrong. We went through it piece by piece. It rapidly became clear that Nathan and I were more than just office friends, that Nathan hadn't called in at work, that the phone had been off the hook.

"So you came over, unlocked the door with your key, and found his body," Button summarized. It was a neat trick. I've pulled it myself in court. You lead the witness along by weaving an assumption into something he's already testified to. With luck, he agrees with your whole statement, thus conceding something he hadn't admitted before.

But I've been around the block myself. "No, Detective, I didn't use a key to get in. I didn't have one."

Button raised his eyebrows. "The de—Mr. Wasserstein didn't give you a key to his apartment?"

"No, he didn't." I was keeping my temper with difficulty.

"Then how did you get in?"

"I followed someone with a key into the front door, and the door to the apartment was open."

"Did that surprise you?"

"Of course it did!" I exploded. "Nobody in New York keeps their apartment door unlocked."

"If you thought the door was locked," Button said insinuatingly, his little sharp teeth showing in a predatory grin, "why did you try it?"

"I don't know." It was the best I could do. "I rang the bell; there was no answer, but there'd been a busy signal on the phone. If he was home, he might have left the door unlocked. Or maybe I just hated to come for nothing, to leave without trying everything. I just don't know," I repeated.

"Okay." Button nodded decisively. "Now, about your friend's social life. Did you know of any lovers—other than yourself?"

"No," I answered. "But it wouldn't have mattered. We weren't seeing each other exclusively. It would have been okay with me if Nathan took out other women."

The predatory smile was back. "But what about other men?" he asked softly.

"What the fuck is that supposed to mean?"

"It means," Button said harshly, "that we got a guy upstairs tied to the bed in what the sex manuals call a D and B position—do you know what that means, Miss Jameson?"

"I live in the Village, Detective. I've heard the term. But it has nothing to do with Nathan! Just because some nut tied him up doesn't mean—"

"Let me finish, please. Not only was your boyfriend tied up, naked, but we found a few souvenirs in one of the night tables." Button opened the door and bent down, picking up a stack of magazines. He tossed them into my lap, saying, "Go ahead, look them over. They've been dusted for prints."

The nightmare deepened. The magazines were graphic. Some were slicks. *Macho. Stud.* Glossy color pictures of young men wearing nothing but leather and erections. Some were pulps. Muddy black-and-white photos on cheap paper. Articles like "Chained and Chastised." "Boys in Reform School." I would have thrown up again, if I'd had anything left to vomit.

"This—this is crazy," I whispered. "Nathan would never have looked at this filth."

"You never saw it before?"

"Of course not! It wasn't there!"

"Oh, you've looked in every one of your boyfriend's drawers, Miss Jameson? In every closet?"

"No. But I didn't have to. Nathan wasn't gay and he—he hated pornography. Said it was inhuman, exploitative, obscene."

"You discussed pornography?"

"A bunch of guys at the office wanted to go to the porno movie house on Court Street," I explained. "They asked Nathan to go with them. He went off on this absolute tirade about porno degrading both the people who make it and the people who see it. He turned some people off. They said he was being moralistic. But that's how strongly he felt about it."

"This wouldn't be the first time a guy has said one thing and done another," Button said. "Besides, that movie house only shows girlie stuff. Maybe he felt differently if boys were involved."

"Why are you doing this!" I cried, nearly in tears. "Can't you see I'm upset? My friend is dead, and you're calling him dirty names."

There wasn't an ounce of sympathy in Button's face or voice. "The dead man may have been your lover, Miss Jameson, but it looks to me like he was somebody else's too. And that somebody else killed him. I want that guy, and I want the truth from you. Did you know your boyfriend was AC-DC?"

"He wasn't!" I screamed. "He wasn't!"

"Okay," he rapped out. "You didn't know. Do you know if he hung out at any special bars or if he had any particular male friends?"

I shook my head, too angry to talk. "What about his clients?" Button barked. I shook my head again. At that moment, I think I hated Button even more than I hated Nathan's killer.

"Look, Miss Jameson." Button's voice went back to being soothing. "I know this is hard on you. But it looks very much like your friend picked up the wrong guy this time. All I want is some cooperation in catching that guy. If you think of anything later, any little thing that could help, just let me know." He handed me a card with his name and phone number on it, then stood up.

"If you'd like me to drive you home—" he began.

The last thing in the world I wanted was to be alone in a police car with Button. The second last thing I wanted was to go home. Face it, the cheerful colors, the instant furniture, the political posters were fun when you were in a good mood, but it was no place to go for comfort.

"No," I shook my head, "I'll stay with a friend in the neighborhood."

When I looked up, Button was staring at me. A steady, sad gaze. The pity in his eyes hurt more than all the nasty things he'd said about Nathan.

EIGHT

A young cop in uniform brought me my purse and tote bag. I thanked him and meant it; I'd have left them there rather than go back up to Nathan's apartment. He also warned me to leave right away. They were bringing the body downstairs in a green bag, and he didn't think I'd want to see it. He was right.

I headed straight for the Promenade. Ordinarily its panoramic view of Lower Manhattan gave me a thrill, but now I had only one thought—getting to Dorinda's apartment.

I followed the Promenade to its end, then up an incline to Columbia Heights. There was a steep hill. I walked down it slowly, my semi-good boots too high-heeled to permit easy navigation. I could see Dorinda's building, once a whorehouse for local sailors, but I didn't dare look up in case there was no light in the window.

Dorinda Blalock's been my friend since our freshman year in college. We went to Kent State before it became a headline. She split in our junior year to go live in the East Village with an experimental filmmaker, the first of a series of men she's followed to various artsy locales. Now she's on her own, living under the Brooklyn Bridge and cooking for a natural food restaurant in the Heights. Dorinda's a pretty good cook, if you can forget you're eating soybeans instead of steak.

When I reached the bottom of the hill, I looked up and sighed with relief. There was a light. I called Dorinda's name in a voice ragged with tears and damp cold. She looked out, waved, and tossed me the key. The buzzer sys-

49

tem in that building hasn't worked since they took the red light off the front door.

I let myself in and ran up the three flights to Dorinda's floor. The corridors are long; not every space in the huge building is developed. I stood, breathless, before the door. At my knock, she came, smiling, filling the doorway with her five foot ten inch farm girl's frame. Her thick braids were wound around her head like something out of *I Remember Mama.* I blurted out what had happened and suddenly began to shiver. I don't know if it was the cold or the events that were catching up with me, but Dorinda helped me take off my clothes and put me into one of her huge flannel nightgowns. She gave me thick handmade wool socks for my icy feet and sat me down in the kitchen while she brewed herb tea. Usually herb tea appeals to me about as much as wet hay, but tonight it was wonderful—hot, honey-sweet, and spearminty. I drank it greedily, letting its soothing warmth flow through my body. There was a warm afghan and a purring cat on my lap. It was as though no cold, no horror, no death could penetrate this place of warmth and comfort.

But I hadn't told Dorinda the whole story. I hadn't mentioned the magazines Button had shown me, the conclusions he'd drawn. I didn't want to. Nathan's death was bad enough; if I talked about the rest, that cold, nasty world outside would penetrate Dorinda's haven. And I wasn't ready for that.

We sat in silence. Dorinda lit a joint and passed it to me. I sucked in the smoke and leaned back, some muscle tension loosening. I stroked the little calico cat, Mignonette. A new addition. The older cat, Tansy, had appropriated Dorinda's lap as though to show the newcomer who was boss. Both cats were purring loudly; it was the only sound in the room.

I broke the silence, haltingly at first, telling Dorinda the whole story. She didn't say much. She's been around, Dorinda, lived with quite a few guys, one of whom was a part-time transvestite, so I knew she wasn't shocked by the basic idea of S-M paraphernalia. Maybe, like me, she found the idea of associating it with Nathan hard to accept. At any rate, she let me talk without comment or interruption.

I was a lot calmer than I'd expected. The initial hysteria had worn off; grief hadn't set in yet. I was in a limbo state of numbness that allowed me to think I was being objective, rational.

"I can't believe that Nathan was—what they said he was. It just seems so out of character, him with those awful magazines. Ropes and shit." I shuddered.

"Sometimes you see what you want to see in a person, you know?" Dorinda replied. She ought to know, I thought, a little cynically. Every starving artist Dorinda has ever picked up was going to be the next Mark Suvero or Robert Motherwell.

"I remember when I found that lingerie in George's drawer," she went on. I wasn't sure I could take another rendition of The Day Dorinda Discovered George Was a Transvestite, but I listened anyway. "I thought it meant he had another old lady. I really freaked when I found out the stuff was his."

I nodded. "But you stayed with him anyway."

"Yeah. He was a pretty nice guy, you know. Gentle. He wanted me to ball him while he wore that stuff, but I wouldn't. That would have been too kinky. But what I'm getting at is, you never know."

"I knew," I said flatly. "Nathan was a sensitive lover. He didn't need to hurt anyone to get his rocks off. That's not the kind of thing you can hide."

"Then what was all that stuff doing there?" Dorinda asked, her gray eyes serious. "Who tied him up? And why?"

"I don't know. Maybe somebody wanted it to look like a gay killing, to hide the real motive."

Dorinda got up. Tansy jumped from her lap, meowing in protest. She went to the stove and put on more water. I stroked Mignonette, my hand lightly touching the soft fur with its pale calico markings. The little cat purred loudly, rubbing against me, her whole tiny body reveling in being caressed.

Dorinda was back with more hot water. She put it on the table and pushed the hand-thrown honey pot over to me. I swirled honey into my mug, also hand-made, and poured water over the herbs. Still silence. The light was soft on Dorinda's long wheat-blonde hair. She had it out of the braid now, and it hung loose over her shoulders, making her look about twelve. A large economy-size Alice in Wonderland.

"Cassie," she began. I recalled Detective Button's pitying tone and thought I heard an echo of it in Dorinda's. It scared me.

"Cassie, listen. You may be right. Maybe somebody did make it look like a gay killing. But if so, there had to be a reason. You don't set up just anybody for a thing like that. There has to be a basis for it."

"No, there doesn't," I retorted. "It's the kind of thing people always believe about a man. Like they always believe a woman is a nympho. Once it's said, your whole attitude changes. You can't look at the person the same way anymore. That's what will be so horrible, Dorinda. People who never met Nathan will read the papers and say, Oh, yes, the fag lawyer that was killed in the Heights. It'll be believed whether it's true or not."

"But if the cops think—" she began.

"That's just it! The cops will waste their time looking for some mythical Midnight Cowboy and all the time whoever did it will be walking around scot-free."

"What can you do?" Dorinda asked.

"I don't know," I answered. I was unbearably tired, but it was only five o'clock. Dorinda offered dinner, but I asked her if I could lie down instead. She took me into the bedroom, turned down the quilts on her bed, and hugged me. Very motherly. A feeling of security came over me.

The bed was warm and comforting. The quilts were homey-smelling, heavy, protective. Yet I lay awake, stiff with anxiety and pain. I remembered my last night with Nathan. How he'd spoken for the first time about his breakdown. How he'd wanted to tell me something else.

How I'd run out the next morning before he'd had a chance. And now I'd never hear it.

My thoughts grew morbid. Nathan's last moments. Had he lain on the bed, his mind flailing in agony, in the certain knowledge that death was coming? Had he been afraid? Or was it like those stories told by people who were clinically dead but recovered—were there beautiful, white-clad illusions to help him into death? And had he thought of me?

I was startled by a touch on my face. It was the little calico cat. She burrowed under the quilts and curled herself up against my chest, purring like a furry toy. I made myself a nest around her, enveloping her in my larger warmth, hugging her as tightly as she would let me. It was good to feel life.

NINE

I awoke early, with a huge heavy lump in my chest. I lay in Dorinda's bed, the little cat still on one side of me, my sleeping friend on the other. My mind a near-perfect blank. I wanted to cry, but no tears would come.

I stayed at Dorinda's for breakfast. My taste buds at least were back to normal; I wished to God she drank real coffee instead of some horrible herbal brew with star anise in it.

Then I trudged up the hill toward the Promenade. The fog was so dense I could hardly see the city. The scene reminded me of a morning I'd spent on Cape Cod. The fog had been so thick I couldn't tell where the crashing ocean waves ended and the rolling fog began. I'd tried to capture it on film, but all I'd gotten were meaningless gray photographs and a skylight filter full of salt spray.

Lousy as the weather was, it was perfect for mourning. I sat on a bench, not caring that its wetness immediately began to seep through my lined raincoat. I wanted to cry, freely, unrestrained by having to maintain composure in front of anyone. But I still couldn't cry.

Slowly, unbidden, images of Nathan came to me. Nathan at a block fair, trying on a George Raft hat and looking, as I told him, like a Jewish hit man. I saw him in that hat, and I laughed and then cried, sobs bursting from me like an exploding boiler. Nathan at the bench, shrugging, wheedling, schmoozing to get one of his kids into a program instead of Riker's. And I'd told Button he didn't have special relationships with clients! What would the detective's sleazy coplike mind think when he found out Nathan had actually had clients to his house? Then, I recalled Nathan in bed, his gentle hands touching me. Finally, Nathan in death, his body splayed and tied by malicious hands.

I must have used thirty Kleenexes. I'd used a few twice. They sat in a sodden heap at the end of the bench. I picked them up and threw them into an empty trash barrel, where they fell, with a muffled, hollow thud.

My grieving over, at least for the moment, I turned my thoughts to the question Dorinda had asked me the night before. If I really believed Nathan had been killed by someone other than a gay lover, what was I prepared to do about it?

Button wouldn't listen to me. Why should he? I had nothing concrete, no evidence that any other motive existed for Nathan's murder.

Motive. If it wasn't sexual, what was it? Not robbery—a robber would have hit Nathan over the head or stabbed him or shot him. Not tied him to the bed and wasted time wrecking the place. Ruining things of value instead of taking them.

No, the cops were right in one sense. The scene had been set to look like the work of a gay pickup who freaked out. The magazines had been planted. The tying up was to complete the picture. Kinky sex gone wrong.

That's a defense, kinky sex gone wrong. Flaherty used it once in a trial. The victim—we defense lawyers usually say "complaining witness," but this was a victim—was raped with a broom handle. It was up to Flaherty to persuade the jury that the woman and his client were into weird sex and things had just gotten out of hand. No rape, just kinky sex gone wrong. It made me sick at the time, but Flaherty just said, "That's the job, Cass. Do it or don't do it."

Now the cops were fastening that kinky sex label on Nathan.

I couldn't let them. I knew the truth, knew that Nathan was not an exploiter, sexual or otherwise. I had to prove it. But how?

Back to motive. Why does someone kill a lawyer? Could the motive lie somewhere in Nathan's caseload?

If so, there was only one case that filled the bill. Charlie Blackwell. Face it, Legal Aid lawyers represent wife-beaters, junkies, muggers, crazies. How often do we pick up a client with heavy mob connections, with information destined for the Special Prosecutor? Information so hot that it puts his own life in danger?

Only instead of Charlie, they had murdered Nathan. Murdered him because he'd talked to Charlie? Because he knew what Charlie intended to tell the Special Prosecutor?

My pulse quickened. I had to get to the office—to Nathan's office—to see Blackwell's file. To see Charlie himself at the Brooklyn House. I stood up from the bench, stretched my stiff muscles, and strode toward the office.

On the way, I bought coffee and the paper. The story was on page 7. LAWYER'S BODY FOUND IN BKLYN HEIGHTS APT. My name wasn't mentioned. I supposed I had Button to thank for that. The thought galled me, but I had to give credit where it was due. At least I wouldn't have reporters calling me all morning, as I had when I arraigned the guy they'd labeled the Bensonhurst Slasher three years ago. When I got to the part where it said the body had been found in a "sunny, plant-filled apartment," my eyes filled with tears. The plants had been my idea. I'd helped Nathan clear a space by the window and fill it with marble chips. Then we'd spent a Saturday in the plant district on Sixth Avenue in Manhattan picking out trees and such. False aralia, schefflera, rubber plants, giant dieffenbachia, palms, a couple of figs—it was a little jungle. The last time I'd seen it, the plants had been ripped from their pots and the dirt thrown over everything in the living room.

The office was like a morgue. Lily, Ramona, and the other secretaries sat at their desks, dabbing at their eyes with Kleenexes. Ramona motioned me into the lunchroom, where the lawyers were.

Flaherty sat at one end of the table, a cup of milky coffee and two Danishes in front of him. His blue eyes were red-rimmed. They teared up as I came over to him. I put my arms around his bulk and kissed him. He squeezed my hand.

"God, Cass, what an awful thing," he said. His voice nearly broke. I set my coffee down and sat next to him.

The others in the room were in better control than Flaherty, but just barely. Bill Pomerantz had the paper open, shaking his head as though he thought they might have made the whole thing up.

Jackie Bohan blew her nose and said, "I can't believe it. Nathan of all people."

"I just hope I don't pick up any fucking burglary cases today," Mario said bitterly. His mouth was ugly with hate. "If I have to represent some fucking burglar the day after a friend of mine gets killed by one. . . ."

Flaherty cut him off. "That's your job," he said, his voice hard. "Don't confuse your grief for Nathan with anything else, okay?"

Mario stalked out of the room, muttering, "Just don't ask me to get 'em out of jail. Not today."

Bill looked up from the paper, a disgusted look on his face. "Christ, what shit this is," he said. "You were right, Pat. They don't actually say it, but they hint like hell."

"What do you mean?" I asked, alarmed. I'd bought the paper because I was afraid of what they might say, but as far as I could see nothing had been said about Button's Midnight Cowboy theory.

Flaherty's voice was bitter. "It's subtle. But it's clear to anyone with a certain type of mind. 'Bachelor apartment.' 'No sign of forced entry.' 'Bound hand and foot on the bed.' It all adds up to 'fag killing,' doesn't it?"

"Flaherty," I said softly, trying to keep it between the two of us. "I was Nathan's lover. Don't you think I would have known if he was—like that?"

He looked at me, an expression of pure misery on his normally humorous face. "I don't know, Cass. I want to believe you, but what about this?" He gestured at the paper. "It does look like he knew whoever killed him. He let the killer in, and he let—" his voice choked, "he let himself be tied up. How can you explain that?"

I couldn't. He went on. "Oh, God, Cass." His voice was achingly tight, and his face was pinched with pain. "I can't help but wonder—did Nathan have a whole side to his personality that none of us knew about? A dark side?"

"That business of having clients come to his house—" Sylvia began.

"It was dangerous," Bill agreed. "Stupid."

"Maybe he was, like, courting death," Sylvia offered. "A death wish. Unconsciously setting himself up. You know what I mean?"

"Whoever did it must have really hated him," Jackie said. "The way his apartment was destroyed. A real psycho."

Flaherty looked at me, an appeal in his vivid blue eyes. Eyes that usually laughed and now could hardly keep from crying. "I feel betrayed," he whispered.

So did I. But not by Nathan. By the people I'd thought were his friends and who now stood ready to throw away everything they'd known about him in life, to erase all that for one moment, frozen by death.

Even Flaherty believed the lies of that last moment, not the truth of the living man he'd known and loved. I got up and walked out of the lunchroom without looking back.

TEN

Nathan's office already had a forlorn, abandoned look. Just my imagination—or Nathan's habitual neatness—I told myself.

There was a little book on the corner of his desk. A paperback, beautifully put together by a small press, with a Japanese brush painting on the gray cover. *Zen in the Art of Photography*. I picked it up. Nathan had written in the flyleaf: "For Cass. You are the Photographer/You are the Photograph. Love, Nathan." I crumpled into Nathan's chair, put my arms down on his desk, and cried.

After a few minutes, I dried my tears and stood up. Then I went to the file cabinet and looked under "B." Blackwell's file was right there. There was nothing in it but the court papers, neatly stapled onto the folder. No notes.

This was serious. I knew Nathan had seen Blackwell at the House of Detention Wednesday; both Charlie and Nathan himself had said so. If I needed to, I could verify the visit by looking at the sign-in register at the jail. And yet there were no notes of the meeting in the file. The meeting had to have been pretty damn significant if Nathan was afraid to commit the details to paper. It's like when you have a client who's giving evidence to the cops. You approach the bench and put the facts of his cooperation on the record out of the hearing of the audience. You don't want the world to know the guy's an informer. Similarly, Nathan didn't want Charlie's file to contain information too hot to handle, in case the wrong people got a look at it.

The blank file was in its negative way a confirmation that I was on to something.

But my mind rebelled at the thought that conscientious Nathan would have kept the whole thing in his head. If he didn't trust a Legal Aid file, fine, but he would have made some notes somewhere, if only to protect himself if Charlie should get an attack of nerves and start denying everything. But where were those notes? I was about to ransack the office when I recalled that Nathan had gone to the Brooklyn House on Wednesday. And by Thursday, yesterday, he was dead. He hadn't been to the office since seeing Charlie.

Were the notes in his apartment? If so, was that the reason for the destruction? No, I decided. The destruction was too wholesale for that. And where would the notes have been? Had the murderer gotten them or were they still there? I decided to call Button, distasteful as the prospect was, to find out.

Then I remembered Nathan's spiral notebook. The one he always carried in his breast pocket. In it he kept such things as grocery lists, to-do lists, phone numbers, book titles, and information about his extracurricular clients. That's where he would have written shorthand notes of his meeting with Charlie. I was sure of it. I'd call Button and ask if such a notebook had been found. If it had, it would confirm my suspicion that something Charlie had told Nathan had been the murder motive. If the notebook was missing, it would go a long way toward disproving the Midnight Cowboy theory. What would a gay pickup want with Nathan's notebook?

Even though there was nothing in it, I took Blackwell's file back to my office with me. I'd get a notice to the warden in Supreme Court and go to the Brooklyn House of Detention as soon as I'd covered my cases for the day.

I called Button before I left for court. By some miracle, he was in. He barked his hello, and I tried to collect my thoughts.

"Detective Button? This is Cassandra Jameson. About the Nathan Wasserstein case?"

"Yes, I remember." There was a hint of dryness in his tone, but I had neither the time nor the inclination to follow it up.

"I've just been in Mr. Wasserstein's office here at the Legal Aid Society and I think maybe something is missing. Did you or your men find a pocket-sized spiral notebook in the apartment?"

"Miss Jameson, you saw that place. Only the Sanitation Department could help it. We haven't been looking for one little notebook. Why do you think it's important?"

I took a deep breath. This was the hard part. "If Nathan wasn't killed by some gay pickup, then it's more than likely he was killed because of a case he was handling. It involved a very heavy witness, and Nathan may have written some notes about a conversation with this witness in the notebook. If the notebook is there, it might have the notes of that conversation, which would lead to the murderer."

"If it contains incriminating notes, why would your hypothetical murderer leave it there?"

"Maybe he didn't know about it. But even if it's gone, doesn't that prove something? It proves that there was something in it the murderer didn't want found."

"Miss Jameson, I appreciate that you're very upset about your friend's death and that you'd like very much for the murderer to be somebody other than a gay pickup, but facts are facts. If this notebook is not in the apartment, and the murderer, whoever he is, has it, then we won't find the notebook till we find the killer, in which case the contents of the notebook will be somewhat superfluous. And all it will probably contain is the street name and phone number of a gay hustler."

I had to confess I hadn't thought of that. "But will you at least look for it?"

"To the extent that we can spare the time," he sighed. "But even you admit the notebook only might be there and only might be important. That's too many mights for me to spend a lot of time and resources on. Anyway, thanks for calling. Let me know if you think of anything else."

Even though the last words sounded like something of a

formula, I was glad he'd said them. I had every intention of
calling him again after I'd talked to Charlie. By that time, I
ought to have the original information, which would be as
good as or better than the notebook itself.

I did one more thing before I left for court. I drafted a
writ to be heard by the Appellate Division for Digna Gonzalez. I'd get her out of jail no matter how many courts I
had to go to.

People were still huddled in shocked bunches as I left
the office. Everyone felt the loss. Everyone felt the pain.

Nathan's murder was also the number one topic of conversation in the courthouse. I wasn't ready to discuss it, so
I just did my cases and left. On the way out of Supreme, I
picked up the notice to the warden that would allow me to
visit Charlie at the Brooklyn House of Detention.

Criminal Court was harder than Supreme. I almost cried
again, talking to Tim, the AP4 bridgeman. "He was a real
gentleman," Tim said sadly. "He really cared about his
clients, and he treated everybody right." It was the best
epitaph I'd heard yet.

Just when I'd finished my cases and was about to step
out the back way to BHD, I heard a voice calling me.

"Yo! Miss Jameson! Yo!" I wheeled around. It was
Tyrone Blake.

"Hey, man, save that 'Yo' stuff for the street corner, will
you?" I told him. "I'm your fucking lawyer, for Christ's
sake. What are you doing here, anyway? Your sentence
date isn't till next month."

"I got me a new case."

"Oh, no! Another car, I suppose."

"I thought the car was legal. Honest!"

"That's the trouble with you, Tyrone. You think a lot of
cars are legal."

"This time I knowed the car was okay. These dudes was
friends of mine. They done called me over to fix they car
on account of I'm the best mechanic in Coney Island. So I
be lookin' in the engine when the cops come down on us.
They all split, Miss Jameson, leavin' me by the side of the

car with a wrench in my hand. I didn't even run away 'cause I knowed that car legal. Only, it ain't."

"This is the story of your fuckin' life, Tyrone. You just blew your probation on the other case, unless you beat this or do some fast talking at your sentencing. When's your next date, and who's the lawyer on your new case?"

I wrote the information down in my own pocket notebook, having caught the habit from Nathan. As I said good-bye to Tyrone, I added, "And stay away from cars. As far as you're concerned, ain't none of 'em legal."

After Tyrone walked away, I turned toward the back door. I was passing the judges' elevator, when I was accosted again, this time by Judge Di Anci. "Wasn't it a shame about Nate Wasserstein?" he asked, with more than a hint of suppressed excitement on his face. "I hear he was tied up when the police got there. Is that true?" I told him curtly I didn't know, but he went on. "Such a terrible thing. A man like that, works for the poor, and one of them kills him. Just goes to show, doesn't it?"

I didn't wait around to find out what it went to show. I muttered, "Have to run, Judge," and ducked out the door, breathing a sigh of relief.

Of the two, I definitely preferred Tyrone.

Normally, I hate entering the Brooklyn House of Detention for Men. It's a big gloomy building that looms over Atlantic Avenue. But today I was so keyed up at the prospect of seeing Charlie that I rushed up to the double-strength front door and knocked eagerly. I was let in by a correction officer. I went to the desk and handed my notice to the warden to the officer there. The notice identified me as Charlie's attorney. I told myself I was not here under false pretenses; the Legal Aid Society was Charlie's attorney of record, and I was a Legal Aid lawyer. Besides, I'd probably get Flaherty to assign me officially to the case on Monday. I signed into the two visitors' books and showed my Legal Aid card, then waited on a bench while they went up to the cell block to get Charlie.

As I waited, I wondered how Charlie would be. Would he have heard of Nathan's death? If so, his paranoia would be totally out of control. But there was a chance he hadn't, in which case he might be willing to talk. Either way, I had to prevail on him to tell me what he'd told Nathan. The thought began to occur to me that knowing the information that had killed Nathan might not be good for my own health, but before I could examine it, the correction officer was back.

He was angry. "What is this, lady, a joke?"

"What do you mean? I'm Blackwell's lawyer."

"Not anymore you ain't. Don'tcha read the papers, lady? Blackwell hung himself in his cell last night."

ELEVEN

$\blacksquare$

$\mathbf{A}$t first I just stood there, numb clear through. On top of everything else, this was just too much. Then, as I grabbed my bag and waited for the iron door to open and let me out, too many thoughts crowded in at once.

Like the fact that I should have seen it coming. If Nathan had been killed because of what Charlie Blackwell had told him, how could the murderer leave Blackwell alive? No matter how much you scared him, Blackwell was dangerously unpredictable. I recalled his nervous, twitching hands, his stammering panic. Poor little guy. He knew it was coming, but he couldn't get out of the way.

I didn't believe for a minute that Charlie had hanged himself. For one thing, he was so single-minded about getting protection. What did he need protection for if he was planning to do the job himself? Plus, I couldn't accept the coincidence. The only two people who knew what Blackwell had to tell the Special Prosecutor died by violence. One day apart. The connection was obvious. I'd have to get back to Button. Maybe he wasn't impressed with the missing notebook, but this would convince him to consider what I was saying.

For a brief moment I wondered how they had gotten through the web of administrative segregation–suicide watch that I'd put around Charlie, then dismissed the thought. The mob had their methods.

Much as I hated the thought of going back to the office, I had to get to a phone and call Button. Reluctantly, I

turned toward downtown Brooklyn and made my way
along Court Street.

As usual, the street was jammed with people. Shoppers.
Office workers. Lawyers. I turned as a familiar voice called
my name.

It was Paul Trentino. Ex-Legal Aid attorney. Ex-lover.
Since we broke up three years ago, I hadn't seen much of
him. Less so after he and Pete Kalisch started in private
practice together. Which was just as well, as ours had been
the kind of office romance that gets messy when it's over.
The people who'd sided with him still treated me with
coolness. And vice versa, I suppose.

He walked up to me, the concern on his face showing
through the mask of politeness he usually wore at our in-
frequent meetings.

"Cass. I'm really sorry. What a terrible thing."

"Thanks, Paul," I said. I had to swallow to keep down
the lump forming in my throat. The sympathy in Paul's
voice was so warm, so unexpected, that it brought back
sharply the reasons I'd been fond of him.

"Hey, listen," Paul said, touching my hand. "I'm sorry. I
didn't mean to get you upset."

I shook my head. "No," I replied, my voice shaky, "it's
not you. It's just—" I broke off. The tears that I'd kept
down through the work day were welling up now, not to be
denied.

Paul looked around at the swirling crowds on Court
Street. Poor guy, I thought. He just wants to say a couple
of polite words to an old friend, and suddenly he's stuck
with a crazy woman, crying on the street, in full view of the
entire Brooklyn bar.

"Let's go in here," Paul said quickly, shepherding me
into a dimly-lit coffee shop. Passing the counter, he led me
to the farthest booth, sat me down, and ordered coffee for
both of us.

Finally the tears stopped. I still snuffled a little, my
breath catching in my throat every so often, but I felt
lighter. As though an anvil had been taken out of my chest.

"Thanks," I smiled at Paul, "I needed that."

He smiled back. It was the first genuine, unrestrained smile I'd seen since we broke up. It felt good to rediscover a friend. Especially now.

"Oh, God, Paul. I feel so damn—I don't know. Fragile. Helpless. Confused. First the shock of losing Nathan. Then the awful things they're saying." Paul nodded, a wry twist to his mouth. "And now, Charlie Blackwell's dead."

"Who the hell is Charlie Blackwell?"

I told him. When I finished, Paul knit his eyebrows in thought and said, "What do the police think?"

"They didn't think much of the suggestion before," I admitted. "But now—"

"Didn't the correction officer at BHD say suicide?"

"Yes, but what if it was made to look like suicide?"

"Or what if this Blackwell heard the news about Nathan and got cold feet?"

"If Charlie was scared, wouldn't he ask for more protection? Instead, he kills himself to save his enemies the trouble?"

Paul shrugged. "Could be. Anyway," he said, looking at his watch, "I'm sorry, Cass, but I really have to run. Important client waiting upstairs."

"That's right," I remembered, "your office is in this building." While we waited for the check, I asked the obligatory question, "How do you like private practice?"

"Love it." The wide smile confirmed his words. "I'm my own boss. I'm building something for the future. For the first time in my life, I feel like a grownup."

"Sounds great," I lied. It sounded awful. Feeling like a grownup has never been my favorite thing. And never less so than now. I would have given anything to go back to the Popcorn Shop in Chagrin Falls, eating popcorn balls and playing beside the waterfall. Far away from robbery, arson, murder.

I gave Paul a warm goodbye. We agreed to have lunch someday and meant it.

Back at Legal Aid, I went straight to my office, skipping the little groups of people around the secretaries' desks, talking about Nathan. I had more important things to do than talk.

I called Button. I told him about Blackwell, who he'd been and why his death was linked to Nathan's.

"You say he hanged himself, Miss Jameson?" Trust Button to go straight to the weak point.

"That's what the correction officer said. But how hard would it be for someone to do it for him?"

"I don't know. I'll talk to whoever's handling the case over here. Thanks for calling."

Before he could hang up, I got in a couple of questions. Did they know yet how Nathan had died? They did. The autopsy report wasn't in yet, but the unofficial word was strangulation. Manual. Any trace of drugs? No, Nathan had been conscious when he died. That news hit me so hard I almost didn't get out my next question. My mind was filled with the thought of Nathan going to his death knowing what was happening every minute. No blessed unconsciousness, no quietly going to sleep and not waking up.

What about the blood on the towel? Not Nathan's. But that was all they knew. There was nothing to show that it might have belonged to the murderer. They would check under Nathan's fingernails to see whether he could have scratched his assailant, but it hadn't been done yet. As to the magazines, there had been no usable prints, even on the slicks. I asked Button pointedly if that wasn't unusual, but he declined the bait. He just said, "Not necessarily," in a bland voice and thanked me for calling.

I took the subway home mechanically, hardly aware of changing to the local at Chambers Street. I stepped off the train at Sheridan Square, the heart of Greenwich Village.

I crossed Seventh Avenue and walked along Grove Street till I came to my little red brick townhouse. I picked up my mail—a letter from Ron. I walked up the long curved, carpeted staircase to the top floor rear, opened the door, tossed my things on a chair and sat down to read the latest from my brother.

hi kid—
big news today. frankie manzoni, the guy i was telling
you about, won his lawsuit. he can move out on his own
with full state subsidy unless the v.a. can prove at a hearing that he's incapable of functioning, which they won't
be able to do. so with any luck at all, your big brother
might finally get his own apartment at the tender age of
34. rick bannister wants to move in with frankie, and
gene kavanaugh and i have been talking about being the
next ones out. he's got the use of one arm, so he does
the dishes. wish me luck.
so how's by you, as they say where you live/ still feeling
the job's a bummer/ too bad, cassie, i thought when you
went to law school that your dreams were coming true.
but i guess there's always room for new dreams, isn't
there, kid/ keep dreaming. i know they'll come true.

loveandkisses,
ron

I felt like a prize bitch. My brother lived in a V.A. hospital in Brecksville, near the Cleveland suburb where we'd
grown up. He was a quadriplegic who typed his letters by
using a stick in his mouth to hit the keys. That's why he
didn't shift and used the slash for a question mark. And
here I'd sounded off to him about my stupid, trivial dissat-
isfaction with being a lawyer. When being a lawyer had
been his dream before Vietnam. Now his dream had
shrunk to being able to leave the hospital where he'd spent
the last nine years of his life.

I pulled a yellow pad out of my briefcase and began to
write. At least this time the problems I burdened him with
wouldn't be trivial ones. I wrote fast and furiously, filling
sheets of paper with large, sprawly handwriting. I wanted
him to understand how I felt, how important it was for me
to find the truth about Nathan and clear his name. Clear
his name—that sounded so melodramatic, like a thirties
movie. But it was true. I didn't want people dismissing
Nathan, using the sordid circumstances of his death to forget what he'd been in life. Like Flaherty was doing.

TWELVE

◼

Burton Stone. He was the key. I'd decided that as I lay in bed the night before, tossing and turning, my mind racing like a motor I couldn't turn off. Try as I might, I couldn't stop seeing Nathan's last moments in my imagination. The chilling knowledge. The futile struggle. The final despair. And if Burton Stone was why, I had to learn everything I could about him.

I took the subway to Times Square. The New York Public Library Annex on West 43rd Street should have everything I want, I told myself, as I walked toward the Hudson, through the neighborhood they'd once called Hell's Kitchen. Now it looked more like Hell's Drawing Room. Fancy restaurants, high-rise co-ops. What they call gentrification. I didn't see any gentry, though. The streets were empty, except for the Communists.

They stood in front of a Depression-style building passing out literature. The youngest of them looked about seventy. Men with wrinkled faces and bright birds' eyes. One woman with white hair and stout old lady shoes. Was this the life Nathan's father had led? I stopped, took a *Daily World,* and gave a dollar to one of the men. He smiled at me. "Intensify the struggle," he said.

"By any means necessary," I answered. I hadn't exchanged slogans like that since my SDS days at Kent. I hadn't cared about anything as passionately since then either. Until now. Until Nathan's killer had to be found.

Much to my surprise and delight, the library still had real newsprint. Not microfilm. I got my hands dirty, but I didn't care. It was nice to have the feel of yellowing pulp, the sense of immediacy a real newspaper brings, unfiltered by the electronic marvels of the 1980s.

When I'd had enough, I packed my notes into my shoulder bag and went out to look for a restaurant. There was a fancy-looking place in the ground floor of one of the high-rises. I took a table near the window and spread my notes on the butcher block. I ordered a bloody mary and a BLT, thinking of Flaherty as I asked for extra mayonnaise. It would have been good to have someone to do this with, to help me unravel the implications I'd read between the lines.

It was a fairly standard if sordid picture that emerged from the articles. Burton Stone, whom even the *News* (but not the *Times*) called The Fixer, was alleged to have taken bribes from various construction companies around the city. In return for those manila envelopes, Stone used his influence with boards, committees, agencies, etcetera. And he had a lot of influence with a lot of people.

Unfortunately for Stone, one of the construction companies used Charlie Blackwell as its delivery boy. Not only did Charlie tell all when he got busted for a petty scam, but he went to the last meeting wired for sound. Of course, Stone was no dummy. Like the others, the last meeting took place in a men's room, so all the tape got was the sound of running water and flushing. So it came down to Charlie's word against Stone's at the trial. Not that there wasn't secondary evidence—Stone's bank accounts, the votes he'd cast on his numerous boards and committees, the clients he'd represented. It all added up. But the only direct proof that he'd ever taken a bribe was the testimony of Charlie Blackwell. Charlie was guarded like the Crown Jewels. Every other edition had a picture of the sharply handsome Special Prosecutor, Del Parma, promising the public that Charlie would be safe until he took the stand. The papers played it for all it was worth, stressing the danger to Charlie, the significance of his testimony. You got the feeling they were all living for the day when Charlie would be killed. Then they could use the headline "Key Witness Gunned Down."

As I read, I sipped my bloody mary and made notes for future activities. Just how well had Charlie been guarded? Where had he been kept? Who had had access to him? If Nathan's insinuation had been correct, Matt Riordan, Stone's lawyer, had supposedly gotten to Blackwell. The question was how. I resolved to find out.

The famous cross-examination had been described in all the papers, but I hadn't copied much of it. I preferred to see it whole, in the trial transcript. There had to be things even a reporter might miss that I as a trial lawyer would pick up. I looked forward to reading it; the papers had reviewed Riordan's performance as though it had been Al Pacino's.

As I ate my sandwich, I mentally reviewed what the papers had said about the outcome of the trial. All had blamed it on the Special Prosecutor, pointing out the flimsiness of a case made out solely by a witness who turns out to be not only a professional informer but a free-lance crazy. As Del Parma himself had tried the case, I figured he'd been good and mad. I hoped he was still mad enough eight years later to tell me what I wanted to know. Having his star witness this time destroyed not figuratively by cross-examination but literally by murder might put him in a talkative mood.

Feeling as though I'd put in a good day, I ordered coffee, put the notes away, and tried to think about something else. It wasn't easy.

One of the things I was trying not to think about was Nathan's funeral. It was to be held tomorrow in Westchester, where his ex-wife and children lived. Should I go?

In the end, I decided not to. Instead, I did something I hadn't done since the last time I spent Christmas with Grandma Winchell in Ohio. I went to church. I'm not sure what impulse brought me there. I guess I needed a ritual. I needed to close something. To say goodbye. To take a piece of time and make it special by filling it with Nathan.

At first the service brought me little more than fresh

pain. My eyes teared up at every hymn, since they all brought back childhood memories. Then I moved straight into guilt. I had left Nathan deliberately our last morning together, knowing he needed to talk but preferring not to accept whatever confidence he intended to share. Because I liked our relationship light. Because there was a limit to what I felt for him. Because I could no more commit myself to him than to my chosen profession.

As the tears flowed silently down my cheeks, I thought of the last Zen story he had told me. Concentration and compassion. Concentration I would use to the utmost to find the truth, that I resolved. And compassion—could I find that for whoever killed him? I doubted it.

I left the church with a sense of something too nebulous to be called peace. But I did feel as if the intense mourning had ended—maybe I'd even stop waking up in tears every morning—and the harder task of adjusting to day-to-day life without Nathan would begin.

Flaherty told me about the funeral. "The rabbi was awful, Cass," he said angrily. "Oily bastard. He'd obviously never even met Nathan."

"What about the family?" I asked. I'd already explained to Flaherty why I didn't go. I couldn't stand the thought of sobbing in the back pew like the Other Woman in a goddamn Bette Davis movie.

"The ex-wife was there," he said. "She looked more disgusted than grief-stricken. And there were the two sons. And Nathan's father."

The Communist. I wished I had gone to the funeral, if only to meet him.

"He was pretty pathetic," Flaherty went on. "A shaky old guy. He broke down at the cemetery. Refused to leave the grave site. Said he couldn't abandon his son when it took so long for them to find each other."

"I wonder what he meant by that?"

"Milt said Nathan and the old man were estranged for a long time. Nathan didn't approve of his father's politics, I guess." So Flaherty knew, I thought. It still struck me as odd. I guess it would anyone of my generation. We, not our parents, were supposed to be the radicals.

The image stuck with me long after I'd hung up the phone. The old man standing beside his son's grave, unwilling to leave lest that leaving become abandonment, forgetting.

THIRTEEN

"**M**r. Parma will see you in a moment, Miss Jameson," the receptionist said. "Please take a seat."

I was on the fifty-seventh floor of the World Trade Center. Looking out the window, I felt distinctly queasy. There are 747s that fly lower than this.

I sat on the imitation leather couch and waited for Parma. I'd pushed hard to get this appointment on such short notice, calling the first thing Monday morning and then taking the day off work. I was glad I had. The Special Prosecutor could give me a lot of information if he wanted to. The trick would be to make him want to.

Maybe the whole concept of a Special Prosecutor is unique to New York City. And Watergate, of course. The thing was, after Serpico blew the lid off the Knapp Commission hearings, it was clear that there were judges and D.A.s up to their asses in corruption. And how are you going to get those D.A.s to prosecute and those judges to convict their own? Answer: you appoint an above-suspicion type guy to be Special Prosecutor, give him a handpicked staff of incorruptibles, let him present all his cases to a Special Grand Jury to be heard by a Special Judge. And so Del Parma's little hit squad came into being. They didn't always get convictions, or even indictments, but the mere mention that they were investigating someone struck fear and terror into plenty of hearts. He got so good at tainting reputations without backing it up with evidence that he was under considerable criticism even from people

who wanted to see corruption unmasked. You can imagine
what the people who didn't thought of him.

"Mr. Parma will see you now." I looked up from the
week-old *People* to see a fortyish woman with dyed red hair
and a generous mouth. As I followed her down the corridor to the master office, I noticed that her straight black
skirt and hot pink angora sweater were just a shade too
tight. Fifteen, even ten years ago, she must have looked as
perfectly ornamental as the girl at the reception desk, but
now it was an uphill fight. There were fine lines around her
eyes and the clothes that once would have been showy now
looked a little cheap. She seemed an odd choice for private
secretary to a man as concerned with appearances as Del
Parma. I wondered why he hadn't traded her in for a new
model.

Parma's office was spacious, carpeted in royal blue with
a vast, white-topped, empty desk. It was a mark of his
status that although there were two spectacular views—one
of the harbor and the other of Lower Manhattan and the
bridges—the desk faced away from the windows. The implication was that the views were purely for the tourists;
the Great Man was too busy to take notice of their panoramic beauty.

The secretary announced my name and slipped away,
leaving me alone with the Special Prosecutor. Parma paced
the room like a cat, all sinuous movement and burning
black eyes. Barely looking at me, he spoke to the room,
and perhaps the world, at large.

"Why can't you people leave me alone? I don't know
anything about Charlie Blackwell's death. I've barely heard
the man's name in the last eight years. Doesn't anyone
understand that?" He gestured theatrically as he spoke.
He still hadn't faced me directly. "You finish a case, it's
over, you go on to the next one. You don't brood about it.
You don't keep in touch with all the witnesses. Okay,
Blackwell's dead. I'm sorry to hear it. But it's nothing to do
with me. There's nothing I can tell you or any other newspaper."

Light dawned. I explained to Parma that I wasn't a reporter. That stopped him pacing, but then he gave me a look of suspicion, as though I'd come under false pretenses.

"But I am interested in Blackwell's death," I added hastily. "And in the murder of Nathan Wasserstein. I think you knew him?" I made it a question, though I knew the answer.

Parma was still wary, but he answered. "Yes, I knew Nathan. We worked together in the D.A.'s office many years ago. I was sorry to read of his death."

"I was a friend of Nathan's. At the Legal Aid Society. He made an appointment to see you the day before he was killed."

"Oh, yes, I remember. I wondered why he didn't show up. Of course, now I know."

"Did he tell you what it was he wanted to talk about?"

"I'm not sure that he did. We arranged to have lunch. I assumed he'd tell me then."

"It was about Charlie Blackwell. He'd picked Blackwell up in arraignments, and Blackwell said he had information for you. And now Blackwell's dead too."

"And you think there's a connection?" he demanded. I nodded. "But, Miss Jameson, are you sure that's what Nathan wanted to see me about?"

"I'm sure," I said grimly. That at least I could make him believe. The rest I wasn't so sure of.

"He told you?" Parma persisted. I wasn't sure who he meant by "he," so I elaborated. "First Nathan told me he wanted to see you about Blackwell, and then Blackwell himself told me he'd told Nathan 'everything,' whatever that meant. So there's no doubt in my mind that Blackwell had information for you and Nathan was the go-between."

"And now they're both dead. That's what you're thinking." He began to pace again, his fine hands darting all over, now pointed at me, now gesturing in the air, now thrust into a pocket, now running through his curly black hair. His whole body emphasized his every word. I'd had a client like that once: he was deaf. "But my God, Miss Jameson, what you're suggesting is impossible. Charlie

Blackwell was a very unstable man. If you saw him, you saw
that yourself. Nothing could be more natural than for him
to kill himself. I'm sure that's what the investigating committee will find—that he hanged himself. And as for Nathan—well, the newspapers said he must have been killed
by someone he knew. Someone he let into his apartment.
Granted, it's a coincidence both of these things should
happen so close together, but, take my word for it, that's
all it is. A coincidence. Probably Blackwell had nothing for
me anyway. You know how people are—any little thing,
they think the Special Prosecutor's the right person to go
to. I wouldn't put much stock in this, Cassandra, really I
wouldn't." He stopped to see what effect his words were
having. They weren't having much. I had my own reasons
for believing Charlie Blackwell wanted to live, and I certainly didn't believe he was the type to cry wolf. He had
information the Special Prosecutor wanted. I decided to
mention that.

"It's a fact, though, that Charlie could have told you a
few things you wanted to know, isn't it? About the Stone
trial?"

Parma didn't like the question. "It's true that I had a few
questions about that trial I could have asked Charlie," he
admitted.

"In fact, you believed Charlie took a dive on that case.
And you wanted to know who got to him."

Parma smiled, his boyish face taking on a paternal look.
"Cassandra, you must go to a lot of movies. It's true I've
always wondered if Charlie hadn't been a less enthusiastic
witness than I wanted him to be, but I certainly wouldn't
allege publicly that he 'took a dive,' as you put it."

"Maybe not publicly. How about privately?"

"I think my private thoughts will stay private," he said
coldly. "And now if there's nothing else. . . ."

"There is." I was crisp and to the point. If he didn't want
to air his opinions, fine, but I still wanted the answers to
some questions. "I'm interested in the type of security ar-
rangements Blackwell was held under eight years ago."

Parma sighed. "Cassandra, all this was a long time ago,

and I frankly haven't got the time to spend on it. However, I don't wish to appear unhelpful, so I'll let you talk to one of my assistants. Mr. Chessler will be able to answer any questions." He looked at his watch. "I'm late for an appointment, so if you'll excuse me." He stood up, called his secretary and walked me out of the room. We shook hands again, and I thanked him with as much graciousness as I could muster.

The red-haired secretary led me to another, smaller office down the hall. I wondered if the assistant would be programmed to give me a different version of the bum's rush I'd just gotten from the boss.

This time there was only one window, facing the Hudson River and New Jersey. From here, even New Jersey looked good.

The man behind the desk was about thirty-two, with thinning blond hair and mild blue eyes behind slightly tinted aviator glasses. He'd taken off the jacket from his three-piece suit, leaving a gray, pin-striped vest and pants, a pink shirt, and a tie of light blue, silver, and pink paisley. Very preppy-looking. He probably had little alligators on his underwear.

He stood up, offered his hand, and said, "I'm Dave Chessler." I shook his hand. They were big on shaking hands in this place. Maybe I should have worn white gloves. He motioned me to a guest chair in front of his desk, which was neither as large nor as tidy as Parma's.

"Would you like some coffee?" he asked. I nodded. Coffee would be nice, and besides, he couldn't throw me out as quickly as Parma had if I were drinking his coffee.

He called for a secretary to get us coffee. I'd expected the usual office instant with powdered creamer, so I was pleasantly surprised to taste a rich dark blend with a hint of French roast. Real half and half. In china mugs, not styrofoam. I decided I approved of Chessler.

When we'd both sipped our coffee, he set his mug on the desk, leaned back in his chair and clasped his hands behind his head. It's a common enough gesture, but it brought Nathan back so sharply that tears came into my eyes. Angrily, I brushed them away, hoping Chessler hadn't noticed.

He had. "What's the matter?" he asked, in a voice that was light and pleasant. Altogether he wasn't the kind of man I'd expected to find among Del Parma's scalp-hunters.

"Nothing. You just reminded me of someone." I quickly turned businesslike. "Mr. Parma said you might be able to help me. I need some information about the Burton Stone trial. Specifically about Charlie Blackwell. He was—"

"Oh, I know who Charlie is. Or was. Of course, that trial was before my time, but I've heard about it."

"Well, I'm concerned about his death. They're saying suicide, but it's certainly possible that he was killed by people who didn't want him to tell your office what really happened at Stone's trial."

"Could be," Chessler said cheerfully. "Of course, it just happened, so all the facts aren't in yet. There's going to be an investigation, though. Maybe something will come out of that."

"So that's what Parma meant," I said. "I didn't know what he was talking about. Who's investigating?"

"Department of Corrections, for one. They don't like the idea that a man can get killed, by himself or by someone else, while he's under their jurisdiction."

"True," I nodded. "It shouldn't have happened either way. Plus," I added, "Charlie should have been on suicide watch, and I read in the paper that he wasn't. I'd like to know how that happened."

"Meanwhile, how can I help?" Chessler leaned forward in his chair, his light blue eyes intent as he waited for me to answer. I was disconcerted by so much receptivity. So many others, even people Nathan had called friends, had been unwilling to hear me out.

"Charlie's dead, and so is the Legal Aid lawyer he told his story to," I said boldly. "I think there's a connection."

"Legal Aid lawyer? You mean the guy killed in his apartment in the—"

"That's the one. Nathan Wasserstein."

"But—I don't know quite how to put this, but—"

"But the police think he was killed by a gay lover. Yes, that's true. I don't believe it. I don't believe Nathan was gay, and I think it's too much of a coincidence that Charlie died the next day."

"In an apparent suicide."

"Oh, come on. How difficult would it be to hang someone in his cell and make it look like suicide?"

"Not very. And I agree that the kind of people who would want to ice Charlie would find plenty of help. Even correction officers, if necessary."

"That's a charming thought."

"That's the way it is. If Riordan's associates got him, they could count on officers at least turning their backs. For a price."

"Why Riordan?" I asked.

"We've always known Blackwell was gotten to at the Stone trial," Chessler answered. "And we knew who did it. Matt Riordan. He and Blackwell ran that cross-examination like it had been rehearsed for weeks." The mild voice was bitter now. "Riordan broke Blackwell on the stand in a hundred different ways. And they were all based on the fact that he knew to the letter every word Blackwell was going to say. He knew because he told Blackwell what the questions would be and how to answer them. Riordan made us look like fools in that case. Lost us a conviction where we should have gotten one. I'd be a liar if I told you this office didn't care what Blackwell had to say to us. If he was going to nail Riordan, we wanted to hear it."

The thought crossed my mind that Chessler seemed to know a lot about a guy his boss claimed he hadn't thought about in eight years. Not to mention being more angry and bitter over the defeat than the man who had been there taking the heat—Parma himself.

"Okay," I said. "I can see you think Riordan fixed the Stone case. But would he kill somebody? Or have the clout to have it done for him?"

The once-pleasant voice grew harsh. "Riordan's a slimy son-of-a-bitch who makes a fortune representing the worst scum in the city."

"I thought I represented the worst scum in the city," I said facetiously. It seemed oddly like betrayal to sit here with a prosecutor and malign a fellow defense lawyer, however unsavory his reputation.

Chessler forced a smile. "Seriously, Ms. Jameson, the man is an unscrupulous bastard who'll do anything for his clients. Like use phony medical records to get a long adjournment and in the middle of that adjournment the chief prosecution witness gets fished out of the East River. Nice, ethical stuff like that."

I was struck by the contrast between the well-tailored clothes, the modulated voice, and the street toughness. Maybe, like the little D.A. the night Nathan and I were in court together, Chessler was working overtime to put a hard shell of experience around an essentially soft nature. He went on. "Your clients may bop old ladies on the head for their purses, but Riordan's clients will burn that lady's house down with her in it and then contribute money to a law-and-order candidate for mayor. Only that candidate never quite gets around to doing anything about arson once he's elected. So getting Blackwell to flip on the stand in order to get a scumbag like Stone off the hook is light stuff for Riordan. So is icing Blackwell if he has to. The man wouldn't turn a hair."

"I see," I said. I wasn't sure I accepted at face value Chessler's assessment of Riordan, but Nathan himself had said the consensus was that Blackwell had been bought or threatened into falling apart on the stand. "But to get back to ancient history, how could Riordan have gotten to Blackwell? Didn't you have him under pretty tight security?"

"Of course. He was in a hotel, under full-time guard. The only people allowed in were members of the Special Prosecutor's staff and Charlie's only relative, his sister."

"So the sister could have been a leak?"

"She was pretty thoroughly interrogated when the fiasco was over." I gathered he meant the trial. "But she's the next thing to borderline retarded, so I doubt she'd have been much of a go-between for Riordan. No, unfortunately, we had to face the fact that it was probably one of the guards. We never got any of them to admit anything, but then Riordan wouldn't pick somebody who couldn't stand up to questioning."

Suddenly he stood up, almost as abruptly as Parma had, and walked over to a bookshelf crammed with papers and transcripts. From a pile on the top shelf he picked up a hefty transcript and handed it to me. It was part of the Stone trial—direct, cross, and redirect of Charlie Blackwell.

"Take this home. Read it. Then get it back to me by, say, Friday. Copy what you want, but don't tell anyone you got it from me. Understood?"

"Why are you letting me have it?"

He shrugged. "It's a public record. You could get it at the courthouse. I'm just saving you a little time."

"But why?"

Chessler leaned back easily against the corner of the desk, and looked down at me with a friendly grin. "Do you always look gift horses in the mouth, Ms. Jameson?"

This time I noticed the Ms. He was steadily rising in my estimation. He was the first person I'd talked to who hadn't dismissed my theory out of hand. I looked forward to seeing him again when I returned the transcript.

FOURTEEN

Maybe it was just the weather, or maybe my mood was thawing along with the leftover snow, but I got up early the next morning and walked to work. Across Bleecker Street, down Broadway—stopping at a coffee shop where they make their own Danish—and onto the Brooklyn Bridge.

When I'd climbed the stairs to the elevated pedestrian walkway, I turned, looking once again at the skyline through the gleaming silver web. It was a picture I never tired of. I'd photographed it many times, in color and black and white, on cloudy days and sunny days, morning and evening.

Nathan had urged me to enter my picture in a photo contest run by the *Phoenix,* Brooklyn's neighborhood paper. We'd had a big fight about it. I wasn't ready, I told him, to have my work judged. Now I wondered, as I stood on the bridge, why I'd been so reluctant. Now waiting for anything, putting anything off, seemed an act of ultimate stupidity.

I walked the rest of the bridge with Nathan. His imaginary company was a comfort, bringing a smile instead of tears.

I didn't feel much like talking to anyone at work. I nodded to the secretaries and stepped into my office. Working quickly, before anyone could come in, I threw the day's case files into my Channel Thirteen tote bag, where the precious transcript already lay. On my way out, I told Ramona, my secretary, where I'd be and tossed my AP4 cases in the traffic cop box.

Kings County Supreme Court is a huge slab of a building with tiny windows that look like shifty, close-set eyes. Inside it hasn't got a lot more character—marble walls the color of used chewing gum, an imitation tile floor so dirty the original color is a mystery, and overall a bureaucratic impersonality Albert Speer would have been proud of.

I took the elevator to nine, sidestepping the airport-style security system and going straight into the hallway.

On the side of the hall, away from the courtroom there are windows, each with a little recessed window seat, where defendants sit and wait for their lawyers, and lawyers discuss pleas with their clients. As Lenny Bruce said, the only justice is in the halls.

I checked into Part C, telling the clerk what case I was there on, and sat in the first row. I took the transcript out of my bag and started to read the direct examination of Charlie Blackwell.

Parma was good on direct—clean and crisp. Straight to the point, yet anticipating what he expected Riordan to ask on cross. Like the way he had Charlie explain his past criminal record—no hedging, no denying his guilt. If Riordan went after Charlie for being a skell, he'd be beating a dead horse. Same thing with Charlie's previous appearances as a People's witness. Charlie was open. Charlie was frank. Charlie admitted he'd made deals in the past, deals that had insured his freedom when all around him were losing theirs. Again, all Riordan could expect to get on cross was a rehash of that seeming frankness. Parma was leaving no chink in Charlie's already thin armor.

When the direct was over and Riordan stood to cross, I could almost see a smile of satisfaction on Parma's sharp, handsome face. Where could Riordan go that Parma hadn't planned for, hadn't planted little land mines for Riordan to trip over?

Nowhere, it seemed. At first. Riordan did what Parma expected. He hit on Charlie's record. He emphasized Charlie's reputation for selling out his grandmother to catch himself a break. Just what Parma had planned for.

Until the flying saucers. They came flying in all right,

straight out of left field. I was laughing silently as I read, visualizing Parma's stricken face as he took in this unexpected development.

Parma peppered the record with objections. They were all out of line, and finally the judge admonished him, but they were designed to give Charlie time to think. The trouble was that Charlie didn't want time to think. He seemed eager to confide in Riordan, like an author pushing his book with a helpful talk-show host. He was more than happy to tell the world, through Riordan, all about his close encounter of the third kind. In detail. Wacky detail.

As it went on, my sick, defense-oriented sense of humor began to subside. I felt sorry for Del Parma. His case was falling apart, and I for one couldn't see what the hell he could do about it. And because of Riordan's curve ball, Burton Stone, who had single-handedly bought and sold large portions of the city I loved, would go free. To continue to traffic in people's lives.

Riordan closed his cross with a couple of questions about Charlie's 730 examinations. The questions were interesting for what they *didn't* say. They were brief and perfunctory, as though it was only the fact of Charlie's having been examined at all that Riordan wanted to bring out. The implication was clear. If the examinations had mentioned flying saucers, Riordan would have used them for all they were worth. Since he didn't, they didn't. In other words, although Charlie had been examined by six shrinks at various stages in his career, now was the first time he had ever mentioned space travel. Very interesting.

The question was, what could Parma do about it? If he used the 730s to show that Charlie's science fantasy was a recent development, he still risked emphasizing Blackwell's general looniness. If he didn't, the jury would get the impression, fostered by Riordan, that the reports backed up Charlie's unreliability.

I was so absorbed that when my case was finally called, I felt as though I'd been rudely interrupted. I wanted to ask the judge, as I'd asked my mother so many times when I was a kid, if I couldn't finish the chapter first.

My client was brought out and sentenced to one-and-one-half-to-four. On a Rob Two reduced from Rob One. First offense, but that doesn't matter anymore. Not when there's a gun.

The kid seemed to accept it. He slouched into the pens without a backward glance. His mother was a different story. She kept wanting to know why her baby couldn't have gotten probation. I explained as best I could about AFOs, armed felony offenses, which involve mandatory jail sentences, but she didn't want to understand.

Finally it came out. This kid was her baby, all right, the youngest of her four boys. All the others had records; two were in the can right now. All had gotten probation the first time out. Why couldn't Robert get the same?

I explained it one more time, gently, I hope, then walked away. What could you say to a woman who had watched four sons, one by one, eaten up by the street?

Then I packed my file and headed for 120 Schermerhorn Street and Part D, the drug part. Jorge Ruiz's hour had come.

I sat Jorge and his girlfriend Alma on the bench outside the courtroom. Alma, thank God, spoke English. I ran through the case again, telling Jorge that he was charged with selling methadone to an undercover cop, that the D.A. had plenty of evidence to back up the charge, and that if he went to trial, he'd probably go to jail. In fact, when Jorge shook his head and blandly repeated, for the hundredth time, *"No culpable,"* I went further. I told him I saw no way for him to win the case. It was true. Never had Jorge given me the slightest hint of a defense. *No culpable* was all well and good, but it wasn't good enough. Not for a jury.

I brought out the heavy guns. I explained in great detail that selling methadone was a C felony, carrying a penalty of up to fifteen years. That got to Jorge. He laughed. He couldn't believe that selling your clinic-given methadone for an easy ten bucks wasn't a God-given right, protected by the Constitution. Or at least a minor offense, like spitting in the subway.

Finally, Jorge agreed to talk. Boiled down, the story was exactly what the D.A. had said it would be. Jorge was approached by a dude looking to score; he pulled a bottle of methadone out of his sock, gave it to the dude in return for ten bills, and then got the shock of his life when the dude flashed a badge and arrested him.

I looked at Alma. She looked at me. Being about ten times swifter than her boyfriend, in Spanish or English, she saw the point immediately. What was there in his story to support a plea of *no culpable*?

Finally, it came out. Jorge wasn't guilty because the stuff he'd pulled out of his sock wasn't methadone. It was orange juice.

We ran through the events of the sale again. Then again. This time I asked Jorge how he knew the stuff was orange juice. The answer was a classic. "Chico told me." Who was Chico? The wholesaler who'd sold him the stuff for resale.

As usual, Alma caught on before Jorge did. She jumped off the bench, let out a tirade in Spanish, stamped her foot and walked away. I looked at Jorge. He looked back at me and shrugged. Until Alma came back, sign language was all we had.

She was back a minute later, red-faced but composed. "This Chico," I began. She started swearing again.

I cut her off. "He's your friendly neighborhood dealer, I suppose."

She nodded. "That pig, he sell to the kids from the school. No good son of a bitch."

"And everybody knows it." She nodded again. "Including Jorge." He might as well not have been in the room.

Again she answered for him. "I tell him to stay away from that bum. He's no good."

"So if Jorge believed this guy when he said the stuff was orange juice, he'd have to be an idiot."

Alma bristled, then nodded. "Tell Jorge that," I urged. "Tell him the only way the jury's going to buy that he really thought the stuff was harmless is if they think he's stupid.

Tell him *I* don't think he's dumb" (sometimes you have to lie) "and I don't think a jury will either. If he goes to trial with that story, he's dead. Tell him."

I sat back and waited. At this point, the ball was in Alma's court. She understood what was happening, if Jorge didn't. She wanted him home, not doing time, when their baby came. So it was up to her to convince him he really was *culpable* and that he should accept probation.

Finally, she turned to me and nodded. Jorge would take the plea. We were both exhausted. Now all I had to do was get him probation.

I'd just gotten back into the transcript when the case was called. I horse traded while we waited for an official interpreter. I got what I wanted, everyone agreeing Jorge wasn't such a bad guy as to deserve jail. Jorge took the plea. He answered all the questions the right way, admitting he'd knowingly sold methadone to an undercover cop, and we set a date for sentencing.

Just as we were stepping out of the bridge, Jorge changed his mind. I could see it coming. The look of cunning as he used his dim brain to figure a way to beat the system, the tensing up as he prepared to throw caution to the wind, the stubborn look of a man determined to do things his own way no matter what the consequences.

The next thing I knew, Jorge was on the record. In English. Not very good English, to be sure, but good enough to be understood. "You Honor. You Honor. Please listen to me. I no wanna plea guilty. My lawyer, she talk me into it, tell me I gotta plea guilty. But I no guilty. I never sell no methadone, You Honor, I swear to God."

Judge Borkman gave me the long, disgusted look of a man who has just spent forty minutes negotiating and allocuting a guilty plea only to see it go down the toilet. I shrugged at him, trying to show it wasn't my fault, but it didn't help. "Plea withdrawn. Date for trial," he said in a tired voice.

I asked to be relieved. I'd done what I could for Jorge. If he honestly thought I was there to sell him out, I didn't see how I could be any use to him. Borkman, still angry, agreed, and I wrote LAR on the file. Legal Aid Relieved. In more ways than one.

I scooped up my things and swept out of the room, hoping to avoid further contact with either Jorge or Alma. Before I got out the door, I felt someone grab my arm. It was Deke Fischer.

"I saw what happened," he said.

"That stupid turkey," I replied. "Do you want to know what that bimbo intends to use for a defense?"

"The guy does seem a bit of a hump," Deke sympathized.

"Understatement of the year."

"On the other hand. . . ."

"On the other hand what?" My voice was cold.

"On the other hand, you jumped off the case pretty fast. Couldn't you have asked for a second call and talked it over with the guy? He just got cold feet, that's all."

"Cold feet, my ass!" I hissed. "The guy's jerking me around, and you're talking cold feet. What he's got is a lot of gall. But not nearly as much as you've got, standing here and telling me how to do my job."

"You're just jealous because I was named supervisor instead of your precious Nathan," Deke said hotly. "Everybody thought he was such hot shit, didn't they? Well, I'll bet even you don't think so after you've talked to Milt."

"Go fuck yourself," I said with venom, then wheeled away from him. Part of me wondered what the hell he meant by his last remark, since Milt Jacobs was head of Brooklyn Legal Aid, but I brushed it away. Just Deke's jealousy, I told myself.

Bill Pomerantz crept up beside me. "Deke on your tail?" he asked blandly.

"Deke's such an asshole," I sighed.

"No argument. But what burned me was what he said about Nathan. He's got a lot of nerve."

"Let's not talk about him." It was easier said than done; I was still trembling with anger as we approached the elevators.

"Where are you going?" Bill asked, pushing the "up" button.

"AP4. You?"

"Tenth floor. The arson trial. Fire marshal should be on." My pulse quickened. "That's Riordan's trial?"

He nodded. "Can't wait to see him on cross."

"Maybe I'll go with you. AP4 can wait." I stepped into the elevator with Bill. But I had no desire to see Riordan's cross-examination technique. I intended to practice my own. On Riordan.

FIFTEEN

You had to be frisked before you could get into the courtroom. That was a standard feature of Riordan's trials. His clients were the type that invited martyrs.

The courtroom was packed. Bill and I barely squeezed into the last row. I recognized quite a few lawyers in the audience, not all of them from Legal Aid. Plus every court buff in the five boroughs.

Court buffs are a weird bunch. They're a little like soap opera fans, except that the soap they follow is real-life trials. They like the drama of it. Of course, they only attend the juiciest parts of the juiciest trials, so they get more drama than is really there. At least I've never seen them at the run-of-the-mill Rob Ones or drug sales that make up the bulk of the trial calendar. Still, they do see the best trial lawyers. They compare notes on their respective skills and techniques, like drama critics comparing Hamlets. Evidently Riordan was a favorite. I could see knowing nods and smiles as he questioned a gray-haired, red-faced fire marshal whose men had apparently failed to dot enough i's and cross enough t's to meet Riordan's standards.

I didn't much care about the substance of the case, so I shushed Bill when he tried to explain it to me. It was Riordan I was interested in. His personality. His integrity, or lack of it. Was he just a hired gun, who'd do anything for a client within the somewhat hazy bounds of the Canons of Ethics, or was he an employee of the mob, who'd do whatever he was told? Right now, of course, he was behaving like a lawyer, methodically taking the hapless fire marshal apart like a jeweler stripping a watch. He picked up each tiny fact with the calipers of his precise questioning, holding it up to the jury, watching the light play on it as he dangled it this way and that, letting the jury see it from every angle. Then he carefully set it down and picked up the next minuscule fact to be similarly examined and displayed.

Whole books have been written about the art of cross-examination. The basic idea is to score points for your side off the other side's witness—who, if your opponent knows what he's doing, has been carefully prepared to block your efforts. Trying a case is like a bridge game. You've got a certain number of tricks you're bound to lose no matter how well you play. Other tricks are sure tricks for you, unless you're a total idiot. The ones in the middle—the ones that could go either way—are what the game's all about. Cross is where you take those tricks. Or lose them.

From what I could see, Riordan was taking every trick that could conceivably have been taken—plus a few that should have gone to the D.A. A fire marshal, after all, is the keystone of an arson case. He's an expert in his field, a professional witness, and he should be able to hold his own with even a skilled cross-examiner. But Riordan was taking tricks off this guy with deuces, pushing the fire marshal closer and closer to admitting his men had made significant mistakes in the handling of their investigation. Either Riordan was really good, or this guy was really bad.

It went on for another half-hour. When Riordan finished, the D.A. stood up for redirect, much to the marshal's obvious dismay. But the judge too had had enough. He called lunch recess fifteen minutes early.

I waited in the back of the courtroom for Riordan, as the crowds milled around. I got rid of Bill with the lie that I had to see the judge about another case. Finally Riordan slung his Burberry over his arm, picked up his Gucci briefcase, and stepped toward the rear doors. I stepped in front of him. "Mr. Riordan, could I talk to you for a minute?"

He smiled. He was even better looking up close. Glossy

black hair, startling blue eyes, a pink face with laugh lines around the eyes and mouth. "Sure, Miss. . . ."

"Jameson. Cassandra Jameson. I'm with Legal Aid here in Brooklyn."

"And you're following this trial?"

It was a natural assumption. What else would I be doing there? But there was a hint of being nice to a groupie about it that turned me off. "Not this trial, Mr. Riordan. It's the Burton Stone trial I'm interested in."

Riordan's smile broadened. In a crack cross-examiner, trained to show a jury triumph when he'd really suffered defeat, that meant he was either rattled or annoyed. I pressed my advantage. "Maybe you've been too busy to keep up with the news, but Charlie Blackwell was found dead in his cell last week."

The smile faded. He said softly, "And what's your interest in all this, Miss Jameson?"

I lied. "Blackwell was my client. He told me a little about the Stone case. I wonder whether he was killed by people who didn't want him to tell Del Parma about it."

"So you're doing what, Miss Jameson? Conducting your own investigation?" I nodded. "Let me give you some advice." He had recovered his poise; the blue eyes were amused. "Leave it to the cops. I'm sure you've always wanted to play Nancy Drew, but don't start with Blackwell. You could be getting involved with some very dangerous people." He opened the courtroom door. "And now if you'll excuse me, Miss Jameson. . . ."

He was gone. I was furious. Nancy Drew, my ass!

On the way out, I saw something disturbing. On a bench outside the courtroom, the D.A. sat with the fire marshal. I could just overhear the D.A. whispering earnestly, "But Mr. Boyce, you were so sure about your facts in the office. What happened?"

It was a good question. Had the same thing happened to him that had happened to Blackwell six years ago? And when Riordan warned me about dangerous people, was he talking about himself?

• • •

That night I had dinner with an old friend, Emily Marks Willburton. After dinner, we walked through the Heights to the former carriage house where she lived. Very picturesque. Very private. Very expensive. Inside it was all antiques—highly polished wood glowed in the light from brass, black-shaded lamps. Her husband, Stan, back early from a bar association meeting, got up from a red, brass-studded leather chair, embraced me, and murmured how sorry he was about Nathan.

I sat on the matching leather couch while Stan went for brandy. Emily sat beside me, her long legs tucked under her like a child's as I told them about the murders and my investigation. It was getting more coherent with each retelling. I wished I could have had it this together when I'd talked to Button.

Stan came in with snifters as I was getting started. He put Emily's and mine on the coffee table and perched on the edge of the red chair, leaning forward, his elbows resting on his knees.

I'd known Emily since she'd taught Appellate Writing at NYU when I was a freshman law student. Now she had one of the best appellate practices in the city. Nearly fifty, she wore her long, graying black hair in a severe bun, which emphasized the classic lines of her face. Her father was Judge Julius Marks, of the Eastern District.

Stan was a complete contrast. Whereas Emily, with her father's encouragement, had gone to Harvard Law School, Stan had pushed a hack by day and attended Brooklyn Law School by night. He had an exclusively criminal practice and headed the murder section of the Brooklyn 18-b panel. He was streetwise and tough, and if anyone could give me an insider's view of Matt Riordan, it was he.

When I finished telling them how Riordan had warned me off the grass, there was silence for a few moments, though each was silent in a different way. Emily sat still, quiet and serene, collecting her thoughts in the same orderly way she wrote her devastatingly thorough appellate briefs. Stan was quiet in the way Nureyev stood still onstage—there was a strong sense of energy contained, of incipient movement.

Characteristically, Stan spoke first. "You want to know whether Riordan's as bad as this guy Chessler thinks he is." It was also typical of Stan to go straight to the point. I nodded.

"I had a case with him once. His client was a big-time drug seller. Major cocaine deal. My guy was a poor slob whose only crime was introducing the undercover cop to Mr. Big. Perfect agency defense, right?" He didn't wait for an answer. I took his word for it. "So Mr. Big cops a plea to three to life. Sale Two. My guy goes to trial. What the hell—he's got no record, all he did was to tell the cop where he could buy dope if he wanted it, he got about fifty bucks and a taste. Well, the upshot is, he gets convicted on a Sale One and is still doing twelve to life."

"That just sounds like Riordan made a good deal for his client," I protested. "Can't blame him for that."

"I don't blame him," Stan said, "though his clients always seem to get a better deal than anyone else's. The thing is, his Mr. Big gets the break of a lifetime while the judge comes down really hard on my poor slob after trial, giving him more than the minimum, making all kinds of nasty remarks on the record. You see, Cass, it was the same judge."

"I get it. He was death on drugs when it came to sentencing your guy, but he treated Riordan's guy, who was the real drug seller, with kid gloves."

"Exactly."

"You think the judge was bought?"

"Who knows? All I know is Riordan gets dream pleas from judges who'd give their grandmothers the maximum."

Emily spoke up. "I've seen several of his records on appeal. He's a good lawyer. He does sail a little close to the wind, though. A couple of his alibis, for instance. . . ." She trailed off, but her meaning was clear.

"Phony alibis," I nodded. "That squares with what Chessler said."

Stan leaned even further forward in his chair, spreading his stubby hands toward me. "You gotta understand how things are done, Cass. It's not that simple. Maybe he says to his client, 'You know, Joe, it would help your case a lot if you had an alibi.' He doesn't say, 'Joe, cook up a phony alibi.' Nothing that crude. But Joe gets the message. The next day there are twenty guys on Riordan's doorstep, ready to swear they were playing poker with Joe. See what I mean? It's a fine line. Riordan doesn't *tell* Joe to fake an alibi, and he certainly doesn't suborn perjury. But he *does* put witnesses on the stand that he's got to have serious doubts about. That, however, is not unethical. That's how Riordan works."

"Just do what you have to do and don't tell me about it," I said with some bitterness. "Like Watergate."

"Right. Which is why I don't believe Riordan himself would get to Blackwell. He wouldn't want to know about it if Stone had it done, but that's a very different thing from doing it himself."

"But," I tried to put this into words, "isn't Stone kind of a special client? I mean, he's not a dope dealer or anything. He was a respected man, a borderline criminal. In that gray area between sharp business practices and outright stealing. Maybe Riordan wouldn't pay off a witness for just any client, but maybe he'd go a little further for a Burton Stone."

"I doubt it." Stan was firm. "Matt Riordan is the consummate professional. Call him a hired gun if you will, but he does a hell of a job for his clients. But even for Stone, I don't see him risking his own professional life by getting to a witness." Emily nodded. It was a strong consensus.

"Okay, so Riordan didn't do the dirty work himself. Wasn't Stone out on bail?"

"My memories are fairly shaky," Emily began, "but aside from the difficulty of anyone who knew Stone getting in to see Blackwell, there's the problem of competence. As I recall the trial, the questions asked by Riordan were detailed. It would be hard for a layman to build a cross-examination like that and then tell Blackwell exactly what to say. It tailored so perfectly with Riordan's defense tactics that it almost had to be planned by someone as good at cross-examination as he is."

"And there aren't that many people, even lawyers, about whom that could be said," Stan added.

"All right. So Riordan planned it and somebody else carried messages," I said.

Stan gave me a wry smile. "You sure want Riordan to be the heavy here, Cass. Look, you're a criminal lawyer. Who would you trust to take messages like that—and get them right?"

I reluctantly admitted that Stan had a point. But I had one too. "If it wasn't Riordan, who was it?"

While her husband and I argued, Emily looked thoughtful. "You know," she said slowly, "what I don't understand is why Del Parma let Charlie Blackwell go into the system at all."

"What choice did he have?" I asked.

"I had a case on appeal," she explained. "My client was arrested and taken straight to the World Trade Center, to Parma's office, for questioning. He didn't get arraigned until *after* he'd made his little deal with Parma."

"And that was upheld on appeal?" I asked incredulously. "Whatever happened to the right to a speedy arraignment?"

"It didn't have to be upheld," Stan cut in. "Parma got what he wanted anyway. But that's a good question—if the Special Prosecutor was so interested in Blackwell, wouldn't they have tried to get to him before he had counsel?"

"If they knew about him," I objected. "He was busted for drugs. They didn't even know he was still alive until Nathan called to make the appointment."

"Maybe." Stan looked skeptical. "But I can't believe Parma wasn't keeping tabs on Blackwell in some way."

The thought was a tantalizing one. If Charlie had been taken to the World Trade Center before arraignment, he might have made his deal before even meeting Nathan.

There would be no need to eliminate Nathan to prevent information from getting to Parma because he'd already have it. And Nathan would be alive. It didn't bear thinking about.

SIXTEEN

"**M**otion granted. The defendant is hereby ordered released from custody on her own recognizance." Justice Harvey Krantz said the magic words that would finally let Digna Gonzalez out of jail. I'd had to go to the Appellate Division to do it, but it was worth it. Not only was Digna free, but it was one in the eye for Di Anci. His father, of course, had excused himself from hearing the case. I wondered idly which way he'd have gone if he'd been there.

I celebrated by stopping at Goldberry's, the fancy natural food restaurant Dorinda works at. Like many Montague Street shops, it's located on the parlor floor of an old brownstone. I climbed the iron staircase, my footsteps echoing hollowly, and found a seat near the window. It was late for lunch, so there were plenty of empty tables.

Dorinda saw me and smiled, then came over to my table. I asked her if she could talk. She looked around at the customers with the eye of a practiced waitress and estimated she'd be free in ten minutes or so. I ordered coffee and asked what there was for dessert.

"Carrot cake. Apple walnut cake. And banana tofu pie."

"What's tofu?"

"Bean curd."

"I'd rather die." I opted for carrot cake and opened the transcript while I waited. I still hadn't finished the last few pages.

Redirect was short and aimless. Even on the printed page I could see Del Parma flailing around, trying to hit the note that would erase the damage Riordan had done on cross. He didn't succeed. And he didn't introduce the 730 reports. The fact that they contained no reference to flying saucers was a negative inference at best. Maybe none of Blackwell's shrinks had ever asked him about space travel.

Riordan didn't bother to recross. No gilder of lilies he.

Dorinda brought the carrot cake and sat down in the chair opposite me, dwarfing it. The chairs were the little wire-backed kind they had at soda fountains in the 1930s. They were painted bright yellow and had white cushions.

"God, this place is a bummer," Dorinda sighed.

"Bad day?"

"It's so damned *artsy*. I mean, look at this decor, for God's sake." I murmured something sympathetic through a mouth full of carrot cake. It was rich and spicy. The frosting was lemony with a tangy edge I hoped wasn't yogurt but probably was.

"And the menus." She went on. "Pure flower child. J.R.R. *Tolkien,* for God's sake."

"Dorinda, you've seen the goddamn menus before. I'll admit line drawings of Tom Bombadil and quotes from *The Fellowship of the Ring* are cloying, but. . . ."

She picked up a menu. It was hand-lettered in a fairly readable approximation of Tolkien's elvish runes. "Listen to this. 'The table is all laden with yellow cream, honeycomb, and white bread and butter. Goldberry is waiting.' I may puke."

"I may join you. There's yogurt in this frosting. I'm sure of it."

That diverted her. "Yogurt is good for you. I made that frosting myself."

"Oh. Well, the cake is fabulous. You know I loathe yogurt. But the question is why this place is getting to you today and not yesterday or the day before."

"It got to me yesterday and the day before. You just weren't here to hear it."

"There's more to it than that."

"Yeah. I made my brown rice salad for Suzanne. You know, the one you like, with the artichoke hearts. She won't use it. Says it's too health-foody. Some natural food restaurant, turning down a dish because it's too healthy."

"Seems to me any place that serves pie made out of bean curd—"

"It's not moving. And it was my idea. When I get my own place. . . ."

"I hate to say it, Dorinda, but you'll get your own place the day I get a job as a professional photographer. Which means never. You need capital to open a restaurant. If you'd find yourself an old man with bread instead of the stray artists you're always picking up. . . ."

"Are you referring to Claude?"

"Who the hell is Claude?"

"This guy I met at a party in Vinegar Hill. We spent the weekend together. He's a woodcarver, and he has wonderful eyebrows."

"Dorinda, for God's sake. Someday you're going to be killed in your bed by some guy with wonderful eyebrows."

She got up to serve coffee to the remaining customers, then brought the pot back and poured us each a cup. I scraped the frosting off and ate the rest of the carrot cake.

"How's the investigation going?" she asked when she came back.

"It looks as though Riordan is still the only person with motive," I answered. "He fixed the Stone case, Blackwell knew it, and Blackwell told Nathan. Now they're both dead."

"But?"

"But I can't prove anything. Oh, I know Riordan's on trial in the building, but he wasn't there for night court. How did he know Blackwell had even been arrested, let alone that he had something to say to the Special Prosecutor? Nathan said Charlie didn't even want the judge to know about that. So how did Riordan find out?"

"Isn't it a public record? Being arrested, I mean?" Dorinda asked.

"Well, sure, but—I see what you mean. Anybody could have seen it on the calendar."

"And you said this guy split on his friends before," Dorinda pointed out.

"So it was a safe bet that he'd do it again. Yeah, that makes sense," I agreed.

"The real question is how did Riordan know that Charlie talked to Nathan?"

"Well, Nathan had to sign a book at the Brooklyn House to see Charlie," I explained. "If Riordan went over there to see his own client, say, he could have seen the signature and put two and two together."

"Maybe." Dorinda looked dubious. "But it seems like a coincidence. Besides, how would he know that Nathan hadn't already called the Special Prosecutor and told him everything on the phone?"

"It's not the kind of thing you say on the phone," I answered crossly. But it was a good question, and one for which I had no answer.

Back at the office, I ran into Sylvia Mintz. On her way out of the elevator, she said, "Cass, I've got a message for you." Trust Sylvia to put it that way, I thought. You have a message. Not telling you what it is, but making you ask. It turned out that Milt Jacobs wanted to see me. She made it sound like I'd been summoned to the principal's office.

When I reached his office, Milt was on the phone. I hovered in the doorway, trying to get his attention so I could tell him I'd come back later, but he motioned me in. I sat in one of the guest chairs and looked around the office. It hadn't changed since the day Milt moved in three years earlier. Still no pictures on the wall, not even posters. No family snapshots. Even the calendar was the one given to all law offices by a major law publisher. Wholly impersonal. Milt could die tomorrow and someone else could move right in without having to clean anything out.

Milt put down the phone and looked at me. Then he picked it up and told Aurora, his secretary, to hold his calls. Whatever he wanted, it was important. And personal.

"I heard you were, ah, close to Nathan." He wasn't looking at me. His eyes were fixed firmly on a blank wall. I didn't know how to make it any easier, so I just nodded.

"Ah, Detective Button was here Monday. You were out on a comp day or something." I nodded again. I'd been seeing Del Parma. "He asked about Nathan's caseload."

I was excited. Maybe I'd been wrong about Button. He might discourage me to my face and then investigate Blackwell behind my back. Which didn't bother me as long as he investigated.

"He was especially interested in a young man named Heriberto Diaz. Does that name ring a bell with you?"

I shook my head, bewildered. What did this have to do with Blackwell?

"Detective Button seems to think Nathan had a special relationship with this boy. He has evidence that the boy had been to Nathan's apartment on several occasions. The boy has a—a history of homosexual relationships."

So Button's found his scapegoat, I thought. Some poor kid whom Nathan had been trying to help and who just happened to be gay. I was exasperated.

"Milt, you know Nathan had clients to his apartment. To get them into programs or to help them get jobs. It didn't mean anything. Okay, so this kid's gay. That doesn't mean Nathan was."

There was a long pause. I didn't know why. It was obvious Milt hated this conversation. Why was he prolonging it?

"Cassandra," he finally said. He was still talking to a point on the wall, but now he was addressing it from much farther away. "I am really sorry about this. I didn't want to be the one to tell you. In fact, I wouldn't have told you if it hadn't been for Flaherty telling me about you and Nathan."

"Yeah, so?" I was more than a little annoyed at Flaherty. He should have consulted me before talking to Milt.

"Cassandra," Milt said it so softly I could barely hear, "the fact is that Nathan was gay."

"What?" I couldn't believe I'd heard correctly. "What are you telling me? Where did you get that idea?"

"It's true." He said it with finality. "He was arrested in a men's room when he was working in Manhattan. His firm hushed it up and put him on sick leave. But he couldn't stop himself. He seemed compelled to go after boys in the most sordid surroundings. He stopped seeing his old friends. Even Sid Rosen and me. Finally his wife had enough and sued for divorce. The firm fired him. He drifted around for a while, then started seeing a shrink and asked me for a job. I knew about the arrest, but I also knew what a good lawyer he was. A good friend, too. So I hired him. Anything he did outside the job I figured was his own business." Milt gave the wall a bleak smile. "He wasn't the first Legal Aid lawyer with an underground sex life. We could run our own Gay Liberation Day parade. The thing is, I hoped he'd be discreet. Not pick up clients. Do you know how bad that would look in the *Post,* Cass? 'Legal Aid Lawyer Having Sex with Seventeen-Year-Old Client'?"

"I can't believe it," I whispered. "Milt, I just don't get this. I was Nathan's lover! Me! Not some kid." My voice began to rise. I cleared my throat and went on. "I just don't know where all this is coming from except from Button's depraved imagination."

"Cass, slow down. Button didn't make it up about Nathan's breakdown. That's a fact. Look, I was there."

"Maybe so." I tried to stay calm. "Maybe Nathan did go through a period where he did things like that. But people can change. He *was* my lover." Milt looked away again. He'd faced me when I'd started talking, but this was too blunt for him. "Milt, I appreciate what you're saying, but I just don't see it. Whatever Nathan did in the past, I know what his preference was when he died. Besides, I think I'm getting somewhere with this Burton Stone case."

"Cass, I appreciate how you feel. I'd rather see any other explanation for all this too. But facts are facts. The police will arrest this Diaz kid, and all I can do is hope to God it doesn't break in the papers. And I'm afraid your running around asking all kinds of questions isn't helping. For God's sake, Cass, don't you see? It's bad enough to think of Nathan making it with one Legal Aid client, but what makes you think this Diaz kid was the only one? Do you want to help the cops rake up more dirt than they've got already?"

I wanted to talk to him. Well, to be honest, I wanted to yell at him. But I could hear the hurt behind his words. He believed what Button was saying about Nathan, and he blamed Nathan. There was nothing I could say. I got up to go.

"One more thing," he said. I turned, not sure I could handle one more thing. "The Department of Corrections is conducting an investigation into the death of a Charlie Blackwell. I understand he was Nathan's client but that you stood up on it the last time he was in court. I told them we'd waive a subpoena. It's tomorrow morning. Nine-thirty A.M. One hundred Centre Street, Manhattan. I'll tell Deke and Flaherty to cover your cases."

Deke. Now I understood what Deke had meant in the hallway outside Part D last Friday. If I knew the truth about my precious Nathan, he had said. But what was the truth—the tender, sensitive man I had known, or this stranger who picked up boys in lavatories?

Once out of Milt's office, I let my defiant facade collapse. It was one thing to maintain a brave front; it was another to hide my doubts from myself.

I was shaken. Button's innuendos hadn't gotten to me because he hadn't known Nathan. But Milt had. Longer than I. If he said Nathan had been involved with boys, then it was true. And if it was true, then maybe Button was right. Maybe he had picked up the wrong boy this time.

I went into my office, shut the door, and slumped into my chair. I felt defeated. My valiant attempt to believe in Nathan was doomed. The Stone connection was a pipe dream. Button was right. A fag killing and a prison suicide. Pure coincidence. I'd been too blind to see the truth. Blinded by the illusion that Nathan had been someone I knew.

A shocking thought struck me. Could that have been what Nathan wanted to talk to me about, that last morning? Oh, by the way, Cass, while you and I have been lovers, I've been humping a client. A teenage boy. I hope you don't mind. My fists clenched. Nathan, goddamn you, my mind screamed, if that's what you were going to tell me, it's a damn good thing you didn't because *I'd* have strangled you. Bare-handed.

There was a knock at my door. A knock so hesitant, so tentative, that I was surprised to see Flaherty come in. He looked at least as depressed as I felt. "You talked to Milt." It was a statement, not a question.

I nodded. Flaherty sat down heavily in Bill Pomerantz's chair. His blue eyes were dull with misery.

"Well," I began sarcastically, "doesn't this confirm what you thought all along? You were ready to condemn Nathan *before* you heard what Milt had to say, so why the long face now?" Somewhere deep inside I was aware that I was lashing out at Flaherty to stifle the hurt I was feeling, but at the time I didn't care. All I knew was the raw bile in my throat. The taste of betrayal.

He didn't rise to the bait. "I kept hoping I was wrong," he said. "God knows I wanted to believe in him, Cass. I wanted to. But, God, I just couldn't. Not after this. How could he behave one way in public and another in private? That's what I don't understand. I feel as though he was a total stranger. A total stranger I wouldn't have wanted to know."

It was a hell of a thought. There was nothing I could say to it. Flaherty shambled out of my office, and I just sat there, unable to move. I'd been denying Nathan's gayness for so long now. It was the keystone of my whole theory that someone else killed him. And it wasn't true.

Unless. Was it possible that he was a Dr. Jekyll and Mr. Hyde, changing his personality so drastically? Wouldn't there be a leak, like light seeping unseen into an incompletely sealed darkroom? Could you lock two separate halves of yourself away from each other so completely?

Even if Nathan had had gay experiences, did that mean he was into ropes and bondage? Could Nathan's past have been a convenient peg the murderer used?

It was wishful thinking. But I clung to it. Because the alternative was too much. It meant wiping Nathan out of my mind and replacing him with a sadistic stranger. Getting cynical about who he'd been and what he'd meant to me.

I couldn't do that.

SEVENTEEN

It was funny, but I hadn't given a lot of thought to the details of Charlie Blackwell's death. For one thing, I'd been busy trying to establish the link between Nathan's murder and the Stone trial, and for another, I just took it for granted Charlie was killed by the mob. It didn't seem to matter exactly how.

But now, as I wandered through the gray halls of Manhattan's Criminal Courts Building Thursday morning, looking for the office of the New York City Department of Correction Investigation Department, I began to wonder. I hoped the investigation would answer some of the questions that were beginning to form in my mind.

It was old home week when I entered the drab little waiting room. It was filled with Brooklyn court officers—Tim, the bridgeman from AP4, Marla Watson, who'd worked the desk, and even the pen crew, Vinnie and Red. Marla was sitting in the only chair.

"Are we it?" I asked Tim. "I mean, are they calling anyone else?"

"They got the Iceman in there now. Pardon me, I mean the Honorable Perry Whalen." He was grinning. Tim was the closest thing I had to a friend among the court officers, who tend as a rule to be hostile to Legal Aid attorneys.

Tim's remark got a smile out of me, Red, and Vinnie, but Marla looked upset. She had twisted the handkerchief in her hand into a wreck. And she hadn't had to answer a single question yet. I was a little surprised; I once saw Marla do a number on a kid who'd decided to go over the wall. Her flying tackle and one-handed cuffing job had been the talk of the Brooklyn Criminal Court. I'd never seen her scared of anything before.

"Shit," she said, "I can't be goin' through this bullshit, you know? I'm only a probationer. If they decide to throw it all on me, I'm fucked. Back to the department store to watch ladies undressing. That ain't no life. Not like this here, where we got a good union."

"Damn right we got a good union," Red Hennessey said. He was tall and skinny, with a huge Adam's apple and a face full of freckles. And, naturally, red hair. "That's why you won't get dumped on, Marla. You got nothin' to worry about. Not if you did things right, you don't."

"Shit, I don't remember what I done. I been in so damn many places since then, AP3, weekend arraignments. How'm I gonna remember one prisoner on one day? Tell me that."

"Marla, think back," I said. "I was traffic cop. We'd just finished a case with three defendants—one in, two out. Vinnie took the in guy back and brought out Charlie Blackwell. He was an older guy, very nervous—"

"Yeah," Tim cut in, "he was so scared I thought he was gonna piss in his pants."

"I approached the bench and asked for suicide watch. It was already on the papers; all the judge had to do was continue it. Then Vinnie took the guy back into the pens." I looked at Vinnie. He nodded curtly.

"I went into the back to talk to the guy, and when I came out—" I stopped, remembering suddenly, "Marla! You're in the clear. I came out, looked at the yellow card to make sure, and it was already written. So whatever went wrong, you wrote the right stuff on the card."

Marla heaved a sigh of relief. "Thanks, Counselor. I been worried as hell since they told us we had to come down here. I sure as hell don't want to go back to no department store."

I turned to Tim. "What exactly do they think happened? I haven't kept up."

"I heard when the prisoner got to BHD there was no

segregation order on his yellow card. So they put him in
with everyone else and in the morning they found him
wearing a necktie."

"Jesus!" I shivered. I had a sudden vision of Charlie
hanging in his cell. Twisting slowly, slowly in the wind.
"Didn't he say anything? He was hot to trot when I saw
him; he begged me to get him suicide watch. Would he just
go into a regular cell without a protest?"

"Don't ask me, Counselor. I don't work at the Brooklyn
House."

"My brother does," Vinnie said. "I asked him when this
thing first came down. He said sometimes if a guy acts
crazy enough, they'll put him in segregation without a
court order. Or they'll even send him to Kings County
Hospital on their own. But he's gotta act wacko. They
don't just do it 'cause he asks nice and polite."

"How could anybody get to a guy in his cell?" I asked
Vinnie. "I mean, they must patrol the place, right?"

"Sure," Vinnie answered. "My brother says it used to be
the C.O.s that did it—punched a clock at the end of the
hall every half hour to show they'd walked the corridor.
Then they started using inmate patrols."

"Inmate patrols!" My mind started racing. "You mean
some other inmate had access to him?"

"They patrol in two-man crews," Vinnie explained. "I'm
sure whoever was on his cellblock will be questioned pretty
closely."

"Yeah," I said mechanically. My thoughts were miles
away. I was visualizing an inmate enemy of Charlie's, os-
tensibly patrolling the cellblock to prevent suicides, reach-
ing through the bars, strangling Charlie, and then stringing
him up to look like a suicide. Which was how it would have
been done at BHD, but how had Charlie been removed
from suicide watch in the first place? I wasn't the only one
who wondered.

"That still don't answer the question who changed that
card," Marla observed. "If I wrote it up the right way, how
come it was wrong when it got to BHD?"

I turned to Red and Vinnie. "You took the card when

you took Blackwell from AP4 to the ninth floor pens, right?" They nodded.

"You know that, Counselor," Vinnie said. "The papers follow the body at all times. We wouldn't take a prisoner up without a card or a card without a prisoner."

"When did Blackwell go up?"

"About a quarter to one. With about six other prisoners," Red answered.

"Did either of you notice what his card said?"

"Hell, Cass, how could they? You can't read every fuckin' card," Tim objected.

"As I recall, Vinnie, you were bringing prisoners back and forth and Red was in the pen. Was one of you there at all times?"

"Counselor," Vinnie's voice was hard, "we was ordered to come here and answer their questions." He jerked his head toward the door behind which the questioning was going on. "But ain't nobody ordered me to answer yours."

"Come on, Vinnie," Tim pleaded. "What the hell. Miss Jameson isn't looking to hurt anybody."

"Oh, yeah." Marla was her old self, a black lump of belligerence. "Look to me like she nailin' me pretty good. If nobody could change the card in the back because Red was there, then it got changed while it was on my desk, and that make me responsible, don't it?"

I started trying to convince Marla I wasn't trying to nail her. Tim was still defending me to Vinnie, and Red was shouting that I was trying to pin the whole thing on the court personnel. The upshot was that when the door opened unexpectedly and the Iceman came out, we were all talking at once. He gave us a frosty smile and walked out of the waiting room, his overcoat on his arm.

I was called next. I guess I ranked after the judge. They would probably call the court officers in order of seniority. Poor Marla. Her handkerchief would look like Swiss cheese by then.

The interview room was tiny, painted a revolting institutional green. The window that faced the little park between the courthouse and Chinatown hadn't been washed since

La Guardia was mayor. There were three men and a female stenographer inside. I didn't really catch names, just that they were biggies in the Correction Department and that the investigation they were conducting was just that—a fact-finding inquiry, not a hearing or a trial. If they felt disciplinary action should be taken against a member of the Department of Correction, they would so recommend. If they felt the matter should be investigated further by the district attorney, they would so recommend. If they felt the whole thing should be quietly forgotten, they would so recommend. I got the feeling their recommendation would be to forget. Quickly.

I told them as concisely as I could what my connection with Blackwell had been and what I'd done for him on his last court date. It wasn't news. They'd had it from Judge Whalen, who, for all his faults, kept the kind of records everyone expects a fussy little man like him to keep.

When I finished my narrative, they began to ask questions. But they weren't the same questions I'd been asking myself. They weren't interested in the changing of the notation on the yellow card or in the motivations that might have led people to wish Charlie out of the picture. They were concerned more with Charlie himself. Had he been nervous? Had he said anything about suicide? Had he struck me as confused? Irrational? Had I known about his past 730 examinations? Had I asked Judge Whalen to order a 730? Why not?

The last question surprised me. In the first place, it had never occurred to me that Charlie was that wacked out. Sure, he was hyper, but as Nathan had rightly pointed out, a man in the business of selling out heavy friends gets hyper. I'd never thought a 730 was warranted. And even if I'd thought so, I wouldn't have asked for it. Charlie was Nathan's client, not mine. Unless he was flipping out pretty badly, I'd have left a decision on 730 to the attorney of record.

I said all this to the three officials. Several times and in several different ways. I didn't like the way they took it. From the questions on Charlie's state of mind, I got the

feeling they were pushing hard to find his death a suicide
From there, the next move would be to find a scapegoat
Preferably one who didn't wear the blue uniform of the
New York City Correction Department. Maybe even one
who couldn't defend himself because he was dead. Their
position would be that it was unfortunate that a disturbed
person like Charlie slipped out of a suicide watch, but the
fault wasn't theirs—it was his lawyer who should have seen
that Charlie was a nut job and ordered him examined by a
doctor. They would regret, they would deplore. They
would whitewash. No inquiry into Charlie's enemies, or the
fact that the Special Prosecutor wanted to talk to him, or
that the yellow card ordering the suicide watch had been
tampered with. Just a nice quiet cover-up with a posthu-
mous slap in the face for Nathan for being so insensitive as
to let his poor crazy client risk hanging himself in his cell

EIGHTEEN

I dressed carefully for my Friday after-work meeting with Dave Chessler. A mauve wool dress with a full skirt and puffed sleeves accented by an embroidered black velvet vest. Tiny silver bell-shaped earrings and a silver pendant hanging from a black velvet ribbon. Black leather boots and matching clutch bag. It might be strictly business, but it didn't have to look that way.

I met him in the waiting area of a fancy bar in the ground floor of the World Trade Center. I was glad I'd dressed when I saw the clothes the other women were wearing. Expensive-looking, tailored, good materials. What the well-dressed female executive will wear. I was of two minds. Part of me envied women whose jobs both permitted and required good clothes, perfect makeup. Yet there was a lurking resentment, too. What did these well-groomed magazine-ad ladies know about the gritty realities of Brooklyn Criminal Court? On the other hand, we all live in worlds of our own choosing. What claim did I have to moral superiority because I'd chosen to work in the pits instead of the towers?

Dave sat me at a tiny table inside the bar and went for drinks. It was still Scotch weather, so I ordered mine on the rocks. He brought it to me along with a bourbon and water for himself.

"So what did you think of the transcript? Did you see what I meant about Riordan?"

"I sure did. Not only on paper, but in person, too. He's appearing on a case in Brooklyn Supreme, so I went over to see him. Say what you will about him, the man is one hell of a cross-examiner."

"It's easy to be if the witness is taking orders from you instead of the prosecutor."

"If I didn't know you better, I'd say that was sour grapes." He didn't answer. I thought perhaps I'd gone too far, so I said, "Actually, you're probably right. I got the feeling the witness in the case I saw didn't exactly come through the way the D.A. expected him to. Riordan got a lot of mileage out of him, too. If he wins the case, it'll be because the witness fell apart."

"Sounds familiar, doesn't it?"

"Not only that. When I spoke to him, Riordan warned me about getting involved. Said there were dangerous people around." I didn't repeat Riordan's crack about Nancy Drew; I didn't trust Dave to understand the seriousness of the insult.

There was a pause. Dave sipped his drink in what appeared to be meditative silence. I figured I'd said everything I wanted to say; it was time for him to speak up. Finally he did. Slowly and a little reluctantly, he said, "There's something I didn't tell you last time, Cassandra."

"Cass," I murmured.

"Cass." He smiled, an unexpected smile that nearly diverted me. "It fits you."

Then he sobered and returned to the topic. "In fact, I'm not sure I should be telling you this now. Parma'd have my head on a plate if he knew I was talking to anyone about it, but I feel you have a right to know." He looked around at the people at the tables closest to us. It looked to me like the usual TGIF pickup scene, but Dave leaned over and lowered his voice.

"I don't know where to begin exactly. For the past six months or so there's been a kind of task force in the Special Prosecutor's office dedicated to one thing—nailing Charlie Blackwell."

"Then everything Parma said about the case being over and done with and forgotten was pure bullshit?" The words didn't go with my dress, but what the hell. You can take the girl out of the pits, but. . . .

"If that's what he said," Dave grinned, "that's what it was. Oh, we did other work, had our regular cases and all, but getting Blackwell in a position where he'd have to play ball with us was our A-number-one priority."

"Why? Sheer revenge? I mean, sure, Parma was mad about losing the Stone case, but why make a big deal now?"

"Don't you read the papers?" Dave looked appalled when I shook my head. It's true; what Dan Rather doesn't tell me, I don't know. "Parma's being considered for an appointment as counsel to a congressional committee. Congressman Gebhardt of Nassau County's going to head a Kefauver-style committee to look into organized crime. If it's handled right, it's the kind of thing that can make a lot of careers. And Del wants it to make his. He wants it so bad he can taste it."

"What's Charlie Blackwell got to do with it?"

"The Stone case was Parma's biggest failure. Oh, we've had a few setbacks—cases reversed on appeal, verdicts set aside after trial—you can't go after the biggies without getting people mad. But the Stone trial was different. It was a slap in the face for Del personally. He started to get paranoid that the congressional committee would hold it against him. So his plan was to nail Charlie and force him to admit he threw the case. This would clear away any suspicion that Parma lost the case through incompetence. Then, if he could get Charlie to give him the goods on Riordan, he'd be scoring a real coup that should impress the hell out of the committee and insure his appointment. Get the picture?"

I nodded. Now it was my turn to be thoughtful. With a nice sense of timing, Dave went to the bar for more drinks. Try as I might, all I could make out of this was that Del had lied in his teeth when he claimed Charlie was ancient history. Which wasn't a crime.

Dave came back, set down the drinks, and said, "The

upshot of all this is that my task force engineered the drug bust your friend represented Charlie on."

"What! You're kidding!" I took a gulp of Scotch. "You mean—but wait—"

"Come on, Counselor," Dave laughed. "You've been around the block. Do you mean to sit there and tell me you never thought of that? We jerked on Blackwell's chain to get him to roll over on Riordan. Happens every day." Once again the contrast between the genteel voice, the mild features, the well-cut clothes, and the tough, streetwise manner grated on me. Which was the role, which was the reality?

I had recovered a little. "Even dealing with the Kings County D.A.'s office hasn't made me cynical enough for your outfit," I told him. "I'm out of my depth here. Let me get this straight. You guys were totally responsible for Charlie being involved in the drug deal. That was a setup to get him in custody because once he was in custody he'd be so afraid of his enemies in prison he'd do anything to make a deal. Right?"

"Right. We were willing to drop the drug rap—or see to it the Brooklyn D.A. dropped it—in return for the truth about Riordan's fixing the Stone case."

"But don't you see what this means? If the only reason Charlie was in jail was because you guys put him there, and you put him there because of his role in the Stone case, then it's one hell of a coincidence if he was iced by someone else for some totally unrelated reason. Isn't it?"

"Is that what the police think?"

"That's what Detective Button said when I told him I thought Blackwell had been murdered. He said Charlie had enemies coming out of his ears and that even if he was murdered, it wasn't necessarily because of the Stone case. But now—"

"Now you know the only reason he was there at all was because of the Stone case."

"Which makes it unlikely that somebody else took advantage of the situation. The connection is clear. And it connects with Nathan too. If someone killed Charlie because of what he knew, Nathan knew the same things."

"Now you see why I felt I had to tell you all this. It supports your thinking about why your friend was killed."

"Yes," I agreed thoughtfully. "If Nathan was killed by someone else, it was one hell of a lucky break for someone."

"For Riordan." Dave's pale blue eyes were grim. I shivered a little. It was one thing to believe Nathan had been murdered because of what Blackwell had told him. It was another to put a name to the murderer.

I remembered what Emily had said. "If you guys were keeping such close tabs on Charlie, how come he ended up in the system at all?"

Dave looked blank. I spelled it out. "If you thought you could squeeze him, wouldn't you have brought him straight to your office instead of letting him go through arraignments? I mean, first of all, every minute he spent in custody was a risk—he was vulnerable as hell in jail. Plus it would have been easier to do a deal without a lawyer in the room, right? So why—"

"You shouldn't believe everything you hear, Counselor," Dave interrupted, an angry, set look on his face. "My office doesn't do things that way, I don't care who told you we do."

I didn't believe him. Maybe *he* didn't, but his colleagues did. Only not this time. But why? Why had Charlie, so important to Parma that he'd been the subject of a private vendetta, been allowed to slip through the Special Prosecutor's fingers just when he ought to have been given the ultimate in protection?

NINETEEN

―――――■―――――

"**I** can't be droppin' no dime on that dude, you dig? Man, he too heavy for me. I don't wanna end up under no pier, you dig where I'm comin' from?"

It was Tuesday morning; Tyrone's old case was on in AP4. I walked up just as Tyrone and the cop started dealing. I knew he was a cop as soon as I got off the elevator; even in plain clothes, he could be nothing else. Steel-gray hair, a face the color of rare steak, built like a longshoreman. But the toughness in his stance wasn't a macho pose, it was a way of life.

I came up behind them and said quietly, "Officer, if you've got something to offer my client in return for information, I'd like to hear it too." As he wheeled around, I held out my hand. "I'm Cassandra Jameson, Tyrone's attorney."

He didn't take the hand. Things were not going to be friendly.

Tyrone, meanwhile, was looking over his shoulder, worried. "Hey, man, like we can't be talkin' here. I don't want nobody to get the wrong idea, you dig?"

I nodded. "He's got a point," I told the cop. "You want to talk, let's go inside." I pointed to the pen area.

The cop, without a word, grabbed Tyrone, threw him against the wall, and cuffed him.

"Whatcha doin' that for, man?" Tyrone squealed. "I ain't *did* nothin'."

"Hey," I shouted. "You can't bust my client."

The cop gave me a malevolent grin. "Can't I, girlie?" he

said. "Just watch me." Then he shoved Tyrone through the pen doors.

I started to follow, but the whole hall had seen it. A middle-aged black man shook his head. "Seems like them cops just do what they please," he said sadly.

"Ain't right," a girl added. Her hair was done in little braids, and when she shook her head, the pink beads rattled.

As I slammed through the door, I turned on the cop. "What the fuck do you think you're doing?"

"Calm down, girlie," he said, grinning. "I got him in here, didn't I? Do you think anybody out there suspects us of talking deal after that?"

He had a point. "Don't call me girlie," I said.

He uncuffed Tyrone, and they started talking. In a foreign language.

"Who's cuttin'?" the cop asked.

"Lotta dudes," Tyrone said, "but the biggest cutting joint, man, it belong to Spanish Nick."

"Where's it at?"

"Man, I done *told* you, I can't be fuckin' that dude up or he do me for sure."

"Tyrone," the cop said softly, "you wanna help yourself here or what?"

That was my cue. "Hold it, officer. What can you offer? And will the D.A. go along with it? Tyrone's got two cases —a promise of probation on the old one, and this new one's open. What are we talking about if he gives you good information?"

"I'll recommend probation on both," the cop answered. I nodded. Best we could do.

"Okay," I answered. "Get me a D.A. to agree to it, and you're on."

When the cop went out to the courtroom, I turned to Tyrone. "That okay with you?"

He nodded. "I can't be *doin'* no time, Miss Jameson. Just keep me out of Riker's, that's all."

"Can you give the cop what he wants?"

"I don't like to be hurtin' nobody, but I gotta help myself, right?"

"Right," I sighed. At seventeen, Tyrone was already starting a career as an informant. I wondered if it would someday get him what it had gotten Charlie Blackwell.

The cop was back, accompanied by A.D.A. Hagerty. Her face was red, and she kept her eyes down, but she mumbled, "He'll get the deal if Officer Brennan tells us the information was good." Then she left.

Brennan laughed. "Stupid bitch wouldn't buy it," he said. "Got on her high horse about how could she make a deal with a criminal? So I picked up the phone, called her supervisor, and he explained the facts of life to her. She doesn't much like the facts of life, does she?"

"I'm not thrilled with them either," I retorted. "I've just been in the system longer than she has." My God, I'm defending her, I realized. Just like Nathan did the night we worked together.

The cop shrugged, and he and Tyrone went to work. The jargon flowed thick and fast. Who was doing tag jobs? Where were the chop shops? Where were they shipping cars? Tyrone knew his stuff. The cop knew he knew it. There was a bond of mutual interest and respect between cop and skell that left me, a mere lawyer, out in the cold. Finally, Tyrone asked shyly whether the cop had heard of him on the street.

"Sure," the cop nodded. "Everybody in the detail knew you was up-and-coming. Somebody to watch."

Tyrone beamed. The cop had just made his whole day.

After Tyrone copped out, I did a preliminary hearing. My client was a thin, wasted junkie with a face the color of oatmeal. He sat in the chair, cuffed hands picking at his worn, dirty pants. His once-white T-shirt had holes in it, as did his high-topped sneakers. He looked as though he'd already done twenty years, and he hadn't even been indicted yet.

The complainant was a blond boy of about twelve. His story was that my guy grabbed him in a schoolyard. He was wearing a St. Christopher medal on a chain around his neck. My guy snapped it off. Then he began to shake the kid, demanding, pleading with him, to have something else —money, a watch, something. The kid had nothing. As he said, "I'm only a kid, what could I have?" But the guy kept shaking him. The way you kick a candy machine when it won't give you your change.

My guy just sat there. No denials. No "he lyin'." He knew it was the end of the line. The case would go upstairs, he'd get three-to-six, and there was nothing to be done about it. And as soon as he got out of prison, the need would come on him again, he'd rob again, he'd do time again. Until he died. "And nothing to look backward to with pride, and nothing to look forward to with hope. So now and never any different." Robert Frost had it right.

I was about to leave the courtroom when the phone lit up. It was Jackie Bohan in AR2, the youth arraignment part. I asked her what was up.

"There's a kid here returned on a warrant," she began. I had to strain to hear her voice. Court must be in session, I thought. "It's one of Nathan's clients. Flaherty said you had all Nathan's cases now."

"Yeah," I admitted. It had seemed like a good idea at the time, but I was getting a little sick of covering Nathan's entire caseload as well as my own. "What's the story?"

"Kid was supposed to be in AP5 last week for sentencing. He didn't show and they picked him up on a warrant. The thing is there are detectives here who want to arrest him on a new charge."

"I'll be right down," I said.

Jackie motioned me into the back, by the pens. "There he is," she said, pointing to a Puerto Rican kid with a face like a Renaissance angel. "The cops who want him are from Homicide. And, Cass," she went on, "one of them is Detective Button."

It figured. I looked at the court papers Jackie handed me. Judge Di Anci had taken the kid's plea. The last adjournment before the bench warrant was marked "For defense counsel to contact Hope House." Just as Nathan had told me the night we worked together. The kid bench warranted the day Nathan died.

I looked at the kid's rap sheet. Prostitution. Button hadn't been bluffing. He had a suspect.

The irony struck me, hard. Here I'd been busting my ass to get to the truth of Nathan's death, researching the Stone case, running to talk to Parma, suspecting the hell out of Matt Riordan and now maybe—just maybe—Nathan's murderer was standing in the AR2 pens waiting to be interviewed by his Legal Aid lawyer.

Me.

TWENTY

It was worse than anything I could have imagined. The kid looked like Dondi from the comic strip—honey-colored skin, big dark eyes, a mass of wavy black hair. He had "chicken" written all over him.

I couldn't think. I especially couldn't think with the kid eight feet away, his huge dark eyes burning into me. I walked to the other side, around the elevator that took the prisoners to the ninth-floor lockup, and sat in one of the chairs they handcuffed female prisoners to. It was as good a place as any.

I tried to convince myself the whole thing was a coincidence, that Button had more than one case, for God's sake, and this kid had probably stabbed some guy in a barroom brawl. But deep down I knew it was no good. Button couldn't have invented a more perfect suspect. This was the kid whose name Milt had mentioned that day in his office. The kid Button had been looking for.

So now what? No way I could represent the kid. Not just because I was Nathan's lover, either. He'd have to have a lawyer from the 18-b panel. The one headed by Stan Willburton, Emily's husband. I jotted a reminder in my pocket notebook to call Stan as soon as I could.

But now? Could I walk into the pen, interview the kid like any other client, and stand up on the case for bail purposes?

I could think of a hundred reasons why not. Conflict of interest. Ethics. Personal feelings. Nobody in the world could blame me if I walked away from this one. I could

comb the courthouse for an 18-b lawyer. I could ask Jackie
to stand up on the case, I could call Milt and dump the
whole mess in his lap.

A large part of me wanted to. I'd been full of energy,
willing to do whatever it took, so long as the evidence led
me away from Button's Midnight Cowboy theory. As long
as I was exploring the Burton Stone–Matt Riordan connection. But now—did I have the guts to look Button's evidence full in the face? To risk the possibility that he'd been
right all along?

To hell with ethics. That was the real question—how
much did I really believe in Nathan? Enough to confront
the facts, whatever they were? Enough to see the kid and
find out for myself what he and Nathan had been to each
other?

Put that way, I had no choice. I stood up, stretched and
yawned like one of Dorinda's cats, and walked toward the
pen. I was ready to talk to Heriberto Diaz.

The pen was empty. The courtroom was nearly so. Tired
of waiting, the judge had called a recess. The summonses
were finished; my case was the only one left.

It was an anticlimax. I was geared up for a confrontation
I couldn't have until the kid was brought back into the
interview pen.

I was standing around uncertainly when I heard a voice
behind me.

"Hey, Counselor." I turned to see Button coming out of
the clerks' office, a smile of triumph on his face. I waited
while he walked closer to me. "We got him, Miss Jameson.
We got the kid who killed your friend."

I had a split second to decide how to handle it. I could
flat-out contradict him, give him my pitch about the Stone
case, and lose him. Or I could concede at least the possibility that he was right and the kid was guilty and maybe learn
something. I wanted very badly to learn something.

"You're pretty sure he's the one, then?" I asked. "You
must have solid evidence."

"That's right, Counselor," he said cheerfully. "We got

this kid nailed. A smart defense lawyer would start working on a good plea."

"Maybe his 18-b lawyer will do just that," I replied. "I can't stay on the case, of course. Even if I wanted to," I added for good measure.

There was a sober look on Button's face as he answered, "Yeah, I don't envy you your job. Imagine having to represent the punk who killed your boyfriend. I couldn't do it, not in a million years."

Neither could I, I thought. Not if I really believed this kid killed Nathan. Perhaps the fact that my guts didn't rebel at the thought of standing up on this kid meant something. I hope I haven't been in the system so long I could just arraign Nathan's murderer and then say, "Next case."

"Look, Detective Button," I said, fixing him with a straight, eyeball-to-eyeball stare, "can I be frank with you?" This was a little like saying "with all due respect" to a judge—whenever you hear a lawyer say that, you know he's about to come out with something highly disrespectful, if not totally outrageous.

The detective cocked his head to one side like an inquisitive Yorkshire terrier, then nodded. I proceeded. "You know how I felt about Nathan. You know I don't want to believe this kid's guilty, but, hell, I'm a lawyer. I can accept facts. If the evidence is there, I can deal with it. Now, I'm going to have to get relieved on this case. So can't you give me an idea of what you've got? I really need to know—not as a lawyer, but as Nathan's friend."

It was honest as far as it went. I really did need to know. And maybe some sense of that got through to Button. He snapped his head up decisively and said, "Where can we talk?"

It was a good question. A homicide detective and a Legal Aid lawyer having a tête-à-tête were bound to cause comment anywhere in the court vicinity. I motioned Button to follow me into the door marked *No Admittance, Authorized Personnel Only*. It led to a corridor off which were located the back entrances to the AR1 courtroom and the clerks' office as well as the room I was heading for. The so-called judge's robing room for the arraignment part. It's a bare little room with castoff furniture—a desk and some old-fashioned benches—as well as the only regularly cleaned bathroom on the first floor. The public bathrooms they just hose out, like a horse's stall.

We each sat on a bench. I put my Channel Thirteen bag on the desk. Neither of us spoke. I was beginning to wonder if Button had changed his mind. I looked at him quizzically. He shook his head. Then I heard a flushing sound. The bathroom door opened, and Cornelia, the court reporter, stepped out. She scurried out when she saw us, but the look on her face told me she was sure she'd interrupted a tryst. Button threw his head back and roared. It was a big laugh, bigger than I'd expected from his small frame.

When we both stopped laughing, he said seriously, "You know, Counselor, every instinct I have plus ten years' experience tells me not to do this. Not to trust a lawyer. Try not to prove me wrong, okay?"

"Oh, come on, Button. You're not giving me anything the 18-b lawyer won't get from the D.A. Besides, if you've really got this kid locked, what's the difference?"

"You know better than that, Miss Jameson. No case was ever so tight a good lawyer couldn't twist things around to his client's benefit."

"Why would I want to twist things around to help the kid who killed Nathan?" The words almost stuck in my throat. Because they admitted, tacitly at least, that maybe Button was right, maybe this kid was the killer. But I said them anyway.

They turned out to be the magic words. "What do you want to know?" Button asked.

"What have you got on this kid?" I countered.

"We've got his name in the book at your friend's apartment building," Button began. "You know, the one people sign in when they're visiting someone. He signed in at eight forty-five on Wednesday night. Time of death was estimated at between eight-thirty and nine thirty."

"Jesus." A chill ran up my spine. This was serious.

"Plus the kid admits being there—well, he could hardly deny it. He says he got up to your friend's apartment, knocked on the door, got no answer, and left right away. But the guy at the desk that night says no, the kid signed in, went upstairs, and didn't come down till after nine thirty. So the kid's lying about the amount of time he spent up there."

I was silent for a moment, trying to turn off the personal feelings and think about it as I would any other case. "Two things," I finally said. "One. If he went up there to kill Nathan, would he have signed his real name in the book?"

"Remember, Miss Jameson, our theory here is crime of passion. When he signed into the book, he had no intention of killing your friend. That came later. After some sexual confrontation in the apartment. So his signing in is no guaranty of innocence."

"Okay. I'll give you that. Two. Would the desk attendant really remember the time? He sees a lot of people. They don't have to sign when they leave, just when they come in. What's so special about this kid?"

"It's a fairly classy building, Counselor. High-rise. Young professionals. How many Puerto Rican hustlers in skin-tight pants, leather jackets, and boots do you suppose this guy sees in a night?"

It sounded good. Too good. A jury would buy it in a minute.

"This statement. Who'd he make it to and when?"

"Warrant officer. Before the officer could even give him the *Miranda* warnings, the kid was blurting it out. It was like he was just waiting to get arrested, waiting to get it off his chest."

TWENTY-ONE

The interview with the kid took a lot out of me. For one thing, it was a good twenty times longer than my usual first interview. That's because I ordinarily cover the high points and leave the rest for later. My theory is that getting the guy out of jail is the number-one priority and the rest can wait. That way I haven't wasted an interview if the guy pleads guilty, skips, or hires private counsel. Besides, the interview goes better the second time. The guy's had a shower; he's cooled down a little from the frantic, get-me-out-of-here arraignment mood; we can talk about what's really important instead of what dirty names the cop called him. Because I save all the details for the second meeting, my first interview seldom goes over three minutes. They don't call me the fastest mouth in Brooklyn for nothing.

This was different. I wouldn't get a second interview.

The first thing I did that was unusual was to go inside the pen. That used to be standard operating procedure, until they put in a fancy little booth that looks like a confessional. Private, but you can't see your client's face. This kid's face I wanted to see.

"You gonna be my lawyer?" he asked. I nodded. I didn't trust myself to talk. Not yet. The kid was small, about my height. His voice was soft, with the merest hint of an accent. He stood, thumbs in his belt, leaning against the wall in a parody of his hustler image. I motioned him to sit, but he shook his head.

"It's okay. I rather stand. If it's okay witch you."

"Sure. Whatever you want. Only thing is, we got a lot to

talk about. I just want you to know that. So get comfort-able."

He nodded, but made no move to sit on the adjoining stool. I didn't like it. It distanced him from me, and I needed to bridge that distance.

I looked at the court papers. The complaint had three a/k/a's. I looked up at the kid. "Which of these names is yours?"

"Heriberto Diaz."

"What do they call you on the street?"

The look he gave me was deliberately blank. As though he had never heard of anything as outré as a street name. Funny, when I was in law school a street name meant the false name a big company would use to trade anonymously on Wall Street. It took me three days in Brooklyn to find out about the other kind.

I pushed him. "Suppose you're playing stickball with your buddies. One of the guys yells, 'Heriberto, here comes a grounder.' Right?" He started to smile.

"Or some dude comes up to you on the corner. Does he say, 'Hey, man, hey, Heriberto, how they hangin'?' " Now the smile was a broad grin. It helped his face a lot. He looked like a real kid, the kind I'd grown up with in Ohio, only a little darker.

"The guys call me Paco."

"Hi, Paco. I'm Cassandra Jameson." I extended my hand in a deliberately formal gesture. He took it, we shook, and finally he sat down on the stool opposite me. "Whatcha want to know?"

What did I want to know? Were you Nathan's lover? Did you kill him? Why? For God's sake and above all, why?

I didn't ask him those questions. I talked about the warrant.

"Look, Paco, they called me over here on this warrant. But the warrant doesn't mean shit now that they've got you tagged for Nathan's murder. You know that's what's hap-pened, don't you?"

He nodded. His eyes were cast down. Then he looked up at me with his puppy's eyes. "They think I done it, killed him." There was wonder in his voice. "Man, how they can be thinkin' somethin' so dumb. Of all the dumb shit. Me killin' him. Jesus!"

"Why is it so dumb, Paco?"

"Hey, you know, like the dude was helpin' me, you dig? He was tryin' to keep me from goin' to the Rock. Why'd I want to kill a guy like that?"

Good question. Button thought he had the answer.

"He was trying to get you into a program, right?"

"Yeah. Like he had this dude to phone my mother and tell me to meet him at his apartment that night."

"What night? The murder? What dude? Go back a minute." I was trying to write it down, but I'm no Archie Goodwin. I can be fast or legible, take your pick, but not both at once.

"My mother told me a guy called from the program. He was supposed to meet me at Nathan's apartment that night."

"Okay. You got the message from your mother. You never talked to the guy yourself?"

"Right. Only my mother. Then—"

"Stop. When did your mother get the message? That same day?"

"Yeah, I think so. I came home around one o'clock. I been out all night with some dudes I know. She told me the guy called then."

"So it could have been that morning. Could it have been the night before?"

He thought. "I don't think so," he answered slowly. "My mother went over to my Aunt Rita's that night. Nobody was home to get the phone. But you better ax my mother."

"I will." I took down her name and phone number.

"What time were you supposed to be at the apartment?"

"My mother say the dude say eight thirty."

"You were there? On time?"

He nodded.

"What happened?"

He shrugged. "Wasn't nobody home, so I booked."

"You don't get off that easy. Back up again. You got to the building when?"

" 'Bout eight thirty. Like I said."

"You signed in the book in the lobby?"

"Right."

"Your real name?"

"Yeah, my real name," he said indignantly. "Whatchou think I am?"

"You went straight up to the apartment? You knew where it was?"

"Yeah. So what? I been there before to talk about my case. About the program."

"I didn't say you weren't. Just asking. You got to the door. Then what?"

"I rang the bell a couple of times. Wasn't no answer." He shrugged again. "I left. That's all."

"How long were you there?"

Another shrug. "Five minutes."

"That's all? You didn't wait any longer?"

"No. I told you, wasn't no point. Nobody home."

"Did you knock? Maybe the bell was broken. Did you call out any names?"

"No."

"You didn't wait a few minutes to see if maybe he stepped out for a minute? Did you call him later to find out what happened?"

"No. I just left." He was sullen. I was shotgunning the questions at him, hoping to deny him time to think. He was lying, and with time to think the lie might get better. I wanted it to stay bad.

"After you left, where did you go?"

"Out."

"Out where?"

"On the street. I walked around."

"Where?"

"Where he lived?"

"Why?"

"No reason." Another shrug.

"What went through your mind when you couldn't get in to the apartment?"

"I didn't think nothin'."

"Come on, Paco. You come to an appointment set up by your lawyer to get you into a program. You get there on time. And there's nobody there. You've gotta think something. Maybe you thought Nathan ducked out on you. Maybe you thought you had the wrong time. Maybe the guy from the program never showed."

"But Nathan would have told me—" he began.

"Exactly. Nathan would have been there even if the guy from the program wasn't. But that's not the point. The point is you *did* think about it. You wondered. Anybody would. And you stayed. You waited longer than five minutes. Anybody would. And you did. The desk guy says you were up there forty-five minutes."

The kid sat in sullen and oppressive silence. There was nothing more for me to say. Either he told the truth now or he didn't. It was only after he spoke that I realized I'd been holding my breath.

"Maybe he's lyin'. Maybe he made a mistake." But there was no hostility, not even conviction, in the kid's tone. He was just trying it on for size.

"No good, Paco. We both know you were there. He's not lying or mistaken. Did you get into the apartment?"

"No!" The kid looked ready to explode. "How many times I gotta *tell* you? There wasn't no answer!" His voice was high, nearly hysterical.

"Okay, I'll buy that," I said in a voice I hoped would soothe him. "You didn't get in, but you did wait around. Where? For how long?"

"You ain't gonna believe me."

"Try me."

He took a deep breath. "When I got to the door, I seen a note. It said for me to wait down the hall on account of because there was another dude in there with him. So that's what I done."

"What did the note look like?"

"It was on that yellow paper you got," he said, pointing at my legal pad. "It was tape to the door."

"How'd you know it was for you?"

A scornful look. "It had my name on it." He didn't actually add "you fool," but he might as well have.

"Which name? Paco?"

"Yeah."

"What did it say? Try to remember exactly."

"It said like he had a client inside and I should go and wait in the laundry room for a half an hour. So I did."

"It said laundry room?" He nodded. "Where is the laundry room?"

"On the same floor. Down the hall."

"Can you see the apartment from the laundry room?" I knew the answer, having been with Nathan once while he did laundry, but I wanted to know how much the kid knew.

"No, it's around the corner, like."

"Right. How long were you there? What did you do there?"

"I lit up a reefer. I sat on a bench like and looked at the machines. I was thinkin'."

"Did you see anybody else?"

"Not in the room. Some people pass by in the hall, but I didn't want them to see the smoke, so I stay quiet."

"So you don't know if they saw you?"

He shook his head.

"You were there about half an hour?" He nodded. "How do you know?"

"Maybe there was a clock in the room." His voice was tentative, evasive.

"What do you mean maybe? You were there, Paco. You tell me. Was there a clock or wasn't there?"

"I don't remember."

"Then how do you know a half hour was up?"

He looked at the floor. Plainly he didn't like the question. I didn't know why till he answered. Then I saw his point. I didn't like it either."

"I had a watch. A friend gave it to me."

"What friend?"

"Na—Mr. Wasserstein." He heard my sigh of resignation and began to talk fast. "He gave it to me! Honest! I didn't steal nothin' from him, no matter what the cops think. I wouldn't do nothin' like that to him. Not to him!"

So far I'd dealt in facts. What time was it? What did you do then? Now we were into the hard part. I had to decide how to go with it. Should I confront the kid, beat him over the head and watch his reaction? Or should I play sympathetic, like I was on his side all the way, but the cops had this crazy idea. . . . I had the uneasy feeling that Detective Button had been thinking along the same lines when he'd questioned me the day I found Nathan's body.

I went for confrontation. The words should have stuck in my throat, but oddly enough, they didn't. I was doing my job, the one I could do in my sleep.

"What'd he give it to you for, Paco?" I asked, my voice as hard as I could make it. "Or maybe I should ask what you did to earn it, huh?"

His reaction was more than I'd bargained for. He gave a hoarse animal cry, lunged out of his seat, and swung wildly at my head. He missed me by inches as he shrieked, "You callin' me a faggot, cunt, I kill you."

TWENTY-TWO

I just sat and watched, like a clinical observer at a psychiatric ward. Or like a zookeeper.

Finally, he subsided into sullenness, muttering, "I ain't no faggot. Motherfucking creep cops."

I hit him again. "I hate to bring this *up,* Paco," I said, in a tone laden with sarcasm, "but you got a sheet here, man, and we both know what it's for. You've been busted for hustling, kid, you'd better face it. The cops aren't making this up."

"Fuck that shit!" He jumped up from the stool again. He smacked one fist into an open palm and spun around, as though his anger was too great to let him stand still. I waited.

"Don't you see?" he finally said in a plaintive, high voice, his back still to me. "That don't mean shit. That's just hustlin', man. That's just to get a little coin, you dig? I get paid. Paid good. Them dudes like young guys. I pretend to like all that shit, but I'm laughin' at 'em all the time. Laughin', you dig? And then I rip 'em off, take like a watch or a ring or somethin'. 'Cause even though they're payin' me, ain't nobody can really pay you enough to do that faggot shit. I wouldn't touch none of them dudes if I couldn't get my bread out of it. I ain't no faggot! No way!"

"So there was nothing between you and Nathan?" I kept my voice flat and steady. If there had been anything, I thought, then Nathan had been degraded by a little hustler who hated his clientele. Laughed at them. No, that wasn't Nathan. He would have seen through this cheap little hooker who used the vulnerability of middle-aged gays. Ripped them off both physically and emotionally.

"Let's get back to the watch," I said in a purposely businesslike tone. "Was it vouchered? Did the cops take it and give you a paper?"

He nodded and reached into the pocket of his tight-fitting denim jacket. I looked at the paper to see if anything else had been vouchered. Vouchering means the item is likely to be used as evidence. In this case the watch would be People's Exhibit One.

For a moment, I just sat there, digesting the implications. The watch was a killer. It could be used two different ways, either of them devastating. Say you accepted the obvious, that the kid stole it. It fitted his record of petty theft, for one thing. Then Nathan caught him at it, they argued, and the kid killed him. Or you bought the kid's story that Nathan gave him the watch. That made them more than lawyer and client, and that was the linchpin of Button's theory. Now you had your gay lover killing. And the way the kid felt about faggots. . . . Whoever represented him would have to keep him off the stand at all costs.

"When did Nathan give you the watch?"

"Last week."

"Did he say why he was giving it to you?"

"Yeah. I was late for an appointment and I told him it was because I ain't got a watch, so he give me his old one. He just got a new one. He showed me it."

That at least was true. Nathan had just bought himself a handsome pocket watch, a gold one with a little cover. He'd been looking for a nice chain. If Paco was going to steal a watch, why not go for the new one? Or even both? Though the D.A. would probably say he'd hoped Nathan wouldn't miss the old one.

"Was anybody else there when he gave you the watch?"

"No. Just him and me."

"Did you show it to anybody? Your mother, your friends?"

"No. I don't like too many people to know my business, you know."

"Nobody saw it before Nathan was killed?"

"I don't know, man. Like I wasn't hidin' it, but I wasn't flashin' it neither. I didn't want anybody rippin' it off me."

"Okay. It doesn't matter anyway." It didn't. If the cops went with the theft angle, they could always claim the actual stealing took place the week before, but that Nathan found out about it the night he was killed. The thing was, I didn't see Nathan reporting this kid to the cops if he'd stolen everything he had, let alone an old watch he'd just replaced. Theft as a motive for Nathan's death didn't cut any ice with me. Particularly in view of the manner of the murder. Burglars don't tie people to beds and strangle them; they hit and run. No, the sex-murder theory was the one to watch out for. It was the theory Button liked, and it was strengthened by the kid's own story. Who would believe Nathan gave a watch, even an old one, to a kid who was nothing more to him than a client?

"You know, Paco," I began, "sometimes people who are up against it—like you are on this case—sometimes they get the wrong idea about what can help them and what can hurt them. Take this watch. I can see where you might be afraid to admit that you took it. You might feel that could get you in a lot of trouble. No," I held up my hand, "let me finish. Don't interrupt. When I'm done, you can say whatever you want to say. Now the thing about this watch is, if you stole it, it's not a big deal. Not compared to murder. But your story that Nathan gave it to you, that's just what the cops want you to say. You understand where I'm coming from?"

He shook his head. "See," I went on, "they think you and Nathan were lovers." Paco said nothing, but he balled his fists. "And if they hear that story about the watch being a present from him to you, they're going to think it was true. See what I mean?" His eyes grew even larger as he nodded, slowly. "Now if you admit the truth, that you stole the watch, the cops can't say you were lovers, can they?"

There were holes in my reasoning you could drive a Corrections bus through, but fortunately the kid didn't notice

them. He nodded. "Yeah," he said, "I took the watch when
he wasn't lookin'. I didn't think he'd need it no more."

I breathed a sigh of relief. I had no doubt that it was the
truth. It was the kid's usual pattern of petty theft, this time
from his lawyer instead of a trick. But it was a much less
potent motive for murder than the other.

I moved back to the murder night. "Let's go back to the
note," I said. "Did it look like Nathan's writing?"

"I don't know. It was printed like." He ducked his head,
and a flush of dark rose suffused his cheeks. He said, so
low I could hardly hear him, "I don't read too good. He
made it simple like."

"But you thought Nathan wrote it?"

"Why wouldn't I? I seen a note with his name on it. I
didn't think about it. Not then. Now I done some thinkin'
and I see how somebody set me up good with that note. I
mean they got me there and kept me there, right?"

"Right. You catch on quick. What happened when you
came back after waiting in the laundry room?"

"There wasn't no note. It was gone. I figured the dude
inside with him was gone, so I ring the bell. No answer. I
knock a few times. No answer. I waited around some more,
knocked some more, no answer. Finally I split."

"Where'd you go?"

"Coney Island. A bar I know." I wondered what kind of
bar, but I didn't ask.

"Did you try to call Nathan?"

"No. I figure I'll catch him later, you dig?"

"While you were knocking at the door, either time, did
anybody pass by?"

"Yeah, maybe, I'm not too sure."

"Did you try the door?" It was almost an afterthought.
To my surprise, he nodded. "It was lock," he said.

This time there was no careful consideration of tactics. I
was so shocked I blurted out, "Paco, you're lying."

"No, I ain't," he replied. For the first time, he looked
really scared.

"Paco," I said softly, "I found Nathan's body and that
door was unlocked. If you'd tried it, you'd have gotten in."

"No, lady," he shook his head. "That door was lock. I know. Maybe somebody come by and open it later, but it was lock when I was there. Cross my heart."

Maybe it was the childish phrase that did it. It's hard to pin down exactly what lawyers mean when they use the hackneyed phrase "the ring of truth," but Paco's statement had it. Maybe it was because saying he hadn't tried the door would have helped him. Saying it was locked hurt him. Therefore it was true.

Meanwhile, there was one more thing that had to be said. "Paco, I can't stay on this case. I can't be your lawyer. The court will appoint someone else, but I'll give them everything I've got and I'll work with them if I can. I believe you. I don't think you killed Nathan."

He was looking at me with a steady gaze, but there was no sign of emotion as I spoke. I wondered if he believed me. Or if he cared.

"The cops will arrest you and charge you with murder after you're arraigned on the warrant. They'll take you to Central Booking and then bring you back here. Do not, repeat *do not,* make any statements to them. You can't help yourself, no matter what they tell you. Understand?" He nodded.

"Don't let them put you in a lineup without a lawyer present—either me or your new lawyer. Okay?"

This time he looked up. His eyes looked enormous. The pupils were dilated with fear.

"Hey, Paco. Try to stay cool, man. I know it's tough. But I really am trying to help you. Please, just hang in there. I'll be doing the best I can."

"Lady, can I ax you something?"

I nodded.

"Can you get me separated in Riker's? Away from the other guys? I don't want to do no more of that faggot shit, you dig?"

Coming into the courtroom was like walking into an icebox. I faced a roomful of hostile glares. I had the last case of the day and the court officers were pissed at being kept waiting.

But if I thought I was unloved by the court personnel, all I had to do was look at Button to see what real hate was all about. He looked at me as though he'd like nothing better than to see me in one of the green body bags they'd carried Nathan out in.

The only break in the general hostility came from the judge. The Hon. Helen Donohue was a former Legal Aid attorney and an old friend. She smiled at me as she dog-eared her paperback copy of *Princess Daisy*. As long as the Hon. Helen had reading matter, she didn't care how long she had to wait for anything.

The bridgeman called the case. Button brought Paco out. He was shaking, a fine shiver that seemed to emanate from a small knot of fear just below his diaphragm. I knew the feeling, but there was nothing I could do to help.

After the long interview, the arraignment itself was an anticlimax. I got relieved, bail was set ($25,000), and sentence date was set on the warrant—the old case—for next Thursday. That was to give the cops time to get him arrested and arraigned on the murder. Then the court officers took Paco back inside. I gave him a smile, but it didn't erase the look of terror on the small, pretty face.

While I was gathering up my things, a harsh voice sounded in my ear. It was Button. "Well, Counselor, I guess Barnum was right. There is a sucker born every minute. And this time it was me. Tell me again how you wanted information for personal reasons, not as a lawyer."

"I got off the case, Button. Didn't you hear what went on?"

"Detective Button to you, Miss Jameson. Yeah, you got off the case. After you told that little bastard everything the cops had on him. Or did you spend two hours with him discussing the weather?" When I opened my mouth to answer, he waved me quiet and said, in a weary voice, "Don't bother, Miss Jameson. I'm not likely to believe anything you tell me after this. It just may be that someday you'll regret that, but that's the way it is. I can be made a sucker of once just like everybody else. But not a second time. Not by you or any other stinking defense lawyer."

He turned on his heel and walked away. I could see his point. From his perspective I'd screwed him—gotten information under false pretenses. But I still felt justified. The information wouldn't be the exclusive property of the prosecution for very long. Paco's 18-b lawyer would have it soon enough. But I could only get it now.

For all the good it would do me. Did I really believe someone had set Paco up, called him pretending to be from the program and then kept him at the scene with a phony note? I could at least find out whether there had been a legitimate call from the program. I could canvass Nathan's building, find out whether anyone had seen Paco at Nathan's door or in the laundry room.

It was with a feeling of optimism, finally, that I left the courthouse. Button's Midnight Cowboy was no longer a bogeyman but a real person. That meant there were facts to be checked, questions to be asked, evidence to be sifted. That meant I could do my job.

TWENTY-THREE

Rick's was packed, especially for a Tuesday night. Wall-to-wall lawyers, court clerks, court reporters. A judge or two. No cops or court officers, though. They had their own bar near criminal court. Just as well. I didn't much fancy drinking with armed people.

Not that Rick's wasn't something of an armed camp in its own right. The D.A.s had their table, and we had ours. In fact, there were distinctions within Legal Aid. The rank and file would be at a back table, cracking peanuts and listening to Flaherty. Milt, Deke, and a few other supervisors usually stood at the bar. So in order to get to where I was going, I would have to pass Milt. I wasn't looking forward to it.

I was right. Milt's eyes narrowed as he saw me coming. "Been in court all this time?" he asked.

"Yeah, Milt." I stopped, resigned to the inevitable. "I got held up on an old warrant of Nathan's."

"An old warrant." He shook his head sadly. "An old warrant who just happened to be his killer." He bit off the last word with a controlled menace that momentarily had me scared. Then I realized there was nothing he could do to me. I could hardly be fired for interviewing a client. I said something to that effect, that I'd just treated the kid like any other client.

Wrong thing to say. "Damn it, Cass!" Milt hissed, between clenched teeth. "Who do you think you're talking to? Since when do *you* do a two-hour interview on just another client? On a Legal Aid Relieved? Don't give me

144

that just another client garbage. You had no business talking to that kid—"

"I got relieved, Milt," I interrupted.

He snorted. "You got relieved," he repeated derisively, "after you got everything you could out of the kid."

"Milt, what's the problem? What difference does it make?"

If Milt had been Del Parma, he'd have started pacing. If he'd been Detective Button, he'd have given me his shark-tooth smile. Being Milt, he spoke very very softly. "You compromised the integrity of the Society, Cassandra. Representing that kid, even for a limited purpose, constituted a total conflict of interest. I can't afford to have my attorneys doing things like that. It makes me look bad. And I don't like looking bad." He was almost whispering.

"But worse than that, Cass. Worse than that. You're opening a can of worms. You're running the risk that the newspapers will get hold of this kid angle. And if there was one kid, maybe there was more than one. Is that all the respect you have for Nathan's memory?"

"Milt, you've got to hear me out." I was talking softly now too, hoping to keep the conversation between Milt and me. "I think the kid may have been framed."

Milt gave me a long, incredulous stare. Then his lip curled in disgust. "Christ," he said, still softly but with venom. "Nathan sure could pick 'em. One of his clients strangles him, and the woman he sleeps with defends his killer." He shook his head and turned his face away.

"Fuck you, Milt," I said. It was a normal tone of voice, but after our intense whispering, it turned heads all along the bar. I didn't care.

"It's all over as far as you're concerned, isn't it? The cops have their suspect. No bad publicity. Let's hope the kid hangs himself in Riker's, like poor old Charlie. That would make things simple for everybody, wouldn't it?"

No answer. Milt's like that. He'd closed the iron door, and I didn't exist anymore. I walked to the back of the bar, barely seeing where I was headed.

"Over here, Cass." The voice wasn't Flaherty's, nor was it coming from the Legal Aid side of the room. I turned to see Stan Willburton in a booth with Roger Morrison, an 18-b lawyer.

"Grab a seat," Roger invited. I put my coat on a hook and slid in next to Stan.

"What was that all about?" Roger asked, signaling the waitress with his free hand. The other was full of peanuts.

It was Stan who answered. "I know you're on trial, Rog, but even you must have heard that the cops arrested a suspect for Nathan's murder and that Cass arraigned him?"

"What is this, Gossip Central?" I asked with a smile. I was trying to keep it light in front of Roger. Stan I could tell the whole story to, if I could get him alone.

"You aren't planning on keeping the case, are you?" Roger asked.

"Of course not. It'll be murder anyway, so one of you bright boys from Stan's 18-b murder panel will get it. In fact," I said, turning to Stan, "I was going to call you. Who can you assign? It's got to be somebody good, somebody who'll really do a job for the kid, not just cop him out."

"Are you suggesting that there are members of my panel who—"

"Who would have copped out Jesus Christ if they could have gotten him two to four concurrent."

Roger laughed, choking on his beer and spraying Stan and me with a fine mist of imported brew. He apologized, mopping himself with a huge white handkerchief. For the first time I noticed how drunk he was. "Roger," I said, "how the hell long have you been in here? You look like you've been putting it away since noon."

"Good old Cass." He gave me a mock bow. "Miss Tact of The Year."

I started to apologize, but he cut me off. "No, Counselor. The witness will answer the question. Yes, I'm tight as a drum. If you were on trial before Hanging Harold Wormser, you'd be smashed too. That bastard is—"

"The Antichrist, the scum of the earth, the worst judge ever to befoul even the corrupt bench of Brooklyn with his presence," Stan interrupted. He went on plaintively, "I know, Roger. Believe me, I know. Cass, don't get him started again. I've had this for two hours already."

"What's he doing to you?" I asked Roger. "In twenty-five words or less," I added hastily, glancing at Stan.

"That's the trouble. It all sounds like such little piddling shit. But it adds up. It adds up and it's burying me. He's nickel-and-diming me to death, and all the time he gives the jury that Will Geer nice-old-codger routine. They love him, and they think I'm a young smartass when all I'm trying to do is get the semblance of a fair trial for my client." Roger took a healthy swallow of beer. "Who just might be innocent," he added morosely. "That's the worst part. Wormser firmly believes that all defendants, without exception, are guilty. If somebody gets an acquittal, he tells the D.A., 'We lost another case.'"

"I hope Paco doesn't get a judge like that," I remarked.

"Paco? That's the kid who killed Nathan? Already you're calling him Paco?" I didn't like the edge of suspicion in Stan's voice.

"Look, Stan, I know this is hard to believe," I said hastily, "but I don't think he did it. I think he was set up."

"Set up?" Stan started shooting questions at me. The way I'd shot them at Paco—"Who by? How? Why?"

Good questions. I took a breath.

"I think somebody got him to the apartment and kept him there by a trick," I began. "A phone call and a note on the door. That way his name would be in the book downstairs, and the desk guy would see him. That way he'd be in the building at the right time. But Nathan would already be dead."

"That's pretty far out, isn't it, Cass?" Stan's tone was patient, but unbelieving. Roger just stared at me through his muzzy haze of beer. "Even supposing you're right, that means somebody knew enough about this kid to set him up —*him,* this particular kid, who I've already heard is a fairy.

That's supposing a lot of inside information, isn't it?" Stan
sat back in the booth, waiting for my reply. Waiting for the
opposition to sum up.

"Well, yes," I admitted. Always admit right away whatever you can't hope to get away with denying. "But it's not
so hard to find things out if you know your way around, is
it? If you or I or anybody in the system wanted to get hold
of—say, a yellow sheet or a defendant's phone number,
how hard would it be? It's all a public record. It's fairly
accessible. Especially for a lawyer." Especially for a lawyer
on trial in the building, I added mentally, thinking of Riordan. He could easily have heard the gossip about Nathan
that must have been rife in Manhattan. He could have
snooped around enough to find a likely patsy in Paco. He
could have gotten the phone number of Paco's mother
from the ROR sheet and made the phony call that lured
Paco to the apartment building. And he'd have known
enough about the ins and outs of the prison system to have
meddled with Blackwell's yellow commit card. Altogether,
Riordan still filled the bill.

Stan shook his head. "It still sounds far-fetched to me,
Cass." I started to explain about Blackwell, but he put up a
restraining hand. "But I'm too tired to argue. Let's discuss
it another time. Have another beer and tell me who you
want assigned to the case. Roger?"

"Yes to the beer," Roger answered. "No to the case.
When the Worm releases me, I'm heading for sun and fun.
I need something to put the roses back into my cheeks."

I was secretly relieved. Roger's an okay guy, a good guy
to drink with, but I wasn't sure about his skills as a trial
lawyer.

Paul Trentino came in with his partner, Pete Kalisch.
Paul plopped his briefcase down and sat next to Roger.
Pete brought over a chair and placed it at the end of the
booth. I signaled Stan with my eyes. As a former Legal Aid
lawyer who'd known Nathan, Paul was disqualified from
representing Paco. But Pete, who'd known Nathan only in
passing, and had become a lawyer after a stint as a court
officer, was eligible. And he was a good lawyer.

I turned to Paul. "They made an arrest in Nathan's case," I told him.

He grimaced. "I heard. How could you stand up on it? Aside from the ethics, how could you stand next to the guy who killed Nathan and make a bail application?" His voice was high with strain. I kept mine as calm as I could.

"I could do it because I don't think he's guilty. I think he was framed."

Stan cut in. "And Cass has decided he needs the best lawyer the county's money can buy. Can you take it, Pete?"

Pete's face was a polite blank. "You'll have to tell me what the cops have got."

"What the cops have got," I began, "is a nice frame." Roger got up, squeezed past Paul, and went upstairs to the men's room. Not surprising, after all the beer he'd drunk. Stan stood up too, said he had to go, and promised to give my love to Emily. Before he left, I whispered, "Thanks, Stan. It means a lot to me to have you in my corner. Even if you don't agree with me. Maybe because you don't agree with me." He gave me a quick kiss and waved goodbye.

I started telling Pete everything I knew or thought I knew about Nathan's murder. It wasn't easy. I found myself turning to Paul, seeking the friendly interest of his brown eyes instead of the cold, noncommittal objectivity of Pete's hazel ones. Expressionless, hard, they seemed to register nothing of what I was saying. Yet I knew that when the questions came, they would be detailed and pointed.

They were. I answered them as best I could, then went on to explain my suspicions about Riordan. Pete cut me off. He wanted the facts, ma'am, just the facts.

When I'd finished—when Pete had finished with me—he got up, put on his raincoat, and walked out the door.

I looked at Paul, astonished. "Is he going to take it, or what?"

Paul grinned. "He'll take it. He wouldn't have bothered asking questions if he wasn't going to."

"How can you stand being in practice with that cold fish?"

Paul shrugged. "He's a damned good lawyer. He'll do whatever it takes for your kid, Cass. Trust him."

But I didn't. Not fully. The only lawyer I really trusted to represent Paco was me. Which was pretty strange coming from a person who didn't even want to *be* a lawyer.

TWENTY-FOUR

"**P**lants don't purr," Dorinda said contentedly, as Tansy sat on her lap, his forepaws kneading her skirt.

"Plants don't spit up hairballs," I retorted, eyeing a suspicious-looking spot on the painted cement floor.

We had just finished dinner—stir-fried vegetables in ginger sauce—and were engaging in a familiar good-natured argument when the television newsman caught my ear. "The deceased, one Charlie Blackwell, met his death at the hands of 'a person or persons unknown.'" I sat up in the rocking chair. Mignonette stood up on my lap and gazed at me inquiringly, but didn't jump off. The newsman went on.

"The commission announced its findings today and urged the district attorney to investigate Blackwell's suspicious death, originally thought to be suicide."

Then Del Parma came on, surrounded by microphones. If the commission's finding troubled him, if he had hoped for a verdict of suicide, there was no sign of it on his face. He radiated vindication, as though he had believed all along Charlie had been murdered and the commission had merely confirmed his opinion.

It was a masterful performance. He outlined his office's efforts to nail Blackwell, making it sound as significant and high-minded as the Abscam investigation. The only thing he didn't mention was its motive. Nowhere was it so much as hinted that Blackwell was intended to be a stepping-stone to Parma's federal job.

Parma went on to praise the commission and to offer the subtle but barbed opinion that "organized crime figures connected with Stone's defense should be carefully scrutinized by the D.A." Reading between the lines, Parma had just fingered Matt Riordan.

"Jesus!" I said to Dorinda, "that Parma's got some balls."

"What do you mean?" she asked.

"*He* sets Blackwell up for the sole purpose of turning him as a witness against Riordan. *He* puts the guy in jail where he gets killed under his very nose, and then *he* goes on TV and starts throwing the blame around. If anybody's responsible for Blackwell's death, it's Parma. If he'd left the fucking guy alone, he'd be alive today." And so would Nathan, I thought bitterly.

"What does all this mean to your investigation?" Dorinda asked.

"Don't know yet. At least somebody besides me thinks Charlie was murdered. That ought to be good for something. But I'm a little confused about this commission. When I was there, they were really into the suicide thing. I wonder what made them decide it was murder?"

The next day was Saturday. A darkroom day. A day away from murder.

It started with a letter from Ron:

hi kid—
sorry about your friend. i know what it's like to lose a friend and i know how long it takes to get over it. don't let that worry you. it never stops hurting in one sense but in another sense peace will come. believe that. i don't completely understand what you're doing with your investigation, but i hope you're getting somewhere. mom and dad wondered why you hadn't written. i told them a friend of yours had died and that you were upset. maybe you could call and let them know you're okay. or not. up to you.
i saw a science program on pbs recently—I've probably earned a phd watching pbs—and the guy was talking about the smallest unit of time. he said it was the period

in which an event of single consequence takes place. somehow i thought of you and nathan. can there be an event of single consequence when people are involved/ i don't think so. it seems that your friend's death is having multiple consequences in the lives of everyone you know. especially yours. i think it's good that you're letting his life and death have consequences in your life. go with it.

ron

I put the letter down and shook the tears out of my eyes. Ron, who'd never met Nathan, seemed to understand so much. Things even Flaherty or Dorinda couldn't seem to grasp. And he didn't even know me very well anymore. Not from one visit a year, at Christmas. Yet he knew instinctively that Nathan's death had a meaning for me that nothing else had had recently. Not since four students had been shot to death at my school. But it wasn't that only death had meaning for me, just that I'd grown such a thick skin doing my job in the pens of Brooklyn that it took a lot to penetrate it. I was a machine. Push the button marked STREET TALK. FOR CLIENT ONLY. Push another one: SYMPATHY. USE ON CLIENT'S MOTHER. Then the one marked LEGAL JARGON. FOR JUDGE'S EARS. I was the keypunch operator of my own mind. Only Nathan's death had shaken me out of that role that I played so well and so unthinkingly. Only that had brought out all the human qualities I'd learned to bury to do my job.

Deke Fischer had been right when he'd chewed me out for dumping Jorge Ruiz. I'd just pushed the CLIENT IS A HUMP button and bailed out. Jorge disappeared from my life as though a trapdoor had opened up and swallowed him. But with Paco, where finding the truth was vital to my understanding of Nathan's murder, I had been patience itself. I would have stayed with him four hours, taking whatever abuse he cared to dish out, to get what I wanted. Ron was right. I was involved. For better or worse.

But not today.

I decided to print up some old negatives from home.

Victorian houses, one of my favorite subjects. There was one in particular, a gingerbread beauty near my favorite pizza joint in Kent. I had full views as well as close-ups of some detail. I wanted to try printing them on high-contrast paper, bringing out just the outlines. To make brief sketches, hints, suggestions—like houses seen in dreams.

I mixed the chemicals at the sink, then carefully carried the filled trays back to the bedroom. My darkroom is under the bed. Which sounds a little weird, except that it's a loft bed, sort of like the top of a bunk bed without the bottom. So there's room underneath for storage or a study or whatever. In my case, it's a darkroom. Tiny, no running water, and I have to step out fairly often to keep from being overcome by hypo fumes, but it works. The perfect New York apartment darkroom.

I was just watching the first print come up in the developer when the phone rang. Watching your picture form on the paper is the most exciting part of printing, maybe of photography itself. Even the pros say if that sight ceases to thrill you, get the hell out of the business. So I was extremely reluctant to pick up that phone.

Finally I did. I popped the picture out of the developer and into the fixer and made a mad dash, hoping it wasn't just some clown wanting me to take home delivery of *The New York Times*.

It wasn't. My instinct had been right. The call was important. It involved Nathan, Charlie Blackwell, and Del Parma's press performance the night before. It was Matt Riordan.

My surprise must have been evident in my voice, for he said, "I guess I'm the last person in the world you expected to hear from."

"Well," I admitted, recovering a little of my poise, "at least you're not trying to sell me a cemetery plot."

He laughed, a rich baritone laugh that went with his face and bearing. Riordan was all of a piece. Smooth as glass.

"Did you see the *Post* this morning?"

"No," I answered, puzzled at first, then realizing what he

was getting at. "But I saw the news last night, if that's what you mean. Del Parma put on quite a show."

"Didn't he then?" Riordan's voice lost its amused casualness. "That slimy ass-kissing little bastard all but accused me of murdering poor Charlie Blackwell."

I didn't know what to say. I could hardly admit that I thought Parma had a point.

"Anyway, Ms. Jameson—or should I say Ms. Drew," the light, bantering tone was back, "I've decided to answer the questions you didn't have a chance to ask me the last time we met. You did want to ask me some, didn't you?"

"A few, just a few, Mr. Riordan," I answered, trying to stay as light as he had.

"Well, how about we meet later—for drinks, say."

"You name the time and place," I said. "I'll be there."

"All right. According to the phonebook, you live in the Village. Is there somewhere near you we could go? Somewhere," he added, "where I'll be safe, that is. I'm not accustomed to being whistled at on the street."

I laughed. "Well, at least now you know how it feels. How about the White Horse Tavern?"

"Fine. Haven't been there in years. Not since I was an undergraduate at Fordham. That was, believe it or not, about the same time that Dylan Thomas was hanging out there. Not," he hastily added, "that I ever saw him."

I was impressed in spite of myself. Somehow I'd expected the Matt Riordan I thought I knew to be full of phony stories, about Dylan Thomas or any other celebrity whose name happened to come up. We agreed to meet at 5:30—a little early, but he had a dinner engagement he couldn't break. As a matter of fact, though I didn't mention it to Riordan, I had a date too—with Dave Chessler.

I put down the phone and stood in thought a moment. Then, remembering, I ran to the darkroom and rescued my print. In spite of its prolonged fixing bath, it looked pretty good. The high-contrast paper erased the evidence of a seedy present—the peeling paint, the tacky curtains—and revealed the stately outlines, the dignified silhouette. Like soft-focus photography of an aging star.

The success of the first print inspired me. I took out another negative, a close-up of a Doric column on another old house, this one now a funeral parlor in Bedford. I got so absorbed in what I was doing I didn't stop to eat lunch till 3:30. I cleaned up the darkroom, made a quick sandwich, and jumped in the shower. As I massaged the shampoo into my hair, I realized how keyed up I was with anticipation. What I couldn't decide was whether the anticipation was for my date with Dave or the long-awaited confrontation with Riordan.

I dressed carefully. Though the days were growing warmer, the nights were still wintry. I put on a wool challis peasant skirt, an embroidered Ukranian blouse, and my black boots. I used a curling iron to make windswept bangs for my normally straight hair and wore enameled earrings with brightly colored birds on them. A touch of perfume and my favorite red-lined black cape and I was ready.

The White Horse was a quick walk through cold back streets. The night was clear and crisp, the day's clouds having blown away. It seemed more like January than April. The last blast of winter, I told myself, before the welcome thaw of spring.

Riordan sat at a window table. For a moment, from the chilly vantage point of Hudson Street, the scene was pure Hopper. A man in a bar, seen through a dirty window. Waiting.

I came in and sat in the booth. Riordan was drinking Scotch, and when I told him I drank it too, he ordered the same for me. I never did find out what brand it was, which was just as well, since I'm sure I can't afford it. It was as far above my usual brand as La Grenouille is from the Golden Arches.

We sat and sipped in silence for a moment, while I adjusted to the dim warmth of the place. Another assumption about Riordan shattered. I would have expected him to abhor silence, to fill it automatically with charming, witty small talk.

Finally he spoke, and it wasn't small talk. "About Charlie Blackwell," he began. Then he broke off and stared at me. "How much do you know about the Stone case?"

"Quite a bit, actually. I've done my homework. Oh, and I was there, for one day, anyway. When I was in law school a bunch of us went over." I smiled at him. "To see the great Matt Riordan in action."

He smiled back. A warm smile. "I hope you weren't disappointed."

I shook my head. "I learned something," I answered. I didn't say what. It had more to do with theater than with law, and I wasn't sure he'd find that flattering.

He went on. "You know, then, that the whole case against Stone rested on Charlie Blackwell's credibility." He smiled. "But as Oliver Wendell Holmes would have said, they were leaning on a weak reed."

Another surprise. Riordan the legal scholar. "Yeah," I agreed. "The papers made a big thing out of it. Parma caught hell for even starting a trial with a witness as flaky as Charlie. Of course, what they didn't know was that Charlie might have been a skunk, but he wasn't all that flaky until you asked him those UFO questions."

"You mean until I planted the answers to those phony UFO questions." He smiled again, but this time the smile was twisted, ironic. "You don't have to be tactful with me, Miss Jameson. I know what everyone thought about that trial. The papers took the line they did because Stone unconvicted was still a powerful man. If he'd been convicted, they'd have eaten him alive like the vultures they are, but since he was acquitted, it was a dirty shame how Parma went after him. That's what happens to losers. Parma took that chance, and he lost. So he paid the price. It's that simple."

"Somehow I don't think Parma thinks it's that simple."

"Parma's a whiner. No, don't defend him. I know he's got a tough job, going after people with power instead of the poor slobs who steal pocketbooks for a living. But nobody put a gun to Parma's head to make him take that job. He wanted the power and the headlines, and he who lives by the headline. . . ." Riordan let his voice trail off and took another swallow of his incredible Scotch, which he drank as if it were water. Not very good water.

"But to get back to our immediate problem. I didn't fix the Stone case. Ironic, isn't it? Parma's been trying to nail my ass to the wall for eight years, and I didn't do a damn thing. Whoever did it is in his own office."

TWENTY-FIVE

I must have looked as boggled as I felt. "Don't look so shocked, Ms. Jameson," Riordan teased. "It shouldn't come as a surprise to someone as smart as you. The tip I got to ask Charlie those questions came from within the Special Prosecutor's office."

"How do you know?" I demanded. He was right. I was shocked. But not so shocked that I believed him. Not until I heard a little proof.

"Well, look at it this way. I didn't plant those questions with Charlie. Take that on faith for the moment. I got them in the mail. Anonymous, of course. But Charlie had all the answers down pat. So pat that I might have prepared him myself. Somebody who had access to him in custody went at him day and night to get that kind of a performance out of him. There was no way I or anybody associated with me could get that kind of access."

"That makes sense," I had to agree, thinking about what Dave had told me regarding security around Blackwell. "But couldn't you—or someone," I hastily amended, "have gotten to him through one of the guards?"

"You've seen the transcript, I assume." I nodded. "Then you know those questions and answers were framed by somebody who knew a hell of a lot about cross-examination." I nodded again. "That rules out Charlie himself, even if he'd been allowed to mail anything that wasn't thoroughly examined. And it rules out the security people, too. It had to be a lawyer, and the only lawyers who could get close to Charlie were Del's own people. And Del himself, of course."

I brushed that thought aside for the moment. It was probably just one of Riordan's ironic jokes. "You say you got the questions in the mail. Didn't you wonder who'd sent them?"

"Of course I wondered. Just as I wondered if they weren't some kind of trap. But, hell, I get paid to defend my clients, not to wonder about things that if the truth were known might get them into even more trouble. I assumed, naturally, that someone, shall we say, favorable to Stone's defense had decided to assist me, and I didn't look any farther."

I probably looked as disgusted as I felt. "Look, Ms. Jameson." The smooth voice was suddenly hard. "Haven't you ever had a client who told you not to worry about his case because the complainant wasn't going to show up in court? And do you always in your touchingly naïve way believe that the complainant just happened to change his mind about prosecuting? Does it ever occur to you that maybe he's not coming in because your client bribed—or in the case of your indigent clientele, probably beat the guy into changing his mind? Do you run to the court with your suspicions? Or do you conveniently suppress them so you can keep your nice liberal conscience clear?"

I was blazing with anger. "At least my clients don't have people thrown into the East River in cement overcoats."

Suddenly he laughed, that big, roaring laugh I'd liked before.

"How refreshingly predictable you are!" he said. "Don't you think a substantial number of your clients would do just that if they had the resources some of my clients have?"

Now it was my turn to laugh, a little ruefully. "I guess you're right," I admitted.

"And if you think about it, you'll see that my keeping silent for eight years is no different from anything any other lawyer would do. Vague suspicions that my client was involved in a fix are not enough to justify my abandoning all pretense of ethics and turning him in to the D.A., now are they?"

I had to agree. I was beginning to get used to being backed into a corner by this sharp-thinking, blue-eyed charmer. "Okay. Fine. So why now? Why after eight years of keeping all this to yourself are you finally talking to someone? And why to me?"

"As to the first question, I find myself revolted by Parma's little farce of last night. I don't much like being accused of murder, Ms. Jameson. I may not take many other things very seriously, but that annoyed me. Plus I like the thought of that oily bastard's face when he finds out the fix came from within his own office instead of from me. As to the second question, why you—why not you? I like you. I liked Nathan. Yes, I knew him when. And I'm beginning to agree with you that there's a link between his death and Blackwell's. I want to help you look for that link. Which is why I think you should see Jesse Winthrop."

"Jesse Winthrop? The guy who writes for the *Village Voice*?"

"Yes. He's written several pieces on the Special Prosecutor's office over the years. I happen to know he's planning a new series to coincide with Parma's new job hunt—the congressional hearings will begin soon and Winthrop wants to give them something to think about. Would you like to see Winthrop—say, tomorrow?"

"Would I? Say when." I was conscious that all this somehow fitted into a larger plan of Riordan's, but for the moment, I didn't care. Aside from the honor of meeting Jesse Winthrop, whom I'd admired for a long time, there was the chance of learning a good deal of inside stuff about the Stone case. And maybe about Riordan, too.

Riordan got up, made a phone call, and came back to tell me I was having brunch the next day with Winthrop. At McGillicuddy's, a pub near the *Voice* office in the East Village.

Now came the charming small talk I'd been expecting earlier. As we finished our drinks, Riordan began to talk about the Village as he'd known it as an undergraduate.

Funny, I usually loathe people telling me how great the Village was in the good old days, but I found myself genuinely entertained by Riordan's stories. So much so that I started talking about myself, my ambitions as a photographer, my growing hatred of criminal law.

He quoted Rumpole, "When you're tired of crime, you're tired of life."

I sighed, then smiled. "In that case, I guess I'm tired of life."

I got back to my apartment in the nick of time. Just as I opened the door, still puffing from the three-flight climb, the bell rang. Dave was here. I buzzed him in, then waited for him to make the trek. It didn't take long.

"You must be in pretty good shape," I told him. "Strong men have been known to faint after climbing up my steps."

He smiled. "I work out a lot. Plus squash three times a week. I need some physical exercise after sitting at a desk all day. What about you?"

I took his coat, a tweedy, academic-looking jacket in a heather green, and hung it on the hatrack that serves as my front closet.

"Not me. By the time I get home from work, plopping down in front of the TV is all the exercise I want. I do hike a little, though, when the weather is good." I thought of the day Nathan and I spent on the Palisades, rock climbing, picture taking, kissing on a bluff. A beautiful fall day I'd translated into some stunning photographs—the ones on Nathan's bedroom wall. I still carried the Swiss Army knife he'd given me as a memento, though I used it for nothing more strenuous than opening wine bottles at office parties.

I shook myself out of the memory and offered Dave a drink. I'd bought bourbon specially for him, so I was pleased when he asked for it. I poured myself a club soda. After two Scotches with Riordan, I was already as high as an elephant's eye. Besides, my own brand would insult my newly acquired palate.

Dave sat on the canvas-covered couch and looked around at my apartment, commenting on the Erté print on the opposite wall. It was the only thing I'd bought in the last five years. Nathan's idea, of course. He'd taken me to a gallery owned by a friend of his, and I'd fallen in love with the print's sophisticated lines. Ordinarily, I'd have stuck with admiration from a distance, but Nathan, who owned two Ertés—one number, one letter—talked me into buying the one I liked best. I still loved it, but I had to admit, seeing my apartment momentarily through the eyes of a visitor, that it didn't go with anything else I owned. The colors were too muted for my bold primaries, and the effect was too voluptuous for my collection of political posters. Like Mae West in a roomful of Gloria Steinems.

"I saw your boss's press conference last night," I began. "He really took the bull by the horns."

"He had to, once the commission came out the way it did," Dave answered, sipping his bourbon.

"Yeah, I wondered about that. I got the impression, when I was there, that they were leaning pretty heavily toward the suicide theory."

"That was before they found out we set Blackwell up. God, was Parma frosted when he heard. He did everything but swear us to secrecy in blood."

"But somebody spilled the beans? Sounds like there's somebody in your office who doesn't like Parma too much."

"Well, face it, the man's out for number one. Always has been. But hell, who isn't?" Dave smiled tolerantly.

"Do you have any idea who tipped them off? Does Parma have any suspicions?"

"If he does, he's not telling me about it. Besides, it probably wasn't that blatant. Somebody started telling just a little too much, and the commission put two and two together."

"Dave, from what I saw of that bunch, they'd have trouble putting two and two together with an IBM computer. If they got sidetracked off the suicide theory, it's because somebody drew them a picture. I'd be interested to know who."

"Jesus, Cass. There you go again looking the gift horse in the mouth." His broad smile took any sting out of the words. "Let's just say somebody did you a big favor and leave it at that."

I got the hint and switched topics. In a way, I admired Dave's loyalty. It was clear he had a good idea about who had said more than he or she should have, but he wasn't going to talk about it to an outsider.

"Anyway, Parma lost no time in trying to implicate Riordan." Dave's smile was knowing. "He didn't name any names. He didn't have to. At least not to anyone who knows what's going on."

"Like you."

"Like me. And Riordan." I dragged out the name provocatively. It worked. Dave was all boyish eagerness. "What do you mean? Did he take the bait? I haven't seen the paper today."

"I haven't either. I don't know what he told them. If anything. He called me this morning."

"You? Why would he call you?"

"I'll overlook the less-than-flattering implications of that question, Mr. Chessler."

He smiled, but his voice was serious. He really wanted an answer.

"He called me because he knows I'm interested in what happened. I tried to ask him questions."

"I thought he brushed you off before," Dave objected. "So why all of a sudden does he want to see you now? Don't you find that just a little suspicious?"

"Well, if you put it that way, yes, I do. But he's really very nice. Not at all what I expected."

"You met him already?" The words were an accusation. "I was hoping I could talk you out of it. Before the famous Riordan charm had a chance to work on you," he added bitterly.

I was surprised. "Jealous?" I asked incredulously. "I just met the man for a drink and we talked about the case. That's all."

"What did he tell you that you didn't know before?"

"That he didn't fix the Stone case."

Dave snorted. "I suppose he told you the Son of Sam

was framed. Jesus, what else would the man say? Did you expect a full confession?"

"I'm not as naïve as you think I am." To my disgust, my voice rose in a defensive whine. "It's just that if he's telling the truth, the whole thing has to be looked at in a different way."

"Any way that points to anybody but Riordan. Can't you see the man is using you?"

"Yeah, and I'm using him. What's wrong with that?"

Dave seemed to sense that I was serious. He smiled and said in a gentler tone, "Cass, forgive me. I just don't want to see you hurt, that's all. I know you're competent and strong and all that, but Riordan is ruthless. He'd tell anybody anything. What else did he say?"

"Not much." I wasn't completely mollified, but I liked Dave saying he thought I could handle things. "He set up a meeting between me and Jesse Winthrop."

Dave's jaw dropped. "Winthrop? That asshole? Are you going to see him?"

"He's not an asshole, he's one of the best investigative reporters around. And yes, I'm going to see him. I'd want to meet him even if he never wrote a word about the Stone case, because I admire him. I'm sorry if you think he's an asshole, but—"

"Cass." Dave held up his hands in a gesture of surrender. "I'm sorry I said that. I agree he's done some good things, it's just that he's got a real bug up his ass about my office, and I get a little tired of reading about how terrible I am. I just think you have to take what he says with a grain of salt."

"At this point, I take what everybody says with a grain of salt," I said pointedly. We left the discussion there while we walked to the restaurant, but I had the uneasy feeling it was unfinished business between us.

The restaurant was called the Cafe Montmartre, and it had a Village-eclectic menu. A little French, a little Italian, a smidgeon of Indian-style curry dishes and a touch of Middle Eastern. The decor was also typical Village—glass-topped tables, exotic blooms, slim, gay waiters. We decided to share two dishes, green fettucine with mushrooms and veal picatta. Dave ordered us a fried zucchini appetizer and a bottle of ice-cold Chablis.

We talked movies. Old movies. I said I didn't think Hollywood had ever really been able to translate mysteries, my favorite reading, into satisfactory movies. He said what about the *films noirs,* those late forties masterpieces about the dark side of American life?

"Oh, I grant you the atmosphere, but where's the detection?" I asked. "It's all camera angles and heavy music and mysterious blondes. Above all, mysterious blondes. I think that's what I've got against those movies. It's so sexist, the Woman as Other. Simone de Beauvoir says—"

"Yes, but the *mise-en-scène*—" Dave interrupted. "The steamy sex. It may be sexist in that the woman isn't portrayed as a person but as a Force, but it's always the man who gets duped by her. He's the sucker. Look at Fred MacMurray and Barbara Stanwyck in *Double Indemnity*— she's leading the poor guy around by the nose."

"Oh, give me a break! He's as bad as she is. Not to mention John Garfield in *The Postman Always Rings Twice.* You can't tell me he isn't looking for trouble."

"But if he'd never met Lana Turner—" Dave began.

"Yes, but is that realistic? The guy's going along minding his own business, totally law-abiding. He meets one mysterious blonde and suddenly he's committing murder. Does that sound reasonable to you, Mr. Prosecutor?"

"Well, I have to admit," Dave said with a grin, "it would take more than a night in the sack with Lana Turner to make me kill somebody.

"But seriously," he continued, "you don't expect realism from a Hollywood movie. The thing is that these movies gave a feeling of gritty truth, not candy-coated sentiment. Did you see *Nightmare Alley*?"

"God, yes. One rainy Sunday afternoon. It gave me the shivers, even with that stupid Hollywood ending. The geek, for Christ's sake."

"Let's talk about something more pleasant. Would you like dessert?"

"Would I? They make a mocha mousse here that I'd kill for."

We ordered mousse and coffee. I finished the last drop of wine before it came. I'd need that coffee.

The first bite of the rich mousse was a gastronomic orgasm. I alternated spoonfuls of mousse and sips of coffee for the maximum flavor.

"To get back to what we were talking about—" Dave began.

"Not the geek, please!" I begged. "I'm eating."

"No, I meant Riordan and Winthrop. Do you really think you should meet Winthrop? I mean, it's clear that all Riordan wants you to do is carry his message about someone else fixing the Stone case. Then Winthrop can use it to beat Parma over the head in print."

"Sorry, Dave, but that prospect doesn't upset me much. I know you're being loyal to Parma, and I respect you for it, but I don't have to be. As far as I'm concerned, the more dirt that gets thrown around, the better. Maybe then somebody besides me will see a link between Blackwell and Nathan."

"But doesn't it bother you to be doing Riordan's dirty work for him?"

"Not as long as I get something out of it."

"But—"

"But me no buts. My mind's made up. I've always wanted to meet Jesse Winthrop, and I'm going to."

He didn't say any more, but there was a spoiled-brat pout on his face for about ten minutes. We didn't even talk about movies anymore.

After dinner, we walked a little, then stopped into a little jazz club for a drink and some music. Dave ordered bourbon, and I had a brandy. I needed something I could sip slowly. We sat close together in the club, barely touching and losing ourselves in the undulating, lush harmonics of the group. Then I put my arm through Dave's tweedy one, and he clasped my hand in his. I was relieved. This was a way to communicate without misunderstandings about Riordan or anything else.

We stayed till the group finished their set, then walked outside. The cold air felt good after the smoky heat of the club. I was about to suggest we go to my place for a nightcap. Very forties and *film noir,* the word nightcap. It makes me think of John J. Malone and Jake and Helene Justus. But before I could offer, Dave asked me to his apartment and steered me toward his car.

I was surprised. First, that he had a car at all. Most of us who live in Manhattan get by without them. Second, that he had brought it to the Village on a Saturday night, when parking would be at a premium. The car itself was my third surprise. Instead of the battered Volvo or VW I was expecting, I saw a low-slung sports car, British racing green. I don't know much about cars, but he'd parked a lot of money on Hudson Street.

"Jesus! This is some car. Aren't you afraid somebody's going to steal it?"

He laughed. "I've got a pretty good alarm system. Anybody touches this thing, and it's going to sound like World War Three."

It was fun zipping around in it, I had to admit. Close to the ground as we were, every corner was an adventure. It felt like we were on a racetrack. We drove across town, down Broadway and then off to the left. An area of former warehouses and present co-ops, so newly gentrified that it didn't even have a nickname. Lower than SoHo, east of Tribeca, it was just waiting for some smart real estate developer to call it something.

There was a garage under Dave's building. We parked and took an elevator to his floor. As we went up, I couldn't help wondering what it cost to live here. Even a studio must run pretty high, with private parking and everything.

Dave's apartment was as unexpected as his car. For one thing, it was no studio. Two bedrooms, one a fully outfitted law office, as I noted on my way to the bathroom. Maybe that explained it, I thought, a little cynically. Parma probably had rules against private practices on the side, but Dave had to have something on the side to afford this place. Then there were the furnishings. No student modern

here—a thick chocolate carpet, a sofa-and-loveseat combi-
nation in a Chinese flower pattern on dark brown background. Chinese vases and lacquered boxes on carved, lacquered tables. Elegant yet masculine. Sunday *Times*
Design Section. Money. Lots of money. I began revising
my estimate. In addition to a practice on the side, Dave
had to have a rich family.

He poured us each a drink. My brandy came in a huge,
hand-blown bubble of a glass. I coveted it. I coveted the
whole apartment. It was so together, so professional. The
apartment of a person who knew what he wanted and how
to get it.

I needed another brandy like I needed a conviction on
my next trial. I'd already had enough so that I kicked off
my boots and ran my stockinged toes through the shag
carpet like a kid testing out the first grass of spring. Still, I
sipped it and let Dave join me on the loveseat, leaning into
him as he put his arm around me. The lights were low.
Probably a dimmer. We began to kiss. Dave was a good
kisser, active and varied. When the lenses on his aviator
glasses began to steam up, he took them off and put them
on one of the Chinese tables. Part of me was worried
they'd leave a scratch, but pretty soon I had other things on
my mind.

Soon we adjourned to the bedroom. That was his word,
"adjourned." It's hard making love to a lawyer.

The bedroom was huge. The oak platform bed with
built-in stereo tables was dwarfed by the size of the room.
There was an exercise bike in one corner. Dave hadn't
been kidding about being a physical fitness nut. And as he
took his clothes off, I could see more muscle under his
shirt than I'd expected. It doesn't do to underestimate
these scholarly types, I told myself with a private grin. The
sight of his unobtrusive but powerful muscles excited me. I
walked toward him and ran my fingers down his back. He
turned and smiled a smile of sweet lechery in the shadowy
light from the living room. We embraced while still half-
dressed and fell on the bed together.

Being half-dressed made it more exciting, as though we

absolutely couldn't wait to enjoy each other. We kissed and groped, panting and writhing on the Bill Blass sheets. Like a James M. Cain novel.

It was as athletic and impersonal as a game of tennis. Thrust and parry, give and take. Match point. We came quickly, then lay exhausted, each on our own side of the bed.

I had never felt so alone.

TWENTY-SIX

We dozed. I woke with a start about an hour later. There were tears on my cheeks. Had I dreamt of Nathan? I didn't even know. I felt a huge emptiness, like an unused room.

I had to go home. I woke Dave, as gently as I could, and asked him for a ride. "Can't you stay?" he asked with a little-boy forlornness that might have touched me earlier that night but now only strengthened my resolve to sleep alone.

I shook my head. "Have to get up in the morning. I'm meeting Jesse Winthrop, remember?" That did it. Dave gave me a sour look, then got up and padded to the bathroom.

We drove in silence. He dropped me off at the door with a perfunctory kiss.

I woke up feeling fuzzy around the edges and slightly seasick. After coffee and a hot shower, I felt better. I was beginning to look forward to meeting the journalist whose muckraking pieces in the *Voice* had been a part of my life ever since I moved to the city. He had a special interest in anything to do with the legal system. I'd often been surprised and pleased at how accurate he was. Usually newspaper accounts of courtroom situations are either dead wrong or totally exploitative or both. His were right on target. I was hoping his analysis of the Stone case would be the same.

I put on designer jeans, a blue workshirt-style blouse softened by a lace-trimmed collar, and Frye boots. It was still a bit chilly, so I wore my handmade South American sweater.

McGillicuddy's wasn't far, so I decided to walk. Actually, it was straight across town from where I lived, except that you can't go straight through the winding Village streets. So I meandered, always heading east and a little north, till I came to Broadway and McGillicuddy's. I got a table by the window, where I could watch the people passing by until Winthrop came. As usual in my chosen city, the people-watching was good. Antiquers, stopping into each of the shops along Broadway, brunch-time browsers and strollers, a few street types left over from the days when this neighborhood was a rundown extension of the Fourteenth street *barrio*.

I looked at McGillicuddy's too. I'd spent a fair amount of time here when I was in law school. Well, not here, exactly. The same place, the same building. But a whole different thing. It had been called Rocky's. There had been no plants in the window then, no butcher block, no quiches and omelettes on the menu. In fact, the place had been downright seedy. Old fight photos of Rocky's ring triumphs. A beer sign with three-dimensional running water. A lit-up jukebox in purple and orange. Occasional live groups. Some pretty damned live. But anyway you looked at it, the place had had an identity of its own. A raunchy individuality. Now it was fungible. Clean and well-lighted and probably terrific omelettes. But no fight photos.

"Been waiting long?" I looked up to see Jesse Winthrop standing at the table, a smile of greeting on his face. He looked like the pictures I'd seen of him, maybe a little older, beard a little grayer, worry lines around the brown, expressive eyes. He sat down, we chatted, then turned to the menus. In spite of all the food I'd eaten the night before, I was acutely hungry. I ordered coffee and challah French toast with ham on the side. I'd have to diet for a week to make up for it, but right now I could think of nothing I'd rather have. Winthrop ordered a bloody mary and eggs benedict.

"I understand you're interested in Charlie Blackwell," Winthrop began. It was as good a place to start as any.

I nodded. "I've read up on the Stone trial." I smiled. "Your account was by far the most thorough."

"And the most biased." He wasn't smiling. "But then I've spent a lifetime trying to expose men like Stone. It made me sick to see Parma take a good clear shot at him and miss."

"Some people seem to think it wasn't Parma's fault. That somehow Stone or someone working for him got to Charlie."

"Some people in Parma's office, you mean." I was startled, then realized he couldn't possibly know I'd been talking to Dave.

"Not just there," I replied, remembering what Nathan had said. "It seems to be a fairly common assumption."

"Carefully fostered by Parma," Winthrop commented acidly. "But that's not important. What is important is that the Stone case doesn't stand alone. It's part of a pattern. And that pattern is what disturbs the hell out of me."

"What pattern? What do you mean?" I took a welcome sip of hot coffee and sat back, prepared to listen. This sounded like hot stuff.

"I don't know if you remember why the Special Prosecutor was appointed in the first place," he began. I nodded, but he went on anyway. "I'm sure you recall what the media said—'fighting corruption in the wake of the Knapp Commission,' and all that." I had to smile; he sounded just like a pompous television commentator. "But that wasn't the whole story. It never is. Somebody benefits, somebody loses. In this case, the governor benefited. He got to appoint his man to a position that would control the prosecution of politicians from New York City. And, naturally, the mayor lost. He lost control of the prosecution of just those politicians and judges. It's no secret that the prosecutors in Parma's office tend to come from the governor's party, and the judges, lawyers, etcetera who get nailed tend to come from the mayor's party. It's also no accident."

"How does Blackwell fit in?"

"Don't rush me," Winthrop said, a smile on his face. "I'll try not to ride my hobbyhorse too much, and I promise to get to the point sometime this morning, but I have to give you the background. In the first place, assuming for a moment that the governor really did want corruption stopped, he picked the wrong man in Parma. Parma's a little hustler, out for himself. Thrives on publicity. In fact, on at least three occasions, his love for public announcements has actually cost him convictions. In one case, evidence was destroyed because the parties involved knew Parma was going to be looking for it. In another case, witnesses were gotten to because Parma announced to the world that they *were* witnesses. Appearances are more important to him than substance. So if the people who appointed him wanted results instead of posturing, they came to the wrong place. That's point number one."

I sipped more coffee. Winthrop took a drink of his bloody mary and went on. "This publicity mania led to another major problem. How many times has Parma called a press conference, announced his intention to investigate or even prosecute someone, and then let the matter drop? There are headlines for a week, the general public gets the idea that whoever was named is a crook, and then—no action. No case. He's done that to a couple of people who might have been guilty as hell if the truth were known, but that's just the point. The truth isn't known. And he's done it to at least one man whose integrity as far as I'm concerned is beyond reproach. Judge Lacey Taylor. You remember?"

"Judge Taylor? Sure, I remember. He's a real hero in Legal Aid circles. Fair to defendants. Willing to stick his neck out if he has to. Willing to stand up to the D.A. and the Policemen's Benevolent Association. What did Parma call him? A judge who was willing to sell his robe to the highest bidder?" I was getting indignant just thinking about it.

So was Winthrop. His voice was taut with emotion. "That dirty slime told the press Taylor's name had been *mentioned* in the Special Grand Jury—mentioned, for

God's sake! He implied a lot of other things, like pending indictments, but those somehow never happened. All that ever happened was that allegations were made and not proved. But that was enough for the party. Taylor, probably the best judge in the city, and certainly the best black judge, was kept off the Supreme Court ballot because the public had heard he was a crook."

Winthrop stopped suddenly and smiled. "Sorry to get carried away." But the smile was on the surface; underneath, Winthrop was still mad as hell.

"But that's light stuff in view of the big picture," he went on. "Do you know how many reversals Parma's had? And how many of those were on grounds of prosecutorial misconduct? And how many cases the special judges threw out for bad Grand Jury practice? How many cases were dismissed for lack of jurisdiction and had to be started over again—or worse, thrown out on double jeopardy grounds? If you look at Parma's record from the standpoint of cost-effectiveness—how many convictions that really stuck versus how many prosecutions that ended in the defendant beating the rap—you'd see a strong and disturbing pattern. Oh, sure, he's made quite a few convictions stick. Mostly cops selling a little dope on the side. In fact, mostly cops. When he gets upward in the social scale, to lawyers and judges, the convictions-that-stick rate drops like a thermometer in January. Does that suggest anything to you, Ms. Jameson?"

"You mean you think it could be deliberate? That Parma lets the biggies off somehow while nailing the small fry?" My mind boggled. It tied in with what Riordan had said, though. And even more with what could be read between the lines.

Our food came. I mulled things over while I ate. The French toast was wonderful. Real maple syrup and the salty contrast of lean ham. I began to regret the passing of Rocky's a little less. I said as much to Winthrop.

He lit up. "You used to come here in the old days?"

"Sure. When I was in law school. My friend Adele and I used to hang out here once in a while. Before it got fashionable. Then she moved to the Upper West Side. Also before it got fashionable."

"There used to be this great group," Winthrop reminisced. "What were they called?"

"The Ray Black Five. If that's the group you mean. One guy played the flute."

"Yes," he said excitedly, "God, yes. That flute would hang over lower Broadway like a red harvest moon."

"Jesus!" I exclaimed. "You really are a writer, aren't you?" He laughed, a little self-consciously. I didn't mention that I had known the group pretty well, having gotten it on with the drummer a few times. Of course, I was younger then, and a black jazz drummer seemed the height of picturesque, bohemian fantasy. In reality, he always brought his laundry over when he came to see me. He said the laundromat near my house was better and cheaper than the one near him. A true romantic.

When we finished eating, Winthrop lit a cigarette, ordered more coffee, and continued talking about Parma. "There's even more to the pattern than just the big shots getting off and the small fry getting nailed," he said. "Like the number of cases where Parma indicted for perjury instead of for substantive crimes, like bribe-taking. Then the cases were tossed by the appellate courts because the perjury was induced by the prosecutor in the Grand Jury. You know the kind of thing."

"I read about it. Wasn't there a case with a lawyer and a law secretary? In the Bronx?"

He nodded. "That was the biggest, but there were others. It got to be a joke. The Special Prosecutor never indicted for substantive crimes. Just perjury—after he'd trapped the witnesses into lying in the first place. The point being that the public never knew whether or not he had any real evidence of corruption. If he did, it never saw the light of day."

"That's true," I agreed. "He never did prove those Bronx lawyers were actually taking bribes."

"Right. Then there are the bad grand jury charges— little things like forgetting to submit exculpatory evidence r to instruct the grand jurors about the defense evidence."

I was once again impressed by Winthrop's grasp of legal procedures and technicalities. He must have been coached constantly by lawyers who knew the ins and outs of criminal procedure. Which may have been one reason his rivals on the big dailies hadn't questioned Parma's methods. They didn't know how deviant those methods were from the way things were usually done.

"And Blackwell wasn't the only key witness to fall apart on the stand. Either Parma has had more than his share of bad luck or—"

"Or he's been sabotaging his own operation all along," I finished. "But what would be in it for Parma? Oh, I know money, but I thought he was so ambitious. He really wants this congressional committee job—would he jeopardize that for ready cash?"

"Maybe he wouldn't have to," Winthrop replied. "Not if he could cover his tracks well enough. Plus if he protected the biggies, he'd be owed quite a few favors. Which is a good thing for an ambitious man to be owed."

My mind was wandering. Two pieces of the puzzle were rattling around in my head. I couldn't shake the feeling that they meant something. But what?

Charlie in the pen, begging me to get him protection. "Better than before," he had said. Where nobody, not nobody, could get to him. Because last time somebody had gotten to him? Somebody supposedly guarding him? Parma himself?

But then why had Charlie told Nathan he had something for the Special Prosecutor? How could even Charlie Blackwell, Master Informer, have informed on Parma *to* Parma? Unless he had never intended to inform. Unless blackmail had been his game. "Get me out of this rap, or I'll tell the world how you fixed the Stone case." Which gave Parma a terrific motive for murder.

"Earth calling Cassandra," I heard an amused voice say. I looked up, blushing, to see a smile on Winthrop's face.

"My wife tells me I look like that when I'm thinking abou a story," he said.

Story. Should I tell Winthrop my thoughts? What coul it hurt, I asked myself. He got it all. Blackwell. Nathar Paco.

"God, this is something," he said excitedly. "You thin this Blackwell character had the guts to put it to Parma?"

"That's the hard part," I admitted. "Charlie was so fuck ing scared. But maybe that's why. He knew he was in ove his head this time."

"Plus I see another problem," Winthrop continued. "I Parma thought Blackwell was a threat to his federal ap pointment, why stir things up in the first place by bustin him? Why not let sleeping dogs lie?"

"There's only one answer to that," I said. I started talk ing fast, aware that I could lose Winthrop completely wit this one.

"It explains why Charlie wasn't taken to the World Trade Center, why the yellow card was changed, why Charlie wa left so vulnerable. Parma meant to kill him from the begin ning."

TWENTY-SEVEN

He was drunk. As usual. He weaved his way down the long corridor toward Part 6, nearly knocking down a pregnant woman, who glared at his tipsy efforts at a courtly apology.

"Not again, Mr. Puckett," I said, resigned. "Plus you're late. Judge Noonan just issued a bench warrant. We'll have to go in and get it lifted."

He started to explain. I cut him off. It would be the same old rambling, boozy excuse. I didn't waste time listening to it.

We went inside. Corcoran, the clerk, looked up from his deskful of papers, a derisive smile on his face. When I asked him to recall the case, he said, "So the old rummy finally showed, eh?" His contempt for Puckett would have been more reasonable, I thought, if I hadn't been able to smell Scotch under the heavy mouthwash odor of his own breath.

The D.A. and I approached the bench. Same old story. Hezekiah Puckett was charged with burglary, and burglary was what he was offered. No plea down to trespass. So no deal. Date for trial, the Monday after next.

"Try to get him here sober, Counselor," Judge Noonan advised. "And if he's late," he warned, speaking loudly enough for my client to hear, "I'll throw him in jail. That I promise."

Which wasn't a bad idea, I thought, cynically, turning back to my client. He'd missed the judge's admonition; he was bending all his efforts to standing up. He swayed

rather a lot. Puckett in jail, I mused, would be a hell of
lot easier to deal with than Puckett out. He'd be on time
for one thing; he'd be reasonably sober, a thing I'd neve
seen, and, best of all, he couldn't wander away from th
courthouse whenever he felt like it, as he'd done the las
time the case was on.

But even with Puckett under control, the case was
loser. He'd been found by the cops on the premises, bur
glars' tools in his pocket. Burg Three was a lousy offer, bu
if we couldn't win at trial, not one we could afford to tur
down, not with a mandatory jail sentence after convictio
for Burglary Two.

"I ain't meant to do no stealin'," was all he would say.

I shrugged. It was his decision, though I'd hoped t
spare him the jail time. I wrote his next court date on on
of my cards, handed it to him, and made sure he put it i
his pocket. I had half a mind to pin it to his coat, the wa
kindergarten teachers pin notes to their kids. Then
watched his dignified weave back down the corrido
toward the elevator.

Next stop, criminal court. I was hoping to get Thoma
Boynton's case dismissed. Then I'd beard the D.A. lions i
their den on Digna's behalf. Her case wasn't on the calen
dar, but if I could get a supervisor to agree to a misde
meanor plea for her today, it would be smooth sailin
when the case was on.

As I sat in the front row in Jury One, waiting for Boyn
ton's case to be called, I found myself thinking back to m
last night with Nathan. "I know I can't save them all," h
had said, "but if I can get one kid into one program. . . ."
It made sense. I couldn't change Digna's life for her, or ge
her kids back, or stop her being poor. All I could do wa
keep her out of jail. And if I did that, it would be enough
There was no point in wishing I could do more. I couldn't

Boynton came up behind me and tapped me on the
shoulder. "When they gonna hear my case?" he asked, fo
the third time in about fifteen minutes.

"Mr. Boynton, *please* just sit down and wait. There'
nothing I can do till they call it, okay?"

"I don't want to be comin' *back* here no more," he grumbled. "Ain't nothin' but a waste of time."

While I waited, I thought about Del Parma. Winthrop's *Voice* article had come out early this morning, Wednesday. I'd read it over breakfast. It really blew the lid off, I reflected admiringly. He'd laid out everything he'd told me about the cases botched by the Special Prosecutor's office, and he'd topped it off with what I'd told him about Riordan, Nathan, and Blackwell. He was within the bounds of the libel laws, but just barely. Parma would have some tall explaining to do to the congressional committee.

And to Detective Button, I hoped. The article should at least get Button thinking. Parma's motive to murder Blackwell stood out a mile, and Winthrop had made the link between Charlie's death and Nathan's very clear. So clear even a cop could understand it.

The bridgeman called Boynton's case. Dismissed. I told Boynton so with a smile, but if I was hoping for thanks I didn't get it. " 'Bout time," he muttered, stalking away. "Waste of my fucking *time*."

Maybe. Maybe not. He'd at least learned how serious his wife was about wanting him to move out and leave her alone. I doubted that anything short of being locked up could have impressed it on him so forcibly. So in a roundabout way, rough justice, Brooklyn-style, had been done. Then why did it leave such a bitter taste in the mouth?

I thought at intervals about Parma throughout the day. A double-agent of crime, playing both sides of the street? So panicked at the thought of what Charlie could do to him that he set the little man up for death, engineering his murder by paid assassins? Maybe with help from court personnel? Somebody, after all, had tampered with Charlie's yellow card. Could Red or Vinnie or even Marla Watson be on Parma's payroll? Or somebody at the Brooklyn House?

As for Nathan's murder, that was easy. If Parma was the killer, he'd learned that Charlie had talked to Nathan because Nathan had called Parma. Personally, as an old friend. But would Nathan call Parma, knowing Parma was the fixer of the Stone case? Maybe out of friendship, to give the man a chance to explain. That would be like Nathan. The only question was how Parma could have known enough to frame Paco. Maybe the same court officer who'd fixed Blackwell's card. . . .

It was a great theory. There was only one flaw in it. A fatal one. At 4:40 P.M. that afternoon, Del Parma was pushed under a moving subway train. He died instantly.

TWENTY-EIGHT

━━━━■━━━━

The next day was Paco's sentence date on the misdemeanor. As I waited for Pete Kalisch, I reflected that a lot of water and not a little blood had flowed under the bridge since that night in arraignments when Nathan had told me about his plans to get the kid into a program. I wished to hell he had. Maybe none of it would have happened, or at least not so easily, had there been no Paco to hang the rap on.

Pete came in about five minutes later. He went up to the bridgeman, signed in to have the case called, submitted a notice of appearance, and then asked for the probation report. I could see the bridgeman shrug, then hand the papers to Pete. He brought them back to the first row and let me read over his shoulder.

I read quickly, trying to pick out the items the murderer could have gotten from the report to use against the kid. Like the fact that he was nicknamed "Paco." That was in the first line. So you didn't have to be his bosom buddy to know that if you wrote him a note it should be addressed to "Paco," not "Heriberto." Also the kid's criminal history was outlined. He'd started hustling at school, putting out for the older boys' lunch money. He'd even been the complaining witness in a Family Court petition against one of those older boys. But the charges were dropped when Paco failed to show up in court.

From school, Paco had graduated to the street, showing up primarily in the Village. There was a string of Manhattan Family Court petitions charging him with petty larceny.

A watch. A ring. A wallet. All from tricks. Just as he'd said,
a little extra payment to take away the shame. He'd been
lucky on the cases—ACDs, fines. Apparently the judges
hadn't liked the complainants. Chicken hawks don't get
much respect in society.

It was all pretty sordid and pretty routine. Until I saw an
adult arrest that sickened me. It started out as the usual
trick-plus-ripoff bag, but the victim had caught Paco leaving with his gold cigarette case and there had been a struggle. According to the report, Paco had gone berserk and
beaten the guy to a pulp. The probation department de-
plored the violence, but they never did get Paco to explain
to them why it had happened. He refused to talk about it.

I was writing it all furiously into my notebook when a
voice penetrated my funk of concentration.

"What's going on here? What's the meaning of this?" I
looked up to see Di Anci framed in the doorway of the
robing room. He was livid, his face distorted with anger,
almost spluttering as he went on, "Ms. Jameson, who told
you you could look at that report?"

Pete stood up. "I did, Your Honor. Ms. Jameson is con-
sulting with me about the case. Her office represented Mr.
Diaz prior to my appointment as counsel."

Di Anci's voice grew deceptively soft and patient. Anyone who knew him would have known he'd all but passed
the bounds of reason. "I don't care, Mr. Kalisch. I don't
care what you thought you were doing. The statute is very
clear. First of all, I am still the judge in this courtroom and
I decide who can see that report. Not," he glared at the
bridgeman, "not the court personnel."

"But Judge, you told us before—" the bridgeman began.
I could have told him to save his breath. Di Anci shouted,
"Silence!" at the top of his lungs. Then he turned to me.
"Ms. Jameson," he said in a voice of deadly calm, "I am
not going to let this matter drop. I am not only going to
take it up with Mr. Jacobs and your bosses at Park Row,
but I am going to seriously consider filing a grievance
against you with the Bar Association. You have violated
the defendant's right to privacy, you have engaged in a

serious conflict of interest, and you have violated the Criminal Procedure Law, which gives the right to see this report to defense counsel only. Which you are not. And for the record, I don't believe for one minute what Mr. Kalisch said about your helping him with the sentence. What you were doing, Ms. Jameson, was snooping. Pure and simple. And I won't have it in my courtroom."

He paused. I guessed it was my turn to launch into a spurious apology, so I did so. Di Anci had no choice but to accept it, but it was obvious to everyone in the room that neither of us meant a word we were saying.

After Di Anci stormed back into the robing room, I went up to the bridgeman. "I'm sorry, Phil. I didn't mean to get you in trouble."

"You shouldn't of looked at it, Counselor," he said in an aggrieved tone. "You know you got no business lookin' over Pete's shoulder like that. It wasn't right."

"Hey, what can I say?" I told him. "If I'd known Di Anci was going to come down on us like that, I wouldn't have done it. It just came out of the blue."

"Yeah," he agreed, "you got a point there. You never know where you stand with that guy. One day he says, 'Give the fuckin' reports'—oh, excuse my language, Ms. Jameson—'to the lawyers and don't bother me.' The next day it's, 'I'm the judge and you can't give 'em nothin' without I say it's okay.' Never know where you stand. Just wish he wouldn't yell on me in front of the whole courtroom. Makes it kinda hard to tell people what they're supposed to do if they seen me get chewed out like that, you know?"

Pete stepped up, finished with the report. "When do you think you'll be able to call it?" he asked.

"We'll bring him down right away. We'll call him after the first calls. Gotta do my first calls first, you know that, Pete."

Pete, himself a former court officer, nodded. That gave us about half an hour. I suggested coffee. And a long talk about the case.

We went to the New Deal Coffee Shop, across the street

from the courthouse. It was small and dingy, the perfect place to duck into for a quick conference.

"Was it worth it?" There was a hardness I didn't like in Pete's tone. Not for the first time, I found myself wishing I was working with Paul. An old friend instead of a disapproving stranger.

I looked straight into his hazel eyes and decided to answer coolness with coolness. Though I felt anything but cool.

"Yes, it was, as a matter of fact. I learned some very interesting things. Like the fact that the nickname 'Paco' was right there for anybody to see. And his pattern of ripping off his tricks. Not to mention the time he nearly killed one of them, who happened to come upon him when he was about to make off with his cigarette case. All of which information would have been of immense help to whoever framed him."

He looked at me appraisingly. "Okay. That makes sense. So you think what—that the murderer just happened to read the probation report and called the kid and pretended to be the guy from the job program? How would the murderer know about that, by the way? It's not in the probation report, since they recommended jail."

"It's noted on the court papers. I saw it when I arraigned Paco. The judge put it down as the reason for the adjournment."

He nodded. "All right. But it still seems far out to me, that someone would go to all this trouble."

"Look at it this way. If someone did, then it paid off. The cops never gave a second's thought to any other possibility. Once they knew about Paco, he was nailed. They never gave the Blackwell thing a chance."

"It's going to be a real bitch to sell to a jury," Pete said gloomily, staring into his coffee.

So he was human after all, worrying about the coming trial just like any other lawyer. I gave him a smile. "That's why we got the best lawyer we could find," I said sweetly.

He smiled back. "Flattery will get you everywhere."

"Everywhere?"

"Well, it's good for a cup of coffee, anyway," he said, putting a quarter on the table and picking up the check.

Meanwhile, back in the courthouse, the prisoners were down. Pete and I slipped in to the pens without going through the courtroom. One Di Anci tantrum per day is my limit.

Paco stood in a corner, smoking a cigarette. I went over to him. "Hi, Paco. Remember me?" He nodded.

"So what's doin' today?" he asked belligerently. "How come I gotta be in court again? This is the third time this week they wake me up at five in the morning to come to court."

Pete explained. "This is your sentence date on the old case. The one Mr. Wasserstein represented you on. The other times you were in court were on the murder case. But you won't be back here again. Today you'll be finished on the old case, and from now on you'll be in Supreme Court on the murder. Understand?"

Paco nodded knowingly. "Goin' upstairs. I never been upstairs before."

"Yeah, well, you're goin' up the hard way, kid." Pete's voice was harsh. "Most people work their way up to murder. You started at the top."

Pete talked to Paco for about half an hour. The iron gates clanged open and shut as the other prisoners went into the courtroom and came back again. Pete didn't learn any more than I'd already told him, but I didn't grudge him the right to hear it first-hand. Finally, he turned to me and asked if I had any questions.

I did. "Don't get mad, Paco, but I have to ask you about this. What about the guy you beat up in the Village last year?"

He looked blank. I tried again. "You know, the guy who caught you taking his cigarette case, so you beat the shit out of him."

The blank look was replaced by a look of animal wariness. "Yeah. Whatchou want to know?"

"I want to know what went down. Why you came down so hard on the guy."

"Like you said, I took the cigarette case and the dude seen me, so I gotta fight with him. No big deal."

"No big deal! Paco, you stomped on the guy. He was in the hospital for three weeks. He lost a fuckin' *kidney*. And you're tellin' me no big deal."

"Yeah, I done time for that. They can't go throwin' that in my face no more. It's finished, man." As if to prove to himself just how finished it was, he walked away from me, to the other side of the cell.

Out of the corner of my eye, I could see the court officer assigned to the pen tense up. Next to me Pete murmured something. Probably telling me to leave his client the hell alone.

But I couldn't let myself deal with either of their concerns. The story was another nail in the kid's coffin. Proof that he was a hothead who would strike out viciously when confronted by a ripped-off victim. Unless there was more to the story. Something that would show why he'd attacked that particular guy. Some personal thing between him and Paco which would have no bearing on his relationship with Nathan.

"Paco, listen to me," I said. "I'm on your side. But that story is a killer. All a jury has to know is that you beat up this guy with no reason, just because he saw you with his stuff, and they'll believe you murdered Nathan for his watch. You want that to happen? You want them to convict you without leaving the fucking *box?* Look, man, you could have hit that guy once and gotten away. Why did you do a number on him?"

"You wanna know?" Paco shrieked, "you really wanna know?" He turned toward me, face contorted. People started rushing into the room. Court officers, lawyers, I recognized Bill Pomerantz. There was a lot of shouting, very little of it making sense. Some of it seemed to be directed at me, trying to get me out of the room before there was trouble. I had no intention of leaving.

"Yeah, I wanna know, Paco," I shouted back above the din. "I wanna know why you nearly wasted that dude. Did it make you feel like a big man, beatin' up on a faggot?"

"You bitch!" He screamed it with all his might, then turned to the wall, clutching his head in his arms.

The court officer turned on me. "Will you for Christ's sake stop tuning him up! We don't want any trouble in here. Let him get calmed down before you talk to him."

"I don't want him calmed down," I said between clenched teeth. "I want him like he is."

He was about to argue, maybe even throw me out of the pens, when Paco crumpled in his corner, sliding to the floor with his arms still wound around his head. Huge sobs racked his body. He rocked himself back and forth on the hard floor like a blind child.

He cried for about five minutes. Pete and I stood and watched. The court officer hustled everyone else out of the pen. Finally, Paco subsided and in a muffled voice said, "He called me names."

"What kind of names, Paco?" I asked softly.

"He said I was—" The voice broke. "He called me his lover. Said how could I steal from him when he loved me and I loved him."

"And that's what made you want to kill him? That he said he loved you?"

Paco raised his tear-stained face. "He ain't supposed to love me," he said sullenly. "Just fuck with me. I ain't got no men for lovers, that's for sure."

Well, I had done a wonderful job. For the prosecution. Before we had had a story which could have given a little boost to the theory that Paco had killed Nathan for the gold watch. Now we had Button's theory on a silver platter. Paco had tried to kill one man who thought he could be his lover. What if he thought Nathan felt the same way? I was sick. I'd been trying to help, but all I'd done was make things even worse.

I went back into the courtroom and sat in the first row. I scarcely noticed what was happening at the bench. Paco stood at the counsel table, head bowed, thin wrists clamped into handcuffs. I woke up and paid attention when the sentence was pronounced.

A year. The maximum. And a self-satisfied little smile

from Di Anci to tell me it was his way of paying me back
for reading the report. Now even if I managed somehow to
clear Paco of the murder, he'd still be in jail. And there'd
be nothing I could do about it. Di Anci had seen to that.

Only one thing could have made me feel worse. On the
way into Supreme Court, I ran into Button. Almost literally. He came bounding out of the revolving door just as I
was about to go in.

He was apparently so preoccupied he didn't recognize
me, just apologized mechanically. I was about to leave it
that way and go right into the building, when he suddenly
said, "Oh, it's you."

"Gee, I love your tone of voice," I said. "As though you
were saying, 'Oh, there's a roach in my soup!'" I was still
pissed off from my encounter with Di Anci. All it would
take was a spark from Button to ignite my anger.

He lit the spark. "That kid who killed your friend—
wasn't he up for sentence today?"

"He got a year. Which really ought to make your day." I
swung away from him, ready to disappear into the revolving door, when I felt a strong hand grip my arm.

"Look, Miss, I'm getting tired of the attitude you've
been copping on this case. I'm not looking to railroad anybody, and I don't need your snide remarks."

I pulled myself free and faced off against him. "Are you
so sure, Detective Button? Are you so damned sure of
yourself that you haven't got a single doubt about that kid?
Not even now that Del Parma is dead?"

"What the hell has Parma got to do with it?" Button was
yelling now. "You trying to give me that shit about the guy
hanging himself in prison again? Is that what you're trying
to do?"

"Oh, Jesus, I don't know why I bother. You don't see
anything you don't want to see. Or maybe it would be too
dangerous for you to see it. It's a lot easier to convict some
Puerto Rican kid with an 18-b lawyer than to take on a big
shot who can afford the best, isn't it? Who knows, there
might even be money or a promotion in going along with
the frame."

For a moment I thought he was going to hit me. His fists were clenched, and his mouth was a taut, thin line. White around the edges. Then he laughed, a soft, bitter laugh that scared me. "You white liberals," he said, "all alike. I got stepped on my whole life in the cops because I was one of Them, because I might be too sympathetic to some poor black kid shot to death by a racist cop. And now I get it from the other side. I'm not liberal enough for Miss Cassandra Jameson. When was the last time someone called you 'nigger,' lady?"

Well, what do you say to that? If you're smart, nothing. I was smart. He cooled down on his own. "All right," he said finally. "All right. Let's have this cockamamie theory of yours. All at once. Right now. I'll be as open-minded as hell."

"Here?" I asked, looking around for the first time at the steps of the courthouse. People had been jostling us for the past three minutes, all but pushing us out of the way to get to the revolving doors.

"Over here," he said peremptorily, gesturing toward the slabs of stone that flanked the steps. I followed him and sat on the cool stone, trying not to think about what it was doing to my beige pantsuit.

I took care of old business first, refreshing Button's memory about the Stone case. Then I moved on to my talk with Riordan and the confirmation I'd gotten from Jesse Winthrop. As I suspected, Button had read the Winthrop article, but discounted it as the ravings of a mad liberal.

I went on to describe how I'd convinced myself Parma was the murderer. Only now Parma was dead.

Button was suitably impressed. "Jesus, lady, who else you gonna link up to this thing? The mayor?"

"Button, it hangs together," I protested. "Three people have been killed, and all three were connected with the Stone case."

"Maybe," he sighed heavily. "But it still looks like one fag killing, one suicide by a flaky skell, and one subway-pushing. Give me one single piece of evidence, for Christ's sake. Just one!" There was a desperate note in his voice that puzzled me.

Then I understood. He believed me. At least a little. Enough that for him to live up to his own image of what a good cop was he'd have to do something. And he wished he didn't feel that way. I smiled to myself. I knew the feeling.

"About that towel. . . ." I began. I was partly thinking aloud and partly trying to give him the piece of evidence he wanted.

"Towel?" Button's voice went so high with indignation that it squeaked. "What are you talking about a towel?"

"The one in Nathan's bathroom. With the bloodstains. It wasn't Nathan's blood, you said. So it may be the murderer's. So why not test it against my client's blood?"

"Wouldn't mean anything. Not necessarily. Could be somebody else came by, cut himself, and used the towel."

"Could be," I agreed cheerfully. I'd learned something about Button in the last few minutes. Push him into a conclusion, and he'd resist like a mule. Let the ideas work on him without pushing, and he'd come around to it himself. I watched him struggle against it, but finally his shoulders sagged and he sighed again, and I knew I'd won. He'd run the blood test, all right. He might never tell me how it came out, but he'd run it. If only to satisfy his curiosity.

TWENTY-NINE

We spun along the spaghetti strands of highway that connect the outer boroughs to Manhattan. I hadn't the vaguest idea which one we were on—I only know them from listening to the morning traffic reports. Backed up on the BQE. Rubbernecking delays on the Major Deegan. I was on my way to Queens, to the Long Island City Greek Orthodox Church where they would lay Del Parma's mangled body to rest.

I looked at Dave, who sat in the driver's seat, effortlessly guiding his little car through the maze of roads, all marked with green signs designating places I had no mental picture of.

Dave turned off the highway onto a city street lined with little one-story neighborhood stores. Gloria's House of Beauty. I thought of Gloria Vinci, with her tough, businesswoman's attitude to life. Sal's Pizza. Nick's Shoe Repair. It looked a lot like Cleveland.

The crowd on the church steps was enormous. Not only had Parma, a political animal, had many friends, but the manner of his death and the Winthrop charges had made his funeral a media event. Remembering the man's lifelong courting of publicity, I thought that on the whole he would have been pleased.

The ornate doors swung open, and the crowds began to file into the church. Inside, it looked like an airplane hangar with pews. I found a place in the back and watched the knots of people. The mayor and his retinue. The wife, blonde and dignified in designer black. Young men from

Parma's office, alike as to their three-piece suits and ambitious, predatory eyes.

Then I saw her. As I'd expected, she sat in the back row. Her face was pale, devoid of makeup. She wore a drab gray dress and a tiny black hat that surely hadn't been out of her closet since 1962. A pillbox, like Jackie Kennedy's. She took her seat in the back with the furtiveness of an amateur shoplifter. The Other Woman weeping in the back row, just as I'd said to Flaherty. Marian Macready, Del Parma's very private secretary. Dave had explained their extra-curricular relationship.

The service was long and tedious. In Greek, except for the florid funeral oration, which praised Parma as a pillar of the Greek community. While the speeches droned on, I looked around the church. It was all gold, heavy and rich. Flat-faced icons hung on the wall, their eyes staring with blank patience at the generations of worshippers that had knelt here.

At last it was over. The pallbearers, one of them Parma's son—about fifteen, with his father's dark good looks and burning eyes—picked up the coffin. I turned toward the aisle to watch it pass and suddenly noticed that Marian was gone. She had slipped out the side door.

I did the same, from my side of the church. I had to run to catch up with the secretary's retreating figure. I called out, "Miss Macready. Marian. Please stop. I have to talk to you." I was out of breath, but I dared not pause to catch it. She halted abruptly, turning on me with a look of implacable hatred on her face.

"Leave me alone." She spat the words out with a venom that shocked me. "I've got nothing to say to you people," she went on.

It took me a minute, but then I remembered that Parma, too, had taken me for a reporter at first. I shook my head. "No, no," I said. "I'm not from a newspaper. I'm a lawyer. I came to see Mr. Parma a couple of weeks ago."

The hatred was gone from her face, but it was replaced by a wariness, a sullen suspicion, that wasn't much more encouraging. She had been badly hurt, and I had to go as carefully as you do with any wounded animal.

"I'm sorry about your boss," I said simply. "But I have to talk to you. It's possible his death was no accident, that it was involved with the death of a man named Charlie Blackwell and Charlie's lawyer, Nathan Wasserstein. You see, Nathan was my lover, so I have some idea what you're going through right now."

There was still a dullness in the red-rimmed eyes, but there was a touch of color in her cheeks. She was coming alive, just a little. I had to wake her up completely.

"If you help me," I said carefully, "we just might be able to nail whoever killed your boss."

"Nail him?" she asked. "You mean put him in prison?" There was a hint of life in the red-rimmed eyes. She looked like she was coming back from a long distance. There was something to live for after all. Revenge. It wasn't a nice emotion to stir up, but it was the only thing that could have penetrated her pain.

"Where can we talk?" she asked in a hoarse voice. She looked around a little wildly, and I realized she'd left the church blindly, with no clear goal in mind.

"We could go somewhere for coffee," I suggested, looking toward the business street Dave had turned off to find his parking space.

She shook her head. "No," she said, "I don't want to be seen like this." She gestured deprecatingly with her hand at the drab gray dress that made her look like a Dorothea Lange portrait. "We can go to my house," she decided.

I nodded my agreement. She turned and walked up the street. Quickly. She had a purpose now. To get the guy who'd killed her lover. I followed, trying not to feel like a heel. She stopped at a red Toyota and unlocked the passenger door, then walked around to the driver's side. I stepped in and closed the door. She started the engine and pulled the car, with negligent expertise, out of its cramped parking space and into the flow of traffic.

After a few turns that left me even more bewildered than before, we turned onto a street of neat little row houses. Light red brick with white shutters, white ironwork fences, and multicolored flagstone walks and patios. Lots of window boxes. Empty now, but by June they'd be filled with geraniums or petunias, depending on how much direct sunlight they got.

We parked the car in the driveway and walked up the stairs to what in a brownstone would be the parlor floor. Marian opened the two-toned green door with keys suspended from an expensive-looking gold ring. I found myself wondering if it had been a gift from Parma.

Inside, the room was as far from the impression I'd formed of Marian as possible. Instead of the vibrant colors she'd worn at our first meeting, the room was all soft blue, ivory, and gold. Elaborate, fake-antiqued, somebody's idea of high-class decorating. There was a wistful quality to it, like the genteel pillbox hat.

I let her putter in the kitchen getting coffee. The kitchen looked homey, with none of the phony touches I saw in the living-dining room. The spiritual center of her home, I told myself, a little fancifully. She should have been the mother of six, preparing huge home-cooked meals which she would set proudly before her brood. "I love to watch a man eat," she would say as hefty sons devoured her offerings. Instead, she'd cooked for one man. Whenever he could plausibly get away from his own dinner table. It seemed such a waste.

She came into the living room and set a tray, laden with coffee pot, glass cream and sugar set, tiny spoons, and two fragile cups, on the ivory coffee table. We went through the ritual of pouring and stirring, then sat in awkward silence for a moment. The intensity that had propelled her home seemed to have dissipated. She looked unbearably weary. I wondered if she'd slept at all since hearing the news.

"I don't know where to start," I began. Then I looked into the troubled gray eyes and began to talk about Nathan. Somehow explaining him to a stranger was comforting. I warmed to the subject and talked freely, telling Marian about Charlie Blackwell and the Burton Stone trial. She recalled the name, nodding her head as I repeated the suspicion that the trial had been fixed.

"Riordan," she said flatly, definitely. "It was that Matt Riordan. Everybody knew what kind of lawyer he was."

"That's what Mr. Parma thought, anyway," I concurred. "But it started to look like it wasn't Riordan after all. Or that if it was him, he had help. From somebody in the office. Somebody Parma trusted."

"Just because Jesse Winthrop printed those lies—" she began hotly.

I held up my hand. "Winthrop was wrong about your boss," I agreed. "But he may have been right, too. There may have been someone in his office who wanted Parma to look bad."

To my surprise, Marian turned white. "That's what he thought," she breathed. "That's why he locked up those files."

"What files? Who locked up what, Marian?"

"Del did," she said simply. "He took a lot of files from the old days and locked them in his office. He said he was going to go through them. I guess he wanted to find out if someone could have been—doing what Winthrop said."

"Jesus!" A chill ran through me. Here was a murder motive—Del Parma about to expose the person who had been sabotaging his cases.

"I can't believe it," Marian said sadly. "We were always a close-knit office. A real sense of camaraderie, if you know what I mean."

"Yeah," I answered shortly. That's how I'd thought of my office until Nathan's murder turned it into an armed camp. Everyone on one side and me on the other. "But it's possible that someone in the office wasn't really pulling for the team. That while your boss was going after the crooks in good faith, somebody who worked for him was doing his best to see that those cases got dismissed or reversed. And whoever did that," I went on, playing my trump card, "made Parma look bad. Made him look like a crook. You don't want him to be remembered like that, do you?" Deliberately, I paraphrased the words I'd used to Dorinda

about Nathan. "You don't want people a year from now to
hear Parma's name and say, 'Oh, yes, the Special Prosecutor who turned out to be on the take.' Do you?"

The gray eyes were hard. "What do you want to know?"

"Did he say anything about the files? The ones he
locked up?"

"He didn't tell me in so many words," she began, a hint
of doubt back in her voice. I nodded encouragement, and
she went on. "But I think he was on his way to meet somebody the night he was killed."

"What makes you say that?"

"Well, in the first place, he broke our date. I was going
to fix something special for him here." Her face glowed
reminiscently. "Blanquette de veau and potatoes Anna.
Asparagus. Fresh. With hollandaise, the way he liked it. It
was sort of an anniversary. When he canceled out," her
face fell, "I thought it was because of *her*." I didn't have to
ask who she meant. Marian must have had quite a few
meals spoiled because of *her*.

She reached for her coffee cup with a shaking hand. I
noticed for the first time that while one of her hands was
perfectly manicured—long nails, red-lacquered—the other
hand had short, stubby, but also painted nails. I ran
through the possibilities. Was she a nail biter who only bit
one hand? A one-handed typist? Hated her left hand? Had
arthritis in the right so that filing the other hand was difficult? Maybe Sherlock Holmes could have figured it out,
but it beat the hell out of me.

She put the cup down and resumed her story. "But if he
was on his way home," she asked, "what was he doing on
the downtown platform of the subway?"

It was a good question. "He lived uptown?" I asked.

"He lived in Glen Cove. On Long Island. Where *she* was
brought up. He took the Long Island Rail Road from Penn
Station. He would have taken the uptown IND. Instead, he
was pushed from the downtown BMT."

"So if he had an appointment," I thought aloud, "it
would have been where? Downtown Manhattan or—
Brooklyn?"

"Not Manhattan," she said decisively. "He would have walked. Nobody would take a train to go two or three stops. Especially not Del. He was a great one for walking." She broke off with a watery smile.

"Okay," I said crisply, businesslike. "So it was Brooklyn. He didn't tell you where or who?"

She shook her head. "I wish I knew," she said simply.

"All right. Let's try another angle. What time did he leave the office that night?"

"It was early, real early. Four o'clock or so. He never left that early unless he had a meeting somewhere. Said it set a bad example if the boss ducked out before everybody else."

"And as far as you know, nobody else left at the same time?" I asked. After all, the likelihood was that whoever was named in the locked-up files was the person who killed Parma, and it was also probable that the killer was an assistant special prosecutor. Of course, if that was the case, why the trip to Brooklyn? This was getting confusing, I told myself.

Marian shook her head. "I'd have noticed. They'd have to pass my desk to get out of the office."

I nodded. The reception area in Parma's office was centrally located, and Marian's office was right next to it. She would have to have seen anyone leaving early.

"Of course," she added, as though she'd been reading my mind, "the files Del locked up were pretty old. They went back to the first year the office was in existence. Most of the assistants we had then are gone now. Went on to other things. Went to law firms. Ran for office. A couple of them became judges. Working for Del was a good start to any career," she finished proudly. I didn't tell her that I for one found it less than a glowing recommendation.

We talked for a little longer, but I'd gotten all I was going to get. Still, I told myself, it was more than the police, still looking for a teenage punk, had gotten. I thanked Marian and got directions for the subway.

As I said goodbye at the door, the pale spring sunlight hit her full in the face, revealing every line. She was forty-

five, at least, used up by loving a man she could never fully
have. And now he was gone. I felt a surge of sympathy. I
wanted to say some healing words, but I didn't have any.
However bitter the blow of Nathan's death had been to
me, he had not been my whole life. Far from it. We'd had a
comfortable, convenient arrangement. I'd liked him enor-
mously, respected him, but I hadn't loved him. Not with
the single-minded devotion with which she'd loved Del
Parma.

She stood in the doorway looking as dried up as a wrinkled fruit, all the youthful juice gone, leaving a shell of
empty promise. Impulsively, I squeezed her hand. Her eyes
filled with tears. She brushed them away. "Just get him,"
she said through clenched teeth. "Just get the mother-
fucker that killed him." I was sure she had never used the
word before, to describe anyone.

THIRTY

J esse Winthrop would have given his left ball to be sitting where I was. In Del Parma's office in the World Trade Center, with the formerly locked-up case files spread out in front of me like a banquet. The names on the cardboard folders read like a Who's Who of corruption. Armand and Nunzio Fratelli—one a criminal lawyer, the other a law secretary to a Bronx judge—thought to have fixed cases up and down the Bronx County Court calendar. Theodore Belsner, who allegedly offered a bribe that was refused by the fire marshal investigating the torching of a Brooklyn apartment building. Judge Bert Margab, stripped of his judgeship and tried for excessive leniency to defendants who invested in his Queens insurance business. And Burton Stone, the Fixer.

Dave had snuck me into his office. On a Saturday afternoon, when all his colleagues were away. So I had the place to myself while Dave sat in his own cubicle working on a Court of Appeals brief.

I knew what I would find in the files. I'd thought it through a hundred times, following the Master's advice. When you have eliminated the impossible, whatever remains, etcetera. I'd been so sure about it that I'd called Button. He hadn't been in, but I'd left a message telling him I was going to the Special Prosecutor's office to look at the files and I'd let him know what I found out. I knew he'd never let Paco off the hook without proof.

I opened the Fratelli file. True to the traditions of the Special Prosecutor's office, the brothers had been indicted, not for bribery, but for perjury. They'd lied to the Special Grand Jury about meetings they'd had with the undercover cop who, posing as a defendant in a case wholly made up by Parma, had offered them a bribe. When the Appellate Division saw the fabricated indictment, they went crazy. Entrapment was probably the kindest word they'd used. I looked through the file to see whose idea it had been to prosecute for perjury instead of bribery. The name that appeared most often was that of assistant special prosecutor Alfonse Di Anci.

My breath came out in a whoosh of relief. It was good, even after all my deductive reasoning, to see it so graphically stated in black and white.

I opened the Belsner file. According to the Court of Appeals, because the bribe had never been accepted, the Special Prosecutor, whose mandate after all had been to prosecute completed acts of corruption, had been without jurisdiction. Case dismissed. And, since no person can be put in jeopardy twice for the same offense, Belsner walked. The assistant who'd recommended prosecution: Al Di Anci.

The Margab case. Thrown out by the trial judge on the ground that the Grand Jury presentation had been hopelessly botched. Grand Jury assistant: Di Anci.

It was almost too good to be true. Had the man made no effort to cover his tracks? It would have taken Del Parma about three minutes to see Di Anci's guilt. Of course, you had to know where to look in which files, and even more than that, you had to know that there was something to look for. Once you did, it stood out like a neon sign. But if you didn't, the sabotage might never have been uncovered. If not for Jesse Winthrop's curiosity, Del Parma's ambition, and Charlie Blackwell's paranoia.

It was Marian who'd started me thinking. Some of Parma's assistants had gone on to become judges, she'd said. Di Anci had been one of them. What if he, not Parma, had sabotaged the cases? As Paco's sentencing judge, Di Anci had seen from the start how the kid's record could be used. And he'd been on the bench the very night Blackwell had been arraigned. Nathan had told him in conference the reason why Blackwell needed to be kept in administrative segregation—because he had an earful for the Special Prosecutor. I recalled how Di Anci had fled from the bench as though he had seen a ghost.

I opened the Stone file. There was a memo concerning access to the material witness Blackwell. Only two people besides Parma himself could get beyond the guards. One of them was Di Anci.

I was so absorbed in reading and thinking that the unexpected voice made me jump. "Interesting, Ms. Jameson?" It was Di Anci's usual urbane, bored drawl, with its overtones of irony. But there was nothing usual in the blunt-nosed gun he was pointing at my chest.

I tried to match his cool. "Weren't you afraid somebody'd find out about you before this?" I asked. "You didn't do much of a job of covering up."

"I didn't have to," he shrugged. "Parma made so many enemies and was under fire from so many sources that he naturally thought all his failures were due to outside corruption. A few of them were," he added.

"But most of them weren't? Most of them were because you were secretly undermining everything he did, making sure indictments would be tossed, witnesses would fall apart, convictions wouldn't hold up?"

He smiled complacently. "Poor Del. He was so intense, so committed. In his stupid way, he thought he could curry political favor with his gung-ho prosecutions. He didn't realize that the people who really count didn't want corruption wiped out. They wanted a show. They wanted a get-tough policy that got tough with their political enemies but not with their friends."

Which was exactly what Jesse Winthrop had said, I reflected. How he'd love to be listening to this.

"And that's what you gave them?" I asked the judge.

"For a price," he agreed blandly. I was indignant enough to want to penetrate that calm, to force some show of emotion out of the childishly smooth face of the man holding the gun on me.

"It must have been quite a shock when you saw Blackwell in court that night," I said.

"It was," he nodded. "Of course I knew Del was trying to nail him, but I didn't know when the Narcotics Division would actually make the bust. I had to think fast—and make a phone call. I am sorry," he began, with a smarmy sincerity that rubbed me raw, "that Nathan had to get caught in the middle. I would, believe me, rather not have killed him."

"It was just one of those things," I said sarcastically.

"Precisely," Di Anci said with a little smile. The smile told me more than words how hypocritical his statements were. Far from regretting Nathan's death, he reveled in it. Maybe it had been necessary, but he had also enjoyed it. The thought sickened and chilled me. Up till then I thought I was dealing with the same Di Anci I had appeared before a hundred times. Now I wasn't sure. It was more than the gun in his hand. It was the sick sadism of his mind that scared the hell out of me.

"If he hadn't been such a conscientious attorney," Di Anci went on, "if he'd only waited a couple more days before going to the Brooklyn House to see Charlie, I could have had Blackwell killed and that would have been the end of it. No other deaths and no reason for anyone to suspect anything more than just another skell hanging himself. Something nobody would lose sleep over."

"You changed the yellow card," I said bitterly. "When you sent me up to Jury One on a wild goose chase. A wild warrant chase."

"There's always a return on a warrant in Jury One," he agreed. "And if by some chance there wasn't, I'd simply have said I made a mistake. You see, it was so much easier for the people who killed Charlie to get to him when he was on the regular cellblock. It wouldn't have been impossible on the suicide watch, but it would have been riskier. And my friends don't like taking risks."

"How did you get in to see Nathan?" I demanded. Talking about him was harder than talking about Blackwell. My throat constricted. But I had to know.

"I mean," I continued, "he knew by that time that you were the one who fixed the Stone case. He'd talked to Charlie that afternoon. So why would he let you into his apartment?"

"Like most civilized men, he found it difficult to believe that other people aren't as civilized as he was. It never entered his mind that I would kill him. It's that simple."

"But he represented Blackwell," I objected. "He must have known it would be a conflict of interest even to talk to you."

Di Anci smiled deprecatingly and gestured with the gun. "He was, shall we say, amenable to persuasion. He'd opened the door, and once he saw this, he really had no choice but to let me in. He still thought he could buy time by talking to me."

"And once you got in. . . ." I trailed off, remembering the horror I'd stumbled on when I turned the knob to Nathan's door.

"Yes," he agreed. The complacent smile was full-moon bright. "Once I was inside, I forced him into the bedroom, tied him up, and strangled him. I had to tie him first, because of the blood flow," he explained with a clinical detachment that made my gorge rise. "If I'd killed him first and tied him later, it would have been obvious from the post mortem. And, since I wanted it to look like a sex case, he had to be tied while still alive. He did try resisting," Di Anci went on, annoyed by the memory. "He was already tied, but he raised his head and bumped right into my nose. Hurt like hell, plus I bled like a pig." The blood on the towel, I thought excitedly. For all the good it did me to know. "After that, the strangling was a pleasure," Di Anci gloated, "a real pleasure. Then, once he was dead, I placed those magazines you've undoubtedly seen in the night table. You see, I knew Nathan when he was a lawyer in Manhattan. He was a hotshot in those days, an arrogant sonofabitch. I wasn't sorry when he got his ass in a sling over those faggots he picked up. And when I saw how he made goo-goo eyes at that little spic he represented. . . . He said he wanted to get the little fucker into a program.

Ha! Program, my ass. He wanted to get him between the sheets."

I tried to control my disgust. "So you called Paco and pretended to be from the program."

He nodded. "Fucking kid came running. He knew what side his bread was buttered on. I put out the note to hold the kid while I killed Nathan, then I waited while the kid came and knocked on the door. I'd removed the note by then. When I heard the kid go down in the elevator, I slipped out myself, leaving the door unlocked to facilitate the finding of the body. I gather it did so, Ms. Jameson?" he asked, his voice thick with amusement. I could hardly bear the thought that Nathan had had to listen to that gloating voice in the last precious moments of his life. I came to with a start when I realized that as things stood, I'd be spending the last few moments of my own life listening to it.

"Why?" I cried hoarsely. "Why did you do it? Just for money? Didn't they pay you enough?" My voice broke with fear and bitterness.

He laughed. Still calm, self-possessed. Not the least bit ashamed or sorry. I'd seen gang-rapists with more remorse.

"The money was good, Ms. Jameson. They don't really pay judges enough, you know."

I snorted. "Most of them get by."

"You think they do the job because of some altruistic motive?" he asked, contempt in his tone.

"No," I answered calmly. "They do it because they want to advance to the Supreme Court. Civil side. Where the bucks are. But at least most of them don't steal while they're on the way up."

"And neither do I. A favor for a friend, here and there. I like to live well. I like to gamble. Sometimes my speculations don't turn out so well. That happened when I was a young assistant district attorney. It so happened the debt could be forgiven if I just saw to it that certain charges were dismissed. They were, and I got my reward. After that, I did more favors. Finally it was suggested that I could do a lot more as a member of Parma's outfit. Parma being the kind of fool who thought that because my father was a judge, I was automatically a good risk, hired me."

"Your father ought to be really proud of you," I sneered.

Now I got my emotional reaction. The pudgy baby face turned red, the face of a tantrum-throwing child. "You shut your face," he said. "I don't need him. I never did. Nothing I ever did was good enough for him. Not my grades. Not the schools I went to. Not my law career or my wife or my kids. Well, fuck him! I've made more money than he'll ever see with his fucking ethics. I fuck his precious legal system up the ass every day of my life, and let me tell you something, Ms. Jameson, I love it. I love watching you lawyers stand in front of me talking about justice and all that crap. I can fucking buy and sell justice, and you want me to give it away for free. It makes me laugh." But Di Anci wasn't laughing. He was shouting, he was gesturing with the goddamn gun, and he looked on the verge of a stroke, but he wasn't laughing. Whatever satisfaction he took from his corruption hadn't made him happy. It was scant comfort.

"Look, you might as well know," I squeaked, trying to distract him, "I'm not here alone. Dave Chessler's with me. So if you try anything, he'll—"

I broke off as I saw Dave quietly slip into the room behind Di Anci. The gun in his hand reassured me. Until I realized it was pointed, not at the judge, but at me.

THIRTY-ONE

Di Anci seemed pleased by the shock on my face. Dave just looked uncomfortable.

"Really, Ms. Jameson," Di Anci said, "did you think my friends would allow me to leave the Special Prosecutor's office without my arranging for a replacement?"

"Carrying on the tradition," I said. I turned to Dave. "I guess that explains your co-op. I thought you must have a rich family."

Chessler gave a short laugh. "My father's a professional alcoholic. My mother works in a department store. But I got a taste for the good things in life when I went to Harvard on a scholarship. And you don't get those things by being honest, Cass. Not when you start from nothing. You either inherit it or steal it, but you don't earn it—not the kind of money I'm talking about."

"Jesus, you guys kill me," I exploded, unconscious for the moment of the irony in that phrase. "I represent the kind of animals who push old people into their apartments and then rip off everything they own. But at least they've got some kind of excuse—their own lives are so empty it makes a weird kind of sense for them to take whatever they can from whoever they can. But you two—"

"Shut up!" Di Anci waved the gun at me. I shut up. It wasn't going to do any good anyway. You couldn't insult people like them. I wished to hell Button had been in when I'd called. I could at least have told him everything I knew and where to find the evidence that would prove it. So that he'd have something to go on when my body was found.

Because I was becoming aware that that was the plan. I was about to become a mugging victim.

"We'll take her downstairs," Di Anci was saying. "Then out onto the street. We should be able to find a deserted place near the river. Then we shoot her, grab her purse, take out the cash and leave the rest. Another mugging. The mayor can give one of his press conferences," he chuckled.

"Except for one thing," I pointed out, trying unsuccessfully to conceal a note of triumph in my voice. "When Dave and I came in, a guard downstairs checked us on a list. So he'll be questioned by the police if anything happens to me." I glanced at Dave, trying to see whether my attempt to split him from Di Anci was doing any good. His face was a blank.

Di Anci laughed. "You must give me credit for some sense, Ms. Jameson. When Dave checked in with the guard, where were you?"

"Waiting for the elevator."

"Exactly." Di Anci beamed. "So the guard only saw Dave. Dave's name was on the list. Not yours. And," he chuckled, "in case you were wondering, my name does not appear on the list at all. Dave was kind enough to obtain a pink pass for me. Which means I can go anywhere in the building. Of course, it's in someone else's name. So when the police come to investigate, they'll find that Dave came here alone to do some research and that I wasn't here at all. Dave will, of course, be deeply upset by what happened to you. I'm sure the *Post* will be able to do a lot with it. 'Lady Lawyer Killed While Boyfriend Works a Few Blocks Away.' Tragic." He shook his head sadly, but the grin on his face spoiled the effect.

I could see it all too clearly. From the utterly sickening "lady lawyer," to the interview with Dave, to comments from my Legal Aid buddies, to a quote from my parents. "We didn't want her to live in New York City on her own." And in a week no one would remember my name. I'd be "the girl who was killed over by the World Trade Center, wasn't it awful?"

Oddly enough, these thoughts, morbid as they were,

gave me a spark of hope. Unlike Nathan, who had invited
Di Anci into his apartment for a talk not knowing that Di
Anci was a killer, I at least knew what his intentions were.
The whole plan depended on my going quietly. And why
the hell should I? Shooting me here in the building, with
guards and Port Authority cops around, when they'd gone
to so much trouble to make it look like I hadn't been there
at all, wasn't Plan A. It didn't even make a very good Plan
B. A shot might be heard. It would be hard to get my body
down fifty-seven floors. It wasn't easy to get blood out of a
royal blue carpet.

I was beginning to enjoy the turn my thoughts were taking. They might have guns, but could they use them? When
Di Anci ordered me to get up from behind Parma's desk, I
laughed in his face. "You don't dare shoot me," I challenged. "You can't make me do anything."

There was, however, one little thing I'd left out of my
calculations. Di Anci lifted the gun up and hit me with it.

I reeled backwards with the force of the blow. My hand
went to my head. It came away with blood on it. As though
from a great distance, I could hear Dave remonstrating
with Di Anci ". . . didn't have to do that."

"What do you want me to do? Let her mouth off like
that?"

"We take her down in the elevator bleeding, and somebody might notice." So much for any momentary thought
that Dave had been concerned for my welfare.

"I shut the bitch up, anyway," Di Anci said with satisfaction. "Christ, that broad can talk."

I fumbled in my bag for a Kleenex to hold against my
bleeding head. Dave gave me a sharp look. Di Anci went
outside to see if the coast was clear for our trip downstairs.
As I pulled the Kleenex out of my purse, I recalled the
Swiss Army knife Nathan had given me. It was still in my
purse, buried under all the garbage I usually carried. Could
I get my hands on it, and bring it out without Dave seeing
me? And even if I could get it, could I open it? Use it? I'd
never done anything but open wine bottles and peel or-
anges with it. Could I use it to stab someone?

The Kleenex I was holding to my cut head was sodden with blood. As I reached for another, I resolved to try for the knife. I plunged my hand into the bottom of the bag, felt something hard, and grabbed it. Dave was watching me closely; I had to work fast. As I brought the knife up, I glommed onto a huge wad of Kleenex and used it to cover the knife. So that what Dave saw was a handful of tissues. I peeled one off, held it to my head, and shoved the rest back into the bag. Then I looked Dave full in the face.

"I'm beginning to believe you're a crook," I said conversationally, "but it's hard to accept you as a murderer. Up to now, Di Anci's the only one who's actually killed. You could turn state's evidence, make a deal, get off lightly. But if you kill me, you're up for murder. Think about—"

There was a chuckle from the doorway. Di Anci. "Wrong again, Ms. Jameson. It's true I killed Nathan and that I had Charlie Blackwell taken care of. But I was at a judges' meeting when Del Parma was pushed under the train. Your friend Dave did that all by himself."

"But—" I began. There were so many buts. They all came down to one big one. But I wouldn't sleep with a murderer. I'd slept with Dave. Therefore he wasn't a murderer. Wonderful reasoning. I settled on a less personal approach. "But Marian said nobody'd left the office at the same time Parma did."

"True," Di Anci said. "We'd thought of that, of course."

"I had a dental appointment for one o'clock," Dave said. "So I told Marian I'd be taking the afternoon off. After I left the dentist, I came back here, waited for Del to leave, followed him into the subway, and—you know the rest."

"Yeah," I nodded. "I saw it on TV. It looked pretty gory. Must have been worse in person. Especially somebody you knew. Somebody you'd worked with for years."

"Don't get sentimental, Ms. Jameson," Di Anci cut in. "It had to be done. Once Parma looked at those files, it was all over."

"So how did you lure him onto the subway platform?"

"Simple," Di Anci shrugged. "I called him up and told him I wanted to see him. He wanted to see me. So I arranged with him to come to Brooklyn. Then Dave followed him and did what he had to do. I'm sure it wasn't pleasant for him, but. . . ."

Dave was looking a little green, but his voice was steady enough. "Del was mad as hell. He didn't even see me. And it didn't take much of a push to knock him off balance. The train did the rest. I just stood back in the crowd, screaming, like everyone else. Then, before the police got there, I slipped away."

"And everybody assumed it was a punk kid. I think I read where some lady gave a description. Short, black kid with a knit hat. Not exactly a perfect description of you."

"No, people don't expect a person like me to commit a crime like that. They see what they want to see," Dave agreed coolly.

Well, I was feeling really bright. I'd figured out the Di Anci part all right, but I'd read Dave wrong from the beginning. When I'd thought he was being helpful, he was really pumping me to see how much I knew. When I'd thought he was personally interested in me, he was just stringing me along, trying to discourage me from talking to Riordan and Winthrop. Playing me for a sucker. I'd been right the first time. Never trust a prosecutor. Always look a gift horse in the mouth.

Di Anci went out again. There'd been a guard in the hall before. Maybe he would be gone by now and we could go downstairs.

It was now or never. I reached into my purse for the knife.

I looked Dave straight in the eye. It was one way to keep his eyes from straying to where my hand was moving, trying to grasp the knife and open it unseen. It wouldn't be easy.

"This explains," I said brightly, "why Charlie was allowed to come through the system. It wasn't Del who screwed up—it was you. You saw to it that Charlie wasn't brought here—and you probably tipped Di Anci that Nathan had an appointment with Parma." As I spoke, my fingers were working on the knife, trying to pry the blade open one-handed, without Dave seeing what I was doing. Also without cutting my finger off.

I went on, "Parma must have been mad as hell when he found out Charlie had passed through the system instead of coming straight here."

Dave nodded, but he didn't answer. It didn't matter. I had the blade open. Now for the hard part. The last physically aggressive thing I had done was pulling Susie Pringle's hair on the school playground when I was ten. Now I was about to stab a man and grab his gun from him. If I could.

I pulled the knife out of the purse, scattering Kleenex all over the place. I lunged forward, the knife held straight in my hand, and plunged it with all my strength into Dave's belly. It went in up to the hilt. My hand, for the second time that afternoon, came away blood. This time it wasn't mine.

Dave cried out with surprise and pain. He dropped the gun with a clatter and clutched his stomach. I jumped out of the chair and got down on my hands and knees, looking for the gun. If only I could get to it before Di Anci came back, I told myself, I could meet him at least on equal terms.

No such luck. The first thing I saw was a shoe, coming right up to the gun and kicking it out of my reach. Then the shoe kicked me in the side. I looked up to see a look of pure pleasure on Di Anci's face. There was mingled in that look no concern at all for the wounded prosecutor.

When he had enjoyed fully the spectacle of me groaning, rolling on the ground and holding my side, Di Anci turned to Chessler. The knife handle stuck out like a novelty-store trick. Like the arrow Steve Martin uses. Except for the dark stain spreading on Dave's impeccable shirt front. Dave grimaced in pain, his eyes wide with shock. I felt sick.

"Don't take the knife out," I advised. "If you do, the blood will really start flowing. You could bleed to death." I don't read murder mysteries for nothing.

Dave nodded.

"Not that your good buddy Al here gives a shit one way

or the other," I went on. "In fact, he'd rather you bled to death than started talking. Wouldn't you, Judge?"

"Shut up, you bitch, or I'll kick you again," was all Di Anci said. But there was a calculating look in his eyes. He was trying to put together a new scenario, one that would fit the knife in Dave's stomach into things. The mugging idea was down the tubes now, I decided. Somehow my dead body and Dave's wound would have to be explained by the same story.

Di Anci turned to Dave. "We'll tell the cops you and the bitch surprised a couple of robbers who were trying to steal the typewriters. They turned on you, you got stabbed, and she got shot."

I opened my mouth to point out just a few of the obvious flaws in that story, then recollected that it wasn't in my interest to help out. But Dave, even in his weakened condition, saw a couple of the same things I had.

"It's her fucking knife, Al," he said in a voice edged with contempt. "It's got her fingerprints on it."

"We'll wipe them off." Dave grimaced; the wiping-off process was not likely to be without pain. I was searching Di Anci's face for some sign that his concentration on the conversation was weakening his attention to me, but there was none. The gun was still pointed straight at me.

"How about we say she pulled the knife, one of the robbers got it away from her, and stabbed me?" Dave suggested. Di Anci nodded. "Okay, but we'll still have to handle the knife. Even if the robbers wore gloves, they'd obscure her prints. The cops shouldn't see clear prints on the knife."

Now Dave nodded. "It's not great, but it's playable. Then how does she get shot?"

"The robbers get your gun away from you. They shoot her. When the cops get here, you're wounded, she's dead. They've only got your word for it as to what happened. You're a prosecutor, a respectable person. Why shouldn't they believe you?"

I was putting my own scenario together while they talked. When they'd wanted me out of the building, my only hope had been to refuse to go. Now that they wanted me here, I had to try to get out. Which made sense. It was the first thing I'd learned as a young lawyer—whatever the other sides wants, you automatically oppose. If they want it, it won't do you any good. So, while Di Anci's eyes flickered, the little wheels behind them whirring away, I began to assess my chances of making a getaway.

Di Anci went on. "I can throw things around a little, make it look like there was a struggle. Of course," he added thoughtfully, "we have to get out of Del's office. The whole thing has to take place in the lobby." And away from Del's private files, I thought. That was the biggest flaw in Di Anci's scheme. He was calling attention to the last place in the world he wanted cops swarming all over.

Dave nodded, but he was looking too weak to come up with any more objections. "Just so we do it quickly," he said. "I gotta see a doctor, Al. Soon."

"Soon," Di Anci agreed. But there was something in his eye, an unholy gleam, that told me the truth. The cops weren't going to find one dead body in Parma's office. They were going to find two. The mythical robbers were going to kill Dave as well as me.

Di Anci moved toward the spot on the floor where Dave's gun lay. He had to lean down to pick it up, so he would use it to shoot me. And Dave? Or was he just going to pull the knife out, thanks to my helpful hint, and let Dave bleed to death? Anyway, that moment when Di Anci concentrated on picking up the gun was my only chance for escape.

As soon as I saw him bend, I ran. I ran as fast as I could through the Special Prosecutor's office. Past the cubicles where the assistants worked, into the reception area where the decorative girl usually sat. Through the door and out into the corridor. Toward the elevators. I could hear Di Anci puffing after me. But he couldn't shoot. He couldn't run the risk. There might be a guard.

When I got to the elevators, I pushed the button and prayed. I stood, pouring sweat and gasping with fear, until one came. I jumped inside and pushed the button for the forty-fourth floor. Just as the doors closed, I saw Di Anci, red-faced and panting, run up and push an elevator button.

I was retracing the steps I'd taken with Dave earlier that afternoon. When I'd thought I was coming to gather evidence against a murderer, not meet him personally. Because the offices weren't open on weekends, there would only be one elevator running from the forty-fourth floor—a kind of transfer point known in World Trade Center parlance as a skylobby—to the first. So that while I was safe from Di Anci on this elevator, which was taking me from the fifty-seventh to the forty-fourth floor, once on forty-four Di Anci and I would be racing to the same—the only—down elevator.

As soon as the elevator opened on forty-four, I flew out of it, running like hell down the corridor, past the sign that said New York State Hearing Room, turning the corner and pushing the down button. Behind me, I could hear the door of Di Anci's elevator, and his footsteps following me. Somehow, the absurdity of the situation chose that moment to hit me. Suppose I saw a guard, I asked myself. What would I tell him? "Help, I'm being chased by an armed judge?"

The elevator door opened. Shaky with panic, I nearly fell inside, pushing the lobby button with fingers slippery with sweat. Then I leaned against the wall and sighed with relief. The doors were closing.

Not for long. An arm thrust itself between the padded doors. An arm with a gun in its hand. The doors flew apart, and Di Anci stepped into the elevator. Despite his panting and sweating, there was a smile of deep satisfaction on his face. This time when the doors shut, we were on the same side.

My eyes clouded over. I saw black spots, just as I had the time I nearly fainted on the subway. It was all over. Di Anci would shoot me in the elevator and come up with a story to cover it later. And why shouldn't he be believed? He was a judge. If he said something, the cops would buy it. I just stood there, exhausted and despairing, waiting for the blow to fall.

Yet Di Anci didn't shoot. Maybe his imagination hadn't yet come up with a scenario to explain the situation. Or maybe it had, but the story didn't call for my dying in the elevator. Anyway, the elevator stopped at the lobby with my live body still on it. Di Anci pushed the button to go back up, but not before I ran for it. The lobby, with its tourists riding the escalator to the special elevators that went to the Observation Deck, was a far safer place for me than a lonely elevator.

My breaking away brought things to a head for Di Anci. If he let me get away, it was all over. If he shot me, he had a chance, however slim, of explaining it away. He shot me.

I felt the bullet rip through my shoulder. It spun me to the side, and I fell onto the carpeted floor of the lobby. The last thing I remember is the acrid dust of the carpet in my mouth. Then I lost consciousness.

I came to only partially, for a few seconds. Through a woozy haze, I looked up to see a familiar face. A neat brown face with bright black eyes. Detective Button.

THIRTY-TWO

For the rest of Saturday I alternated between sleeping and throwing up. By Sunday, I'd stopped throwing up, but I still fell asleep every five minutes. Mostly because staying awake involved pain. My head throbbed, my shoulder hurt, every muscle in my body ached. I couldn't figure out why until I thought about the tension I'd felt in that office with Di Anci holding a gun on me. My whole body must have been clenched like a giant fist.

I was in one of my rare moments of consciousness—wishing I weren't—when Button came in to my hospital room. There was a broad grin on his face and a bunch of daffodils in his hand.

"Hi, Counselor," he said cheerfully. "How you feeling?"

"Rotten. Thanks for the flowers. Sit down and tell me what happened. I sort of lost interest in the proceedings. How did you manage to turn up in the nick of time, like the cavalry?"

"Well, to start with, I got the message you left at the precinct. I didn't much like the idea of you snooping around the World Trade Center on your own, so I came to see what you'd find."

"You didn't know?" I was pleased by the admission. But my triumph didn't last long.

"As a matter of fact, I did," he admitted. "You see, we found that spiral notebook you were telling us about."

"What!" I sat up in bed. Bad move. A sharp pain shot through my shoulder, and the blood drained from my head. I sat back gingerly, still eager for the news. "Did Nathan write notes about Charlie in it like I said?"

"Better. Under the notes of his interview with Blackwell, there was a notation for an appointment. 'Thurs. 9:00 Di Anci. Apt.' So we can put Di Anci in your friend's apartment at the time of the murder."

"But where has the notebook been all this time? How come it wasn't found before?"

Button looked abashed. "To tell you the truth, Miss Jameson, my men have been too busy to really search the place. In fact, we didn't find it. Mrs. Wasserstein did, when she went over there to pack up a few of her ex-husband's things for her children. 'Course, we did ask her to be on the lookout for it."

"What else have you got on Di Anci?"

"His blood matches the blood on the towel. But so does a lot of other people's. Your kid's, by the way, doesn't."

"Has he made a statement? Has Chessler?"

"Counselor," Button gave me the look he reserved for when I was being exceptionally stupid, "the man's a lawyer. Both of them are. They haven't admitted to anything beyond the basic pedigree. Name, rank, and serial number. That's all I'm ever gonna get out of those two shysters."

"Button." I was suddenly suspicious. "You will be able to prove a case against them, won't you?"

He nodded, but his heart wasn't in it. "I think so," he said. "But it's all circumstantial. We'll never get him on Blackwell unless one of the people he used cracks, and I don't see why they should. As for Chessler, we're setting up a lineup on the Parma pushing, but after the half-assed descriptions those witnesses gave us, I don't hold out too much hope. It's going to be an uphill fight. Of course," he added, "we've got Di Anci for shooting you."

"And me for stabbing Chessler?" I asked, only half-joking.

Button threw back his head and laughed his rich laugh. "Hell, no, Counselor. Chessler's afraid to talk about it. He musta fell on that damn knife!"

The nurses came in with lunch. If you could call it that.

It was gray and mushy, and I found myself thinking of the gruel I'd read about as a kid in *Oliver Twist.* It was a measure of my improved health that I could hardly wait for Button to leave so I could wolf it down.

That night I called my parents in Chagrin Falls. I thought they ought to know their only daughter was in Beekman Downtown Hospital with a broken collarbone and a cut head. I think I left them with the impression that I'd been mugged. I assured them the shoulder would be all right after some physical therapy. As I hung up the phone, I could hear my mother starting to say, "Doug, I knew we shouldn't have let—"

I could finish it. "I knew we shouldn't have let her go to New York." As though nothing bad ever happened in Cleveland. I could also appreciate Dad answering, "Betty, New York's a city same as any other. It's just bigger, that's all." But my reminiscent smile turned sour as I recalled Di Anci's original plan. If it had worked, my mother might be saying those words to a zealous reporter, and they'd be used as a kind of epitaph.

The next morning, Monday, I called everyone I knew on the phone. It was time for company. I needed to hear a human voice that wasn't telling me it was time for my medicine.

The upshot was that by visiting time my room was packed. Jackie Bohan, Mario, Bill Pomerantz, the whole gang from Legal Aid. Even Milt Jacobs dropped in for a minute, carrying a potted plant. Soon the room was full of flowers and paperback mysteries, and Legal Aid shoptalk.

"I always knew Di Anci was a crook—" Mario said.

"But you didn't know he was a marksman?" Bill asked coolly.

"I gotta admit," I said thoughtfully, "when my mother warned me against the kind of people I'd get mixed up with as a criminal lawyer, I didn't think she was talking about the judges."

"Your mother's never seen you before the bench," Mario retorted. "Face it, Cass, every judge in Brooklyn is secretly envious of Di Anci."

Finally, I turned to Bill and asked quietly, "How's Flaherty? Still mad?"

Bill nodded. "He didn't say so, but I got that impression."

"Guilt, I suppose. He feels bad that he didn't agree with me about Nathan. And now that I've been proved right. . . ."

Bill didn't say anything, but there was an odd look on his face. I got the feeling there was something he wanted to say, but not here and now. Not with everyone around, and not with me in a hospital bed.

After they left, Emily came in, bearing a huge bouquet of lilacs. I unashamedly buried my nose in them. "Spring!" I said in rapture. "Just what I need—a roomful of spring. Thank you."

Emily sat by the bed. I brought her up to date on what had happened. "But you know what's funny," I said at the end, "I feel sort of let down. I mean, I did it. I found out who killed Nathan and why and I proved the whole homosexual story was a lie, and yet I feel kind of empty. Why?"

Emily smiled. "How do you usually feel at the end of a trial?" she asked. "Even if you did a bang-up job? Even if you won?"

"Same way, I guess," I agreed. "Elated, if I won, but underneath a little hollow. My nights are my own again, I can sleep again. No more last-minute investigations, no more surprise witnesses. My life isn't filled with The Trial —but it's not filled with anything else either. It's kind of hard to go back to watching television."

"You were involved with this thing, Cass. As much as with a trial." She looked at me appraisingly. "Maybe more so. You held nothing back, gave it all you had. Like you did in law school with all those causes you used to get involved with. I haven't seen you like that for a long time." She smiled. "It looks good on you."

Later that evening, Paul Trentino came in. More flowers, anemones this time, purple and red. He had news about Paco.

"Pete talked to Judge Tolliver. As Acting Administrative

Judge, he gets whatever headache cases are going around. And, boy, is this one a headache."

"Please don't use the word headache," I smiled, pointing to my stitches. He grinned.

"Can you imagine the affidavit we could write?" he chortled. " 'The defendant is entitled to be resentenced before a different judge in that the original sentencing judge had framed him for a murder he did not commit.' The last thing Rosy Tolliver needs is that affidavit in his court. He's agreed to vacate the sentence and release the kid pending a new probation report. Of course, Paco may still have to do jail time on the old case, if the report isn't good, but at least he'll be out for now."

"When's it on?"

"Friday. In Jury Four. I'll have some very discreet papers drawn up, and Tolliver will go along regardless of what the D.A. says."

"Good," I said with satisfaction. "I'll try to be there."

After Paul left, I found myself thinking over what Emily had said. It was also what Ron, my brother, had written me. Involvement. But that had been for Nathan. Could I keep it up, transfer it to other cases, other causes. I wasn't sure, but I knew the feeling I'd had in the past few weeks, of being taken out of myself, was a good one. One I wanted to prolong.

Dorinda couldn't come until the next day. Working. She brought a strawberry jar, planted with herbs—curly parsley, trailing rosemary, spiky chives, blue-gray sage, and on top, fragrant lavender. She told me proudly how practical it was—I could take it home and use the plants for cooking. I refrained from telling her how few people sprinkle fresh herbs on TV dinners.

Dorinda was bursting with excitement. "Cassie, wait till I tell you," she began, out of breath and rosy with the cold. "Suzanne had this fabulous idea—"

"Suzanne? The woman who runs Goldberry's? I thought you didn't get along."

"That doesn't matter now," she said impatiently. "She wants to display local artists' work in the restaurant. Sell it.

So I said I had this friend who takes really great photographs—"

"Dorinda! You didn't!" I was torn between two equally strong, equally neurotic, reactions. One was that my pictures were no good and would never sell in a million years. The other was that they were too good to waste on a dinky little neighborhood restaurant.

Before I could express either or both of these feelings, I caught myself. They were both stupid. The pictures were fine, neither as bad as my fears, nor as good as my hopes painted them. And I had to start somewhere.

Dorinda and I spent a very happy hour deciding which pictures I should mount and frame. The Palisades series I had done for Nathan. My Brooklyn Bridge shots, the ones I hadn't entered in the contest. They were printed on high-contrast colored paper, so that they looked like lithographs. Some brownstone portraits, done by season, to show snow, and spring blossoms, and fall leaves. My Victorian houses from home.

I felt a sense of real exhilaration. Finally putting my money—or my pictures—where my mouth was.

That night I was sitting up in bed, doing a crossword puzzle, when the door opened and Matt Riordan walked in. He was dapper in a three-piece charcoal suit with faint stripes of cobalt blue. His tie matched the stripe perfectly.

For the first time in three days, I was conscious of how I looked. My hair felt like a doll's synthetic wig thanks to the spray-on shampoo I had to use. I had no makeup on, and I was wearing an old nightgown topped by a flannel shirt I'd appropriated from Ron when he got drafted. It was faded and soft as a baby's blanket, and I loved it. It gave me a feeling of warmth, of security, of home. But it made me look like a shopping-bag lady.

He handed me a wrapped package. Clearly a book, but what kind? What sort of book would the elegant Matt Riordan choose for me? He was looking at me with amused appraisal. Waiting for my reaction. A kind of test? If I didn't like it, would I be forever branded as a philistine? I took off the brown wrapping.

It was a 1930 first edition of *The Hidden Staircase*.

"Riordan, you prick," I said, laughing. "You *knew* that Nancy Drew crack you made would tune me up, didn't you?"

He nodded, grinning. "It did, too. I don't know when I've seen anybody get as mad as fast as you did."

"And then you warned me about dangerous people. At first I thought you meant yourself."

"I am pretty dangerous," he said with a leer. "But this time I meant other people."

"So what's new in court? What are they saying about Di Anci in Manhattan?"

"Haven't the cops kept you posted?"

"No," I frowned. "For some reason, I can't get hold of Button."

Riordan grimaced. "There's probably a good reason for that, Cass. The rumors aren't too good, I'm afraid."

"What do you mean?"

"Well," he began, with uncharacteristic hesitancy, "you know Di Anci's out on bail—"

"What!" My mind flashed to the memory of Di Anci's denial of release to Digna Gonzalez. And yet he, who had cold-bloodedly killed, was free on bail.

"He hasn't been charged with the murder yet," Riordan explained. "Rumor has it he won't be."

"What the fuck are you talking about, he won't be?" My voice sounded shrill.

"Well, the D.A.'s office is going over the Special Prosecutor's files. Interesting problem of jurisdiction. The Special Prosecutor was appointed to prosecute corrupt officials, but who prosecutes corrupt Special Prosecutors? Anyway," he went on, seeing my impatience, "they've got the goods on Di Anci and Chessler, but what they'd like to do is turn them and get all the guys they were fixing those cases for. The biggies. Starting with my old client Burt Stone."

"Let me get this straight," I said through clenched teeth. "Those fuckers are going to play *Let's Make a Deal* with the guy who killed Nathan? No wonder Button couldn't face me," I added bitterly.

"Cass, listen," Riordan said. I had never seen his face without at least a trace of humor, a sense of irony in the blue eyes or a wry twist to the mouth. Now it was totally serious. "The case against Di Anci on the murder is shaky. So the D.A. can try him and Chessler for murder and maybe lose him *and* the heavies they were fixing cases for. But if they make a deal, they've at least got Stone and a few more guys like him."

"So he'll do what? Cop to Man One, do two-to-six? Jesus!"

Riordan's voice was soft. "The plan is to go for a prosecutor's information and make it Man Two."

"Man Two!" I was screaming now, my voice ragged with tears. "He'll fucking walk on Man Two! I've got guys doing three years for a goddamn nickel bag, and that scumbag can kill three people and walk on a Man Two?" I began to sob, deep, raw sobs. As I had that morning in the fog after Nathan died.

Riordan said nothing. No soothing words. No "please don't cry." No pat on the shoulder. But no looking away, either. No embarrassment. He just sat there. It was enough.

THIRTY-THREE

"**I** knew it couldn't be Del Parma," Dorinda said complacently, "because of his suits."

"His suits?" I sounded like Jerry North feeding straight lines to his wife, who, come to think of it, was also a cat freak.

"Because he was so into his appearance," she explained. "His image. If he'd been fixing his own cases, the last thing he'd have done was try the Stone case himself. He'd have made somebody else do it, so they'd look bad instead of him." Before I could answer, she got up to serve coffee to the other patrons. Being a waitress gives you good exit lines.

I turned to Bill Pomerantz, who was just finishing his country egg salad on five-grain bread. "Maybe I should have talked to her earlier," I said. "I would have saved myself a lot of trouble."

It was Thursday. I'd been out of the hospital for two days. Not quite back to work yet, but I'd go in tomorrow to see Paco released.

Bill looked uncomfortable. I was reminded of the feeling I'd gotten in the hospital, that he had something to say to me. "What is it, Bill?" I asked.

"I've never talked about this to anyone at Legal Aid," he began, quietly but firmly. "I know people gossip about me. Speculate. Well, it's true. I'm gay. I live with a friend in the Village. I've even seen you around, Cass, though I've tried to make sure you didn't see me. I'm not ashamed," he explained. "I'm not in the closet either. I just don't like people knowing my business. Which is why I could understand Nathan."

"What are you talking about?" Oh, God, Bill, I prayed silently, don't take it all away from me now. Don't tell me I did all this for nothing.

"Look, Nathan was bisexual. I hope that doesn't turn you off because I happen to think Nathan was a hell of a guy. He'd walked through the fire, if you know what I mean. But it's no good pretending he was something he's not."

"And the episodes in the men's rooms?" The words didn't hurt as much as I'd thought they would. Somewhere along the line I guess I'd learned to accept the truth, whatever it was. Flaherty hadn't. He never would. That was why he hadn't come to see me in the hospital. Nathan was lost to him, and maybe I was too.

Bill pursed his lips. "Look, Cass," he said firmly. "It's not easy for a guy to repress something his whole life and then reach a point where it won't repress anymore. Lots of people do crazy things when they first come out. But they mature as they accept themselves. As Nathan did."

That was a help. I pushed my luck. "He wouldn't have made it with a client either, would he?"

"I don't know, Cass. Why not ask the kid?"

"I want the truth, Paco," I said flatly. "Not the bullshit you've been handing out."

I faced him across the table at the New Deal Coffee Shop, near the courthouse. The deal with Judge Tolliver had gone down, the murder charges had been dropped, and Paco was out pending his resentence on the old case.

Paco looked down at the half-eaten jelly doughnut in front of him. "No, you don't," he mumbled.

He had a point. I didn't really *want* the truth. But, like the Stones said, you can't always get what you want. Sometimes you get what you need.

"Paco, I need to know."

"Wasn't what you think," he muttered, still focused on the doughnut.

"Don't tell me what I think. Just tell me how it was."

He looked around the nearly-empty restaurant, then crouched forward conspiratorially. I was reminded of Charlie Blackwell, with his yellow teeth, stinking breath, pathetic secrets.

"I knew the minute I seen him what he was," Paco whispered. "I seen too many of them dudes not to. So I told him if he get me cut loose, I pay him back. You know?"

I got the picture. I nodded. It was hard. I wanted to tell him to shut up, that I'd changed my mind, that the old lie would be better after all. But I didn't.

"When I was released, I went home with him."

"Just that once?" I asked, grasping at a straw.

"No, lady." Paco shook his head. "I seen him a lot after that."

The bitterness of the truth welled up inside me. "Did you give him a discount, or did he have to pay the full price?" I demanded. "And when did you steal his watch?"

"Shut your fucking mouth!" Paco screamed, hitting the formica-topped table. "I told you it wasn't *like* that. That first night, nothin' even happened. He said I ain't owed him nothin' for gettin' me out. Wasn't no money, wasn't no hustle. Wasn't no stealin' the watch. He give it to me." Paco's voice cracked. He was near tears. I was ashamed of what I'd said. He'd hurt me with the truth I'd asked for, and I hurt him back. And yet the hurt was bringing out things we both maybe needed to say and hear.

"You loved him, didn't you?" I asked, keeping my voice soft and low.

His face twisted, tears falling from the long, lush lashes down his cheeks. "Don't say that, lady. It ain't right to love like that."

"That's not what Nathan thought," I said.

Paco sniffled and wiped his hand across his face. There was a look of surprise on his face. "No," he agreed, "he said it was okay. He even said—" he choked again, then swallowed and went on—"he said I was okay. See, I never met nobody like him. My mother, my brother, they all thinkin' something wrong with a guy who fucks other guys, you know? Like, they can dig the money I got, but that's all. But Nathan, he says it's okay even if no money. Just to do it 'cause you like somebody. That's okay."

I nodded. Encouraged, Paco went on. "That's why he give me the watch. Because he like me. I'm gonna miss him a lot, you know?"

"I know, Paco, I know."

So we sat there for a moment in silence. Nathan's lovers. The irony of the situation began to hit me. I'd pushed hard to find the truth about Nathan's death because I hadn't wanted to believe he'd been gay. I was wrong. Yet I'd been right, too. The ropes, the magazines, the implication of exploitation in his relationship with Paco—these I'd been right about. I *had* known the essential Nathan, after all. The gentle lover. Did it matter so much whom he'd loved?

I wondered what would become of Paco. Another lover? Probably the best thing that could happen to him. To become a trick, in the Fran Lebowitz sense of the word. He'd get security and an education from the right sort of lover. More than a semiliterate dropout with a sheet could get from any other line of work. What a probation report! Recommendation: a long-term, live-in affair with a middle-aged queen. Paco would never find another Nathan, but the closer he came, the better.

After I left the coffee shop, I walked to the Promenade. I had to think. I stood at the railing, looking out over the harbor. Boats—red tugs and yellow ferries—scudded along the water. A gull flew at me, its tiny pink feet tucked protectively under its breast.

I thought of Ryokan. One of Nathan's favorite Zen stories. Ryokan lived the simplest kind of life in a little hut at the edge of the village. One day, while he was out, a burglar came to the hut, but he found nothing to steal. Ryokan returned home and surprised the thief. "You may have come a long way to visit me," he told the burglar, "and you should not go away empty-handed." Whereupon he took off his clothes and gave them to the thief, who put them on and slunk away.

Ryokan sat naked outside his hut, looking at the moon.

"Poor fellow," he said, "I wish I could have given him this beautiful moon."

There it was. Why Nathan died. Not just because he got in Di Anci's way, but because the caring, the compassion, that made him Nathan left him wide open. Di Anci had said that Nathan had been too conscientious about seeing Blackwell right away. He had also been too generous with Paco, allowing himself to be set up through the boy. And he had opened the door to Di Anci, knowing him to be a crook, but not suspecting that he could be worse. He had wanted to give them all the moon.

Monday morning. Pre-trial butterflies. I had to start picking the jury in Hezekiah Puckett's case at ten.

I was on my way to the Promenade to plan my strategy when I noticed the headline:

JUDGE FOUND SLAIN

There was a picture of Di Anci. I bought the paper. His body had been found in the trunk of a car in Bay Ridge. He had been shot through the back of the head. Police were calling it a "gangland-style killing" and linking it to the fact that he had agreed to turn State's evidence in the corruption cases.

Burton Stone the Fixer had fixed again.

It didn't bother me. Perhaps conventional justice had failed. Street justice hadn't. It seemed a fitting ending, Brooklyn-style.

I walked on to the Promenade. Di Anci was dead, but Puckett was alive. Alive and in need of a defense. Which I didn't have.

I stood at the railing, looking out over the harbor, trying to figure out how to cope with a hopeless case and a drunken client, when the lines of a Phil Ochs song ran through my head. "Show me the whiskey/stains on the floor. . . ." I could hear Baez' clear, diamond-hard voice singing. ". . . Show me a drunken man/as he stumbles out the door. And I'll show you a young man/with many reasons why/and there but for fortune/may go you or I."

Hezekiah Puckett. There but for fortune. That was the

key, I realized. That was how to convince a jury of twelve sober citizens that my client was no burglar, just a pathetic old drunk who'd needed a place to sleep it off. Trespass at most. No intent to steal, just as he'd said. Just the sad, sordid, day-to-day compromises of a man who measured out his life in Thunderbird bottles.

My mind raced ahead to the trial. Voir dire—jury selection—the part of the trial some defense lawyers call the most important. The part where you choose the jurors, where you first expose them to your defense, where you sell yourself and your client.

Could I do it? Could I take twelve people with jobs and clean sheets—in both senses of the word—and *show* them the life of Hezekiah Puckett? Bring them to the point where they could look at his red, watery eyes, his shaky hands, his loose, working mouth and say, There but for fortune? If I could, I would win the case. It was as simple as that.

The beautiful part was, I realized with mounting excitement, that all the negative things about Puckett, all the things I'd hope to hide from a jury, were now aspects of the man to be revealed, to be displayed as evidence of what he was—and was not. I could hardly encourage him to come to court drunk—not that he'd needed much encouragement in the past—but if he did, it would simply constitute proof that he was an alcoholic, not a criminal. Would he sit on the park benches in front of the courthouse with a bottle in his hand, in full view of prospective jurors? Let him; they'd see for themselves how pathetic he was. Would he ramble on the stand? So much the better. They'd understand how a mind like that would be incapable of forming an intent to steal. They'd hear his own story, and after they'd seen him, they'd believe it.

I began pacing up and down the Promenade. Only I wasn't on the Promenade anymore; I was in Part 6, standing before the jury box. I'd use the Phil Ochs lines, in voir dire and on summation. There but for fortune would be my theme. We could all have been Hezekiah Puckett.

I strode along the Promenade, lost in thought, my mind

asking questions of invisible jurors, my hands making the sweeping gestures I would use in the courtroom, my internal voice eloquent. Suddenly I stopped short.

Damn, I thought. Damn, damn, damn, damn—like Henry Higgins. I'm *good* at this! I'm fucking *good.* I began to laugh. Goddamn it, Nathan, I laughed in shocked surprise. I'm good, just as you said I was. What a revoltin' development *this* is. Here I've been spending all this time and energy trying to convince myself that this is not my life, and all the time I'm really good at it. Does that mean you were right about the other thing, Nathan? Involved is involved. Because I can get it up for Hezekiah Puckett, I have more to put into my photographs? Concentration and compassion strike again.

It was my own personal piece of the moon.